THE VOICE ON THE PHONE

A familiar male voice came on the line, this time not muffled by a mask. "You fucking bitch. I told you to stay away. I'm through with holding back on you. You're gonna get yours. Do you hear me, bitch?"

"Louis," Karen said, "what's the matter with you? What are you doing this for anyway? What are you trying to prove? How did you get my number?"

Louis disconnected.

Karen knew that the cops could trace calls. But had Louis been on long enough?

She hit *69.

There was a long succession of rings with no machine kicking in.

Then the call went through. Someone had answered. She heard breathing.

Karen sucked in a draft of air. "Hello," she said.

"Who this?" asked a man with a Latino accent.

"Karen. Put Louis on."

"No Louis here, lady. This is a pay phone."

"A pay phone?"

"Yeah, 33rd and Third. I be passing by."

Louis had called her half a block from her apartment. He was in her neighborhood. He could be right outside her door.

TOO RICH TO LIVE

LAWRENCE LIGHT

LEISURE BOOKS  NEW YORK CITY

A LEISURE BOOK®

June 2005

Published by

Dorchester Publishing Co., Inc.
200 Madison Avenue
New York, NY 10016

ISBN 0-8439-5546-5

Printed in the United States of America.

Visit us on the web at www.dorchesterpub.com.

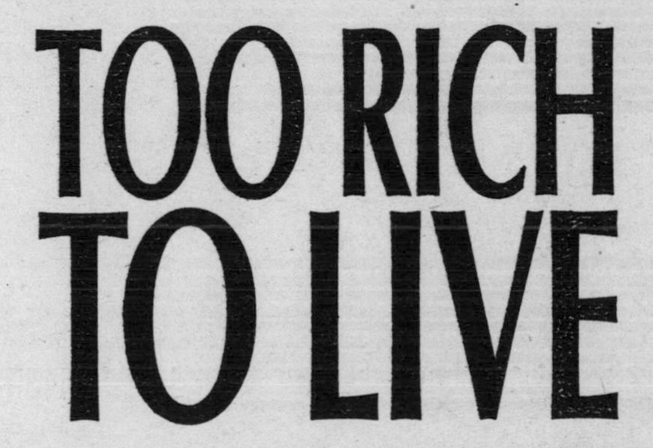
TOO RICH
TO LIVE

Chapter One

Edward Danton stood in his tuxedo, listening to the hubbub of the museum benefit dinner. He never used to be the guy who would kill someone. He'd once had a pleasant smile, but now every smile was a pretense. His favorite movie used to be *Ordinary People*, but now it was *Dangerous Liaisons*. And he had been in love once, but now couldn't remember how that felt.

If Edward Danton hadn't fallen in love, hard and early, he wouldn't have become a killer. Maybe a Wall Street bigshot, where he could have simply terminated people's financial security. Not a killer.

Tonight, Danton was going to kill a member of the Billionaire Boys Club. And the Billionaire Boy wouldn't see Danton coming. Danton stood among the other tuxedoed waiters at the Metropolitan Museum of Art's June fund-raiser. They clustered among the tables set up around the Temple of Dendur. In the Great Hall, the cocktail party rolled.

The other waiters buzzed quietly among themselves as if passing secrets. They were glad to be there because a steady catering gig sure beat working in the reality TV show that was the New York restaurant world, where contestants regularly got ejected.

Danton said nothing and thought only of the small vial that rode in his jacket pocket, weighing it down.

Chef Emily crossed the small bridge over the reflecting pool that flanked the temple. She had a wry smile for Danton. "The dinner's late getting started. Think they'll blame that on me?" She often complained that female chefs were as welcome in the dining business as female quarterbacks in the NFL.

"Caddy Redmon's to blame. He's late, as usual."

She laughed. "Isn't he running for the Senate?"

Danton nodded. "He's lost my vote. Let's start a revolution. We'll kill him. After we humiliate him."

Chef Emily asked Danton if he could baby-sit on Saturday. "Phil has to work." Emily's husband also was a chef.

"No problem. Tommy's not sick of me?"

"My son's going through a difficult phase. You're an angel for coping."

Hyperactive Tommy had a shriek that could break all the lights on Times Square. Danton would have liked to swing Tommy by his heels and smash his obnoxious little skull against the wall. "He's a great kid," he told Emily. "We play lots of games."

She headed back toward the food prep area in the American Wing, watched over by stern portraits of George Washington, who looked as though he were having trouble holding down a supper of Valley Forge campfire gruel.

Danton returned to scrutinizing the long, empty head table where Caddy Redmon, chairman of the Met's board, and the other swells would sit in majesty. Resplendent in its silverware and crystal settings, the table sat right in front of the temple, which was an assemblage of sandstone walls and columns from 15 B.C., honoring the fertility goddess Isis. Above the temple entrance were images of vultures, wings outspread. High-society types, preferring old money to new, liked to dine amid antiquity.

"Are you sure you can handle the head table?" Krapp, the headwaiter, asked him for the fifth time. "We're late starting. There's pressure." Krapp had a stopwatch for a brain and wanted every detail executed perfectly. Catered dinners didn't generate individual tips for waiters, hence their stipends depended on how important people assessed the service the next day.

"Let me see. Is it take from the left and serve from the right? Or take from the right and serve from the left?"

Krapp didn't enjoy being teased. "Chef Emily insisted you do the head table this time. Don't screw it up."

Krapp's eyelid was twitching, which happened when he felt stressed. Danton would have liked to grab one of the exquisitely crafted forks from the nearest table and jam it into his damn eye.

Outside the museum's massive slanted window, the last light from the orange sun made the Central Park trees glow, as if afire.

"If I do screw it up, I'll tell them I'm you."

Krapp's face twisted. "Don't screw it up," he grumbled and stalked away.

Danton slid his hand into his right jacket pocket, the one with the vial.

Chapter Two

Karen Glick needed to make some changes. Impending divorce did that to you.

One was an address change. In New York, cheap rentals in nice buildings were as scarce as true love in a sports bar on Super Bowl Sunday. After looking at several over-priced apartments the size of Roach Motel rooms, she finally accepted her grandmother's offer of a nice little studio in Murray Hill. Gran owned several tenement buildings. Oh, Karen could have stayed on in the luxury co-op she'd shared with Tim, with its Viking range, wrap-around patio, and courtly doorman. Her investment banker husband had offered to take care of the co-op's maintenance charges, which roughly equaled her monthly gross salary. But she had a good job and would pay her own way, if in a smaller apartment. Karen let him keep the co-op and settled for a chunk of their investment portfolio to squirrel away in an individual retirement account.

Karen also needed a job change. She was sick of writing personality profiles of executives for *Profit* magazine—even though she was good at it. One of her few stand-out stories had the hard-charging Jack Welch, General Electric's retired chairman, confessing that whenever he thought about his brutal worker layoffs, he suffered daylong crying jags. But her subjects seldom were this colorful. They tended to be M.B.A. plodders, adept at PowerPoint presentations.

Her latest such story concerned the buyout firm of Redmon, Dengler, Strongville & Morgan. This bunch, who called themselves the Billionaire Boys Club, at least had a smidgen of flair. One partner, Cadmon Redmon, was running for the U.S. Senate. Before they started their firm in the late 1980s, they had made their names at Dewey Cheatham, where Tim worked now.

Karen longed to be an investigative reporter, one of the knights errant of journalism. Maybe this was her way of getting back at her PowerPoint-adept husband. Maybe she simply was tired of being so damn nice to these boring, over-paid executives as she tried to coax some vestige of life from them. *Wow, you have a five handicap? How fascinating*. Maybe it was that nobody ever heard of nice profile writers like Karen Glick, while top-flight investigative reporters had a footlight-bathed renown.

Like her best friend at *Profit*, Frank Vere, one of the world's foremost investigative reporters. So she approached him with her ambitions. The tough part, he told her, was getting a lead to a good story. Powerful bad guys didn't send out press releases advertising their slimy deeds. Next, she would have to burrow through subterfuges, denials, and cover-ups to prove her case. Finally, she would have to defend herself when they filed libel suits. Luck helped, Frank had said.

Then she got some luck. Whatever pagan deity ruled the fates came knocking on Karen's door in the form of the U.S. Postal Service, an agency best suited to delivering astronomical credit card bills. Her windfall was better than a Powerball lottery win or a lifetime supply of bathroom products.

The postman gave Karen a box of documents showing the Billionaire Boys Club to be a cabal of tax cheats. There was no return address.

"My father always says that to get rich, you've got to be a criminal." Karen stood over her kitchen table, talking into the phone. She came from a family of unreconstructed 1960s leftists. "The Billionaire Boys Club has enough money to choke a donkey. And still . . ."

"And still they evade taxes." Frank, on the other end of the phone, was impressed by apparent proof that could level four of Wall Street's most prominent figures with the thoroughness of a thermonuclear strike. "We have to authenticate the documents, of course. This could be an elaborate hoax."

Covering the tabletop was the load of tax and bank documents, going back two decades. By Karen's assessment, the Billionaire Boys had paid very little in taxes on what she estimated as their collective $20 billion net worth.

"So all four of these yahoos are sticking it to Uncle Sucker." Karen picked up Baxter "Butch" Strongville's most recent statement from First Caymans Bank and

Trust, which recorded deposits last year totaling $350 million. Strongville's latest tax return showed he had earned a mere $25 million last year as an RDS&M partner. None of the Billionaire Boys' salaries or capital gains, as they'd reported to the Internal Revenue Service, could account for these huge disparities. "And Uncle Sucker has no right to go poking into an offshore bank account. Right?"

"Right," Frank said. "See, I don't understand why they do this. I mean, why take the risk of getting caught?"

"They figure they're too clever to get caught," said Karen, who knew something about the super-wealthy species from being married to a wannabe billionaire. "To them, the more marbles you've got, the higher your score."

"But if how many marbles you have is such a secret, then why bother?"

"I'm simply quoting my soon-to-be ex-husband, who wants to have carved on his tombstone: 'He had more money than God.'" Tim Bratton, who idolized the Billionaire Boys, itched to be rich like an acute case of psoriasis.

"I hope these outrageous bastards are happy," Frank said. He could have been referring to Tim. Frank and Karen had spent endless hours discussing her husband's failings.

"Well, money can't buy you happiness. But it sure can make you comfortable when you're miserable." Karen sifted through the documents. "I guess whoever sent this stuff to me somehow knew I was working a story on the Billionaire Boys."

Frank chuckled grimly. "I once started out investigating a tip on how the Billionaire Boys were screwing investors in a company they took over."

"Oh, yeah? What happened to the story?" The overhead tenant, whom Karen had dubbed Bigfoot, clumped thunderously along the ceiling. This had never happened at the sound-proofed Bratton-Glick residence.

"Couldn't nail it down," Frank said. "They're a take-no-prisoners group. I heard they left Dewey Cheatham, which is a rough place, in the 1980s because they were too rough for the older partners. You'll be following Caddy Redmon tonight at the Met's big fund-raiser. I wouldn't bring up the tax stuff unless there's an opening. Not until we can authenticate the documents."

"He's agreed to let me tag along. I'm just starting the reporting process, so I haven't met him or any of the others yet. You said you've met Redmon?"

"Yep. He's a world-class salesman, a real silver-tongued talker. Not to mention world-class womanizer. They say he could talk Queen Elizabeth into handing over the Crown Jewels."

"My grandmother is good at anagrams," Karen said. "Like, when you scramble the letters of someone's name to form new words—"

"I know what an anagram is," Frank said. "She did a couple on me. Remember?"

"Well, I told Gran I was interviewing Cadmon Redmon. She took out a legal pad, did a few scratches, and said his new name was Nerd Commando."

"You're wearing your new LBD, I trust, the one you bought before you left Tim?"

One reason Frank made such a good friend and such a good reporter was his amazing ability to observe and remember. Most guys wouldn't know or care about what clothes she bought. Tim was in the most-guys school. "Correct-o. Time for me to get dressed."

"Have fun."

After she hung up, she wrestled the new Little Black Dress from out of her jammed clothes closet. Luckily, it hadn't wrinkled in the move.

Chef Emily surveyed the salads as she might a Renaissance masterpiece from the Met's permanent collection left outside overnight in the rain. "The arugula is going to wilt. The beets are going to bleed into the Stilton."

"Since our guests will all be drunk as lords from their prolonged cocktail party, they won't notice," Danton said.

"I'll notice," she said. "Damn Redmon. What kind of a politician would ruin a salad?"

"He has given a lot of money to the museum," Danton said. "He can do what he wants." Redmon had endowed an exhibit on medieval torture devices, which bore his name.

Emily shook her head and moved over to the long table where her helpers were ladling melon soup into bowls, beneath the famous Gilbert Stuart portrait of Washington. "That damn Redmon," she said. "Why don't you spit in his soup for all of us?"

"Sounds like a good idea," Danton said. He eyed the cash-green soup and felt for the vial in his jacket pocket.

Chapter Three

Karen waited outside her new building on the side-walk. And waited.

Her husband had never failed to keep her waiting. She took to calling him "the late Tim Bratton." He wasn't amused. His perpetual excuse for the delays involved his need to please top Wall Street people, a task far more important than pleasing his wife.

Caddy Redmon had made truckloads of money despite his constant lateness. His partners at the firm, Karen had learned, would start a meeting to get people warmed up, and Caddy would sweep in to dazzle them with his salesmanship. According to his chief aide for his Senate campaign, Caddy's oratorical gifts rivaled those of Bill Clinton. His womanizing gifts did, too.

In her LBD, Karen did look glamorous tonight. But she wasn't dressing for Caddy Redmon. The point was to pass among the society swells. The choker of fresh-water pearls that Tim had bought for a birthday earlier in their marriage would work. Ditto for the Chanel True Red as a lipstick. She used to think that her mouth was too large for such a dramatic color. Yet for a soiree like the Met fund-raiser, her dark hair and clear complexion made it acceptable. She opened her Judith Lieber minaudiere and checked her micro-sized tape recorder, lying next to her lipstick, pen, and notebook. She snapped shut the jeweled purse in the shape of a scimitar. Tim had, late in the marriage and less than kindly, called it evidence of her "cutting wit."

With the sunset, the sky had turned an intense royal blue. Karen called this "the blue hour," that time between day and night when the air was alive with magic possibilities.

A black, shark-sleek limo cruised up to the curb. The super-rich now seldom rode in limos, which had found déclassé favor among middle-class wedding- and prom-goers.

The back door popped open and a tall, broad-shouldered, older man named Ron stepped out. She recognized him from photos as one of Redmon's bodyguards. He had a ruddy outdoorsman's complexion and had combed his hair into an old-fashioned pompadour.

Redmon, seated inside with a cell phone to his ear, gave Karen an impossibly white smile and waved, as to a dear friend.

"He'll only be a moment, miss," Ron said with a curiously avuncular warmth. He was a few years older than Karen's father. As a retired New York cop, Ron had the right to carry a firearm. Ex-cops were popular as bodyguards with the Billionaire Boys, who each had two armed men on duty every waking minute.

Jimmy, the other bodyguard, vaulted onto the sidewalk, closed the door behind him, and gave Karen the up-and-down look. Short with rubbery lips and a suspicion-filled soul, Jimmy had a gumbo-thick Southern accent that did not charm. And Karen enjoyed Southern accents.

"Open your purse for me," Jimmy commanded, rather than asked.

"Do you need to use my lipstick, Jimmy?" Karen smiled sweetly at him.

The edges of Jimmy's over-large lips pulled downward. "How do you know my name?"

She turned to the older bodyguard. "Ron, tell Jimmy I respond best to the word 'please.' "

"Jimmy, Jimmy, Jimmy, there you go again," Ron said. "We'd better work on those people skills." To Karen, "I'll inspect your purse, miss." He peeked inside. "Nothing lethal here."

The car door opened again, and disgorged a woman with a sour expression. She gave Karen a no-nonsense handshake and introduced herself as Rona Ziegler. Karen had only talked to Redmon's top political operative on the phone. Her voice was hard to forget.

"Caddy's on a call with the President," Ziegler rasped, her throat smoke-cured by years of Marlboros. "The President is excited that Caddy is running." She fished out a cigarette and lit it. Clearly, she couldn't smoke in Redmon's presence. "Particularly since Caddy will finance his own campaign and be beholden to no special interests."

"The President? Impressive." Karen didn't think it wise to add that the President had sold himself to those interests with the abandon of a skid-row hooker. "Say, aren't we a little late for the Met shindig?"

"Everyone understands how busy Caddy is." Ziegler sucked on the Marlboro like a diver from an oxygen tank about to give out. "We have a lot of the regular art patrons there at the Met tonight, and big political figures also. He's like John F. Kennedy to them. They admire his incredible oratory."

The door opened and Redmon himself sprang from the car. He switched on a 1,000-watt smile for Karen and enfolded her hand in both of his. "Karen, I've been looking forward to meeting you," he said with a salesman's sincerity. "You have a reputation as a fine journalist." His eyes drank her in like straws.

"Glad to meet you, too." When she was small, her otherwise nonreligious father had read her Genesis to make the point that the serpent was a salesman and she never should trust salesmen. But Redmon's melodious baritone and soothing delivery would make you believe if he told you that the rattle in the car you were buying meant nothing and would disappear.

When everyone was inside the cavernous limo, Redmon kept talking to Karen, grinning all the while. The youngest-looking of the Billionaire Boys, he had a country-club handsomeness that must have eased his hobby as a ladies' man. His eyes had flickered to somewhere south of her chin, and not to her pearl choker.

Redmon straightened his tuxedo's silk lapels, which sported an American flag pin. "I hope my fellas here"—he gestured at the bodyguards sitting across from them—"weren't too hard on you," he said. "We've had some security concerns."

The car moved into traffic, smooth as water on glass.

"Security concerns, how?" Karen said.

"We don't need to go into that," Ziegler said.

Redmon waved dismissively at his campaign aide. The bodyguards were staring out the bulletproof, tinted car windows at the New York streetscape spinning manically past. "I want Karen to understand the burdens of being both a Senate candidate and a financier."

Redmon reached inside his jacket and retrieved a black envelope. He handed it to Karen. "This came in yesterday's mail."

She examined the letter. It was addressed to Redmon at the Billionaire Boys' buyout firm, and marked PERSONAL; the white-ink handwriting was that of a fine calligrapher. She removed a single sheet of stationery, also black, from the envelope. There was the same elegant penmanship. As she read, a tiny tickle went up her spine. It said:

Dear Billionaire Boy: You and your pig pals think you are too good to pay taxes. You despoil the environment. You keep the world's poor living in misery. You, the whoremonger, with your narcissism, and the other three will die soon. You will die first. The signature: "Vampyr."

"Have your heard of this Vampyr?" Redmon sounded controlled and cool.

"Of course. It's a radical, anti-capitalist, anti-globalist group. They first appeared at the 1999 World Trade Organization meeting in Seattle, where they started a street riot. Since then they've gone underground, turned to terrorism. They've set off bombs, killed some people."

Redmon nodded and took back the letter. "There's no actual telling if this is from some crank or not. We sent a copy to the police as a precaution."

"We'll keep you safe, sir," Ron said, all silver-screen sheriff.

"No one will stop me from my quest to bring integrity, untainted by special interests' campaign contributions, to the Senate," said Redmon, trying for Jimmy Stewart in *Mr. Smith Goes to Washington*.

For this middle-aged roué, Karen thought, it was more like Rod Stewart asking if you thought he was sexy.

Since the Vampyr letter had raised the matter, here might be what Frank described as an opening. "What's this about not paying taxes?"

The limo finally turned onto Fifth Avenue just north of the museum. Caddy lived on Fifth. He and all the Billionaire Boys were FOPs—people who insisted on living either on Fifth or Park.

"The real question is: What's best for this country?" Redmon simply ignored her tax query, an old trick of a practiced interviewee.

"Are you going to release your tax statements?" she asked. Politicians often did.

"You're not here to talk about his personal life," Ziegler said.

"Since when are his tax statements his personal life?" Karen shot back.

"You see," he said, spreading his hands, "I have a deep and abiding love for this country, which allows anyone to seek his fortune. I came from nothing, and look at me today." He launched into a little set piece that extolled the virtues that made America great. And while the sentiments sounded hackneyed, Karen had to admit that he delivered them well. "You have to believe in what this country stands for," he concluded, "and to stand up for it."

"Politics," Karen said, deciding to postpone the tax matter for now, "is a nasty game. You're rich. Why bother with the hassle?"

Redmon gave her one of the most bogus smiles this side of a tobacco ad. "I'm a good public speaker. No, I'm a *great* public speaker. Do you realize the power of great oratory? It inspires, like a vision of wonderful tomorrows. Think of Henry V speaking to his troops before that big battle: 'To be or not to be, that is the question.' Think of Roosevelt rallying the nation to war after Pearl Harbor: 'We have nothing to fear but fear itself.' Think of Kennedy rousing America to send a man to the moon: 'One small step for a man, one giant step for mankind.' "

"Those quotes aren't quite—" Karen began, but Jimmy interrupted her.

"We're here, sir."

Someone at the curb opened the car door and Nerd

Commando hopped out, high-intensity grin in place. Ron followed Karen out.

"At home," Ron said, "he likes to listen to tapes of his speeches. He closes his eyes, smiles, laughs."

Redmon bounded up the long sweep of steps to the museum's front door. His entourage kept pace. Karen was good at running in heels. The Met's fortress façade loomed over them with its Roman columns and medieval gargoyles. A small group of well-dressed well-wishers greeted Redmon at the door and ushered him inside to the Great Hall. The swirling mass of tuxedos and gowns froze at the sight of him; then the crowd broke into applause. Redmon expertly worked the room, gripping manicured hands, kissing Botoxed faces. His eyes, seemingly searching for a prize, never were still.

Karen noticed that Ziegler was whispering her raspy comments into his ear as dazzled supporters approached.

"Aside from the high-society ones, he doesn't know everyone's name," Ron explained to Karen. "Rona Ziegler whispers the names to him."

"So she's the Hoarse Whisperer?" Karen said.

A waiter sounded a dulcimer to announce the delayed dinner.

Burbling with well-modulated remarks and laughter, the swarm of New York's social deities moved past the artifacts of antique divinity—mummies, jackals, and cats. Redmon had the finely dressed guests gathered about him. They skirted the reflecting pool and approached the Temple of Dendur, a magnificent monument from a previous empire. The temple, which loomed over an array of white-linen-covered tables, could've been a tacky ice sculpture for all the notice the moneyed folks paid to it.

Everyone took places at the tables. Karen was moving off to the side with Ron and Jimmy when Redmon clasped her hand. "You're sitting with me at the head table."

"The head table?" Karen was flustered.

Jimmy appeared pained.

His smile alight, Redmon said, "Yes. You're my date." He led her by the hand to the dais, as he would a girlfriend.

Karen decided not to make a fuss. She recognized all the worthies at the head table. Redmon seated her between himself and Thad Stuyvesant, whose family had made its first money in spices during the 1700s and today owned shopping malls. Stuyvesant, who seldom shopped at a mall himself, had distinguished silvery hair and the high polish of a good tea service. He introduced himself pleasantly and asked who she was. "Caddy always has such nice young women."

"I'm Karen Glick, from *Profit* magazine."

"Oh." Stuyvesant drew the word out for several syllables. To him, a reporter held all the appeal of a blood-thirsty wolverine. He turned to the heiress to his left, Barbara "Biddy" Croton. Biddy's husband, a sometime tennis pro, was off sailing the world with his boyfriend.

Karen, immune to snubs, ate her salad in silence. It was delicious, even though the arugula was wilted and the beets were bleeding into the Stilton. The Met benefactors, adrift in the arms of Bacchus, didn't seem to notice. Karen was the only one listening to the museum director welcoming the guests when the salad plates were snatched away and replaced with bowls of melon soup.

The guests chatted amongst themselves, boasting about their possessions and status while pretending not to boast. Jimmy and Ron sat at a table to the side with other retainers. Jimmy kept scanning the crowd. Ron was staring into space. Outside, the sun had set.

Karen glanced around and noticed the waiter for the head table, who stood beside the bodyguards. At first, she thought he was merely intent on the head table, checking to see whose glasses were empty. Then she realized he was staring fixedly at Redmon. The waiter's mouth hung open like a predator's, ready to bite. And his eyes burned. Lucifer eyes.

Redmon patted the back of Karen's hand. "Switch with me and talk to Kay-Kay," he said. "I need to bend Thad's ear." He whispered into hers: "And I can't stand Kay-Kay."

Karen shrugged and changed seats with Redmon. The soup in front of her looked scrumptious. It had a flat crouton holding a gob of caviar. Katherine "Kay-Kay" Chapin, who owned a high-end real estate agency, was busy chatting to the man seated beside her. Karen lifted her spoon.

Kay-Kay Chapin didn't hate the press. "Your magazine ought to stick it to Caddy and his pals with a good exposé," Kay-Kay said to Karen with barely perceptible slurring.

About to take her first sip of soup, Karen hesitated. She put down the spoon and complimented Kay-Kay on her diamond necklace. The society doyenne, about ten years older than Karen, had a well-boned patrician prettiness, despite brining herself for years in the hedonism that infinite money made possible.

"Caddy will try to get you into bed," said Kay-Kay, who also was unaccompanied this evening. She and her husband had fewer and fewer common interests lately, Karen knew; he was currently in rehab. "You're young enough for him."

"Great," said Karen, who spent more time than she should examining her face for the first lines. "But I have no interest in Caddy Redmon other than as a story subject."

"Good for you. Not everyone can say no to him." She put her hand to her bejeweled décolleté to show that included her. "The only one of the Billionaire Boys who has stayed with his first wife is Frederick Morgan. Mercedes is still a lovely girl. She used to be a dancer."

Karen asked, "Why are the other three not here?"

"This is Caddy's charity. They each have their own, except for Dengler, who doesn't like giving money to anyone. They're so competitive. Morgan always tells people how he's descended from J.P. Morgan." Kay-Kay, more partial to Captain Morgan, finished her cocktail, then turned to the wine.

"Among the four of them, Caddy's the intellectual lightweight, right?"

Kay-Kay took a slug of wine. "Caddy is deeply shallow. But he could read from the U.S. tax code and make it sound like the Gettysburg Address."

"The tax code, huh? Do you think he cheats on his taxes?

"Why not? He cheated on all his wives."

Karen dipped the spoon into the soup again.

A roll suddenly dropped into her soup bowl. "Excuse me, madam," said the waiter behind her. "How clumsy of me." He grabbed the bowl. "I'll get you a fresh one."

"I'm not the madam; I'm just one of the girls," Karen said. "Don't worry about the roll. I can still eat this soup."

But the waiter, the one with the burning eyes, was walking off carrying the bowl.

"More wine, please?" Kay-Kay called after him.

Redmon touched Karen's bare arm. "How about after my speech we get out of here. I'll give you a real interview. In private."

She was tempted to answer with one of her grandmother's lines: I'd rather be dipped in dung and french-fried. Instead, Karen responded with a polite smile. "I have to get in early tonight. Let's pick this up tomorrow."

"Well, if we leave the dinner early, you can get back and have plenty of sleep."

She had to admit that his inviting baritone would probably make Queen Elizabeth weak in the knees. "My editor and I have scheduled a talk tonight after the party," she lied. Karen would sooner talk to a telemarketer this evening than to her editor.

"Your editor wouldn't mind if you missed it. I'm sure he's reasonable," Redmon purred.

Her editor, Gene Skeen, had many qualities. Reasonable wasn't one of them. "Well . . ."

The waiter put a fresh wineglass in front of Redmon, who, displeased at being interrupted, glared at him.

Holding a bottle, the waiter said, "Mr. Dengler wanted you to have this malbec before your speech, sir. He sent it over specially."

"Simon and I trade fine wines back and forth," Redmon told Karen. "I usually have just one glass before I speak, but what the hell." He gestured for the waiter to go ahead.

The waiter popped the cork and poured a half-inch of the other Billionaire Boy's wine for Redmon to taste. "Excellent," Redmon said. "Pour some for the lady."

"I'll get another glass, sir."

"I can use the old glass," Karen said. But the waiter already was retreating.

"More wine, please," Kay-Kay said.

As he got up to speak, Redmon paused and, with lips brushing Karen's ear, said, "You'll change your mind after you hear this speech."

At the podium, Redmon became a fine creature. He drank in the applause as he had the malbec, then gave a longer version of the same speech Karen had heard in the car. Only now he delivered it with stagy verve. "I have a deep and abiding love for this country."

"That's controversial," Kay-Kay murmured to Karen, who was discreetly dabbing her ear with her napkin.

"Which allows anyone to seek his fortune."

"Particularly if they have no scruples," Kay-Kay said.

"I came from nothing."

"And a lot of people have nothing left, thanks to him," Kay-Kay said.

"And look at me today."

"I'd rather not," Kay-Kay said. "Where's my wine?"

But shortly after Redmon had misquoted Henry V, Roosevelt, and Kennedy, his delivery slackened. He began slurring, worse than Kay-Kay. "And I'm running for the Senate cuz people in this state would be better off with a self-made rich guy like me. People say I'm not that smart. Well, I did pretty damn well for an idiot, right? I bet I got a helluva lot more money than you clowns. Why? I tell them what they want to hear. The guys with the Ivy League degrees, they're easy to smooth-talk into their damn graves. Doesn't matter if what I say is true."

Muttering had started in the audience. The museum director hovered near Redmon, wondering whether to stop him and how.

"And really," Redmon continued, "a lot of you out there wouldn't be sitting in those high-priced chairs except you belonged to the Lucky Sperm Club. You got your money handed to you on a silver spoon. You never faced fear of failure cuz Daddy's moo-lah always was propping you up. You don't produce anything. Indulge yourselves all day long. Bunch of useless leeches. And they say I'm not smart."

It took a drunkard's bravado. "Sit down, Caddy, you're plastered," Kay-Kay called out.

"You oughta know, you damn booze hound," Redmon bellowed at her. The director murmured to him and clutched his sleeve. Redmon shook free. "Don't touch me, you queer."

At that moment, Redmon stopped. The guests held their breath. He seemed to realize what he had been saying. He spread his hands imploringly. Shame contorted his face.

Then he folded in on himself. He grabbed his chest and hunched over. He fell hard. Redmon lay on his back and twitched. His legs flailed like a dying bug's.

Karen scrambled to his side, losing a shoe. She felt for a pulse in his neck. None. Redmon's jaw had pulled to the side in agony. Blood frothed from his mouth and nose. His eyeballs bulged and were stitched with red. She started CPR, pressed down with the heel of her hand on his chest bone. A powerful grip on her shoulders yanked her backward.

"Let me keep trying," she shouted.

Ron, who had pulled her away, kept clamping her shoulders. "Let Jimmy do it," he yelled. Jimmy knelt beside the billionaire and pumped his chest. Ziegler hovered nearby, witnessing the end of her lucrative paychecks.

Amid the cacophony of panicking guests, Danton ran for the set-up area.

"This is a catastrophe," Krapp was wailing as he wrung his hands beside the reflecting pool, his spastic eye in overdrive.

Danton slammed a fist into that twitching eye. The headwaiter collapsed into the water.

Danton met Chef Emily at the door. "What's happening?" she asked him.

"Your kid's a monster," he said and kissed her cheek before resuming running.

He should be elated. Why wasn't he happy?

Chapter Four

Louis looked repulsive: the twisted teeth, the leprous skin, the greasy ropes of unwashed hair down to his large shoulders. How great, he thought, that extreme ugliness had the same effect on people as a sudden burst of fire. When he entered the Templar Media building's lobby, the security guard, usually drowsy with boredom, gave an involuntary squeak.

Louis told the guard that he was delivering an important letter. He carried a black envelope with white-ink hand lettering.

Despite the nice June weather outside, Louis wore a long Burberry raincoat that was buttoned up. The guard, fascinated by Louis's grotesque appearance, made him display a photo I.D. The September 11 hijackers all had photo I.D. Louis signed in as Josef Stalin—the guard matched his signature to the bogus I.D. Louis got waved through. He rode the elevator up to *Profit* magazine's floor. The other people in the elevator car cringed, then pretended he didn't exist.

Louis was the only one to get off at the seventh floor. "Jesus," someone said as he left.

He approached the woman who manned the magazine's reception desk. She jumped from her chair, but managed to give him a smile. Her nameplate said ROSE. A nice person, no doubt. Louis didn't know many nice people.

"I'm here to see Frank Vere and Karen Glick," he told her.

"Are they expecting you, sir?"

"No. This is a surprise. This is about the Billionaire Boys Club. I'm from Vampyr."

Her kindly smile wavered. "Vam . . . ?"

". . . pyr." Louis's right hand slid into his raincoat pocket and, through the slit in its side, he felt the deathly cool metal of his automatic weapon.

"So he came from nowhere and simply vanished," Karen said. It was the morning after Redmon's death. She was seated in the magazine's glass-enclosed conference room with two editors: Eudell Mancuso, her boss until two weeks before, and Gene Skeen, her new superior, who had hijacked Eudell in one of his political maneuvers.

"How is that possible?" Skeen's harsh, nasal delivery made it seem that Karen was at fault for somehow not knowing. "He worked in this catering outfit for months, and no one knows zip about him?"

"Only that he gave his name as Ward Mixon,"

Karen said. "Maybe Frank will get more from his police sources."

Skeen regarded her haughtily down his long nose. "Why should Frank Vere be involved in this story? The Billionaire Boys Club has had trouble with him before. You were supposed to do a good story to show their human side. I don't know what to say about these documents that purport to show they're tax cheats. I'm skeptical—such a charge has libel suit written all over it."

Rasmussen, the copy chief known as the Razz, stood out in the newsroom on the other side of the glass, behind Skeen's back, and made monkey faces at him. Usually, Karen would find that funny. Not this morning.

"Don't you see that this is all connected somehow, the murder and the tax dodges?" Karen said. "Vampyr's letter to Redmon referred to tax cheating, so odds are there's a link."

"What about this Vampyr bunch?" Eudell asked.

"Could be anybody claiming to be Vampyr. Maybe just some nut who has nothing to do with any radical politics," Karen said. "The cops apparently aren't sure, Frank has heard. The Billionaire Boys have a lot of enemies. They've rode over lots of people on their way up. They each have round-the-clock bodyguards."

"The bodyguards didn't do Redmon much good, did they?" Eudell said.

Massaging her temples, Karen said, "They didn't expect poison. They usually expect someone with a knife or a gun." She'd had very little sleep. Alone in her bed, visions of two faces kept spooling through her mind on a diabolical continuous replay: the waiter's, alive with hate; Redmon's, dead, agonized.

Frank Vere entered the conference room, carrying a legal pad full of notes. Scrawny and gawky, he wasn't a handsome man. His Adam's apple bobbed as he spoke. But he conveyed a sense of always being in the know. "Anyone want to hear what the cops say now?"

"Tell us, honey," Eudell said. A large black woman of indeterminate age, she had a maternal affection for her reporters, Frank the star in particular.

Frank sat down at the table next to Karen. "This Mixon guy," he said, "had an elaborate fake work history in food service. Police interviews with co-workers here find that he came to New York in January and got close to Emily Bourdain, the head chef for the Met's catering service. She got him the gig with the caterers. He baby-sat for her. He kept pushing her to handle the head table, and she relented for the dinner last night. She said he was a very sweet guy." Frank pulled an eight-by-ten glossy out from under the legal pad. "This is a photo of Mixon, taken from Met surveillance cameras last night."

"Where did you get this?" Skeen demanded, as if Frank had stolen it.

Frank said, "This was e-mailed to me from a source in museum security."

Karen examined the picture. She recognized him: Mixon was a nondescript fellow with a mustache and thin hair combed neatly. But he wore a friendly smile. He was nothing like the man she'd seen, the one with the hate sparking off him.

"That's not a real smile," Karen said. "It doesn't match his eyes. His eyes look tense."

"Cause of death established?" Eudell asked.

"Redmon definitely was poisoned from the wine, but we have no word from the lab about the nature of it," Frank continued. "Whatever the substance was, it first hit him like a fast-action intoxicant—shattered his inhibitions, let him make a fool of himself." Frank paused. "The poison also was in his soup."

"In his soup?" Karen asked. She had that feeling in her spine once more, the one she'd gotten reading Redmon's threat letter from Vampyr.

"Mixon must've slipped the poison in the wine bottle after he uncorked it," Frank said. "He couldn't exactly dump it in an empty wineglass in front of Redmon. With the soup bowls, he must have placed the poisoned one at Redmon's place setting."

"Tell me about it," Karen said. "I changed places with Redmon and almost ate his soup. Mixon snatched the bowl away in time."

"So he isn't all bad," Eudell said.

Frank nodded. "He knew what he was doing. We have a lot of work to do on this story."

"Excuse me," Skeen said. "There's no *we* about this. The story belongs to Karen Glick and Karen Glick alone."

"You've got to be kidding," Eudell said.

Rolling his eyes, Skeen said, "You're surely aware of the trouble Vere got into with Frederick Morgan's wife, Mercedes? We can't afford to have him on the story."

Karen turned to Frank. "What trouble with Morgan's wife?"

Monte the mail boy opened the conference room door. "Man out front to see you, Frank and Karen. Uh-huh." A dimwitted if sweet middle-aged man, Monte was part of Templar Media's program to hire the handicapped. Monte's mail cart, which he proudly rolled around the newsroom each morning, was outside.

"This is a meeting," Skeen barked at him. "Get out of here."

First passing his hand over his bald head, Monte said, "Miss Rose out front called both your desks, Karen and Frank. But you weren't there. Uh-huh." He spoke to Skeen. "This man, he says he's a vampire. Uh-huh. Miss Rose wanted me to find you, Karen and Frank."

Frank and Karen exchanged a look. "Vampyr?" Frank said.

"We should talk to this character," Karen said.

Eudell stood. "I'm gonna alert building security. How'd he get up to our floor? We can talk to him, but these people are dangerous." She grabbed the phone on the conference table.

Frank, first to spot everything, said, "Well, he got into the newsroom."

One of the ugliest men Karen had ever seen this side of a horror movie was barreling across the cubicle-filled newsroom. A large guy, he wore a long raincoat and a weird expression. People recoiled as he passed. The Razz did a triple take.

The visitor from Vampyr shouldered past Monte

and strode into the conference room. "Hello," he said through hideous teeth.

"You will have to remain waiting in the reception area until we're ready to receive you," Skeen said. "No one is allowed in this newsroom without authorization."

The Vampyr man opened his raincoat, with a flasher's shameless panache, to reveal his intense-looking gun. "Here's my authorization."

For Karen, the world became a slow place of underwater motion. People's mouths elongated to form words. Sound rolled forth as from a foghorn. The mortal thump of her heart was the loudest noise. Her mouth had never been this dry. She doubted she could speak.

Eudell spoke first, with the outraged cadence of a dauntless soul used to facing down bad people. "What the hell do you think you're doing? You get out of my newsroom, hear?"

The Vampyr ignored her. He shucked his raincoat onto a chair, then removed the wicked weapon that rode in a holster around his waist. "A Tec-9," he said. "It's really good at killing a lot of people at once."

He thrust the gun muzzle at Skeen's face and Skeen jerked backward so violently he fell off his chair. The Vampyr laughed at him. "Get back in your seat."

Skeen whimpered and obeyed.

Karen noticed that, inexplicably, the Vampyr wore fashionable blue jeans—Jejunes, the label of hip-hop artist LaZee Boy, who hadn't recorded in a while but was always in the society pages with some hot young babe. The Jejune brand had distinctive gold-thread stitching and cost enough to mount a minor insurrection.

Bill McIntyre, the editor-in-chief, appeared at the door of the conference room. The staffers throughout the floor had stopped their work and were watching, unsure what had happened. Monte hovered just outside the door, looking troubled but as clueless as the people out of earshot.

"Mr. McIntyre," the Vampyr said. "You served in Vietnam. You know about guns. You can recognize this."

McIntyre, a Southern newsman of the old school, always radiated the joking unflappability of someone who had weathered much. Except for today. His hand was on his fringe of white beard. "What do you want?"

"A Tec-9," the Vampyr said. "I can take out a few dozen of you in no time with it. Nothing like a mass killing. You'll make the news, not just report it." He spoke through those nasty teeth with the intensity of man on a sacred mission.

"What do you want?" Bill repeated with more vehemence.

The Vampyr pulled a black envelope from the rear pocket of his blue jeans. "For you to deliver a letter. This is to the next Billionaire Boy on our list."

Plucking the letter from him, Bill said, "Okay, I got your letter. Now why don't you just get on out of here?"

"No," the Vampyr said. "That's what *you're* going to

do. You're going to evacuate this entire floor. And if you don't do it in five minutes . . ." He waggled the gun.

Calvin Christian, the managing editor, had wandered up to the door. The magazine's second-in-command, he was Skeen's mentor and wore a bow tie. Witnessing the threat, Christian emitted a yelp and almost knocked over poor Monte in his haste to flee. The puzzled staffers outside swiveled their heads to watch him sprint for the fire stairwell.

Bill made a sweeping gesture to take in his people in the conference room. "I'm taking them with me."

The Vampyr shook his head and his greasy hair swayed. "No, the woman of color"—he indicated Eudell—"will go with you. The other three stay."

"Listen to me, you," Eudell said, "I go nowhere without the others. They stay, I stay."

The staffers outside had begun to move closer. They muttered among themselves. Karen heard someone say, "Get security."

The Vampyr swept the gun arund him, pointing at the newsroom. "You stupid woman. I will pull this trigger and everyone will die." He eased back from her defiant face and said to Bill, "You just wasted thirty seconds."

Bill stepped over to Eudell, took her by her fleshy arm, and said, "Come on, Eudell. I want you out of here."

As they passed the Vampyr, Eudell said to him, "You hurt my two reporters and I'll hunt you down in hell. You hear me, boy?"

Bill shouted out to the staff: "I want everyone to move for the fire exits. Right now. Move quickly, but don't run. I want no one hurt."

The people shifted from one foot to the other, unsure that this bizarre order made any sense. Journalists don't take orders easily.

"This man has a gun," Bill declared. "Do what I say. Now."

Everyone began to move.

Mike Riley, who always advertised himself as brave at cards and cowardly at all else, asked loudly, "What about Karen and Frank?"

Skeen leaned across the conference table and waved a hand to get the Vampyr's attention. "What about me? Can I go, too?"

"Shut up," the Vampyr said, more interested in the evacuation.

As Bill shepherded them out, people looked back over their shoulders at the glassed-in conference room. Wendy, her parrot perched as always on her shoulder, was crying.

Frank, whose eyes had never left the Vampyr, now shifted them over to Monte. The mail boy was still standing at the door uncertainly while the crowd walked toward the exits.

"Monte," Frank said, "you go with the others."

"Can I take my mail cart, Frank? Uh-huh."

Skeen slumped in his chair.

"Take your mail cart, Monte." Frank remained calm. He watched Monte trundle off with his precious cart. Then Frank resumed his scrutiny of the gunman.

The Vampyr nodded with satisfaction as the last

back disappeared through the exits. "Now, let's talk about what's truly important—death and taxes."

Karen's thoughts wafted to her friends. How they had such wonderful times together, cooking, drinking, laughing. Most summer weekends found them in Mike's Hampton Bays house, which he had won in a card game. They prepared great feasts, the women in the kitchen, the men outside around the grill except for Frank, a superb pastry chef, who was with the girls making dessert. The summer breeze carried the smell of barbecue. Out in the blue hour.

"The only things that are inevitable," the Vampyr was saying. He marched back and forth as might a professor in a lecture hall. "Death and taxes. Karl Marx said that."

Karen wanted to interrupt and say that Benjamin Franklin had said it. But her tongue lay paralyzed in her mouth. Oddly, she wondered if misquoting had become an epidemic.

The Vampyr ranted on. "Do you know what taxes do? They take from the rich and give to the poor. At least that's what they should do. But the rich get so obscenely swollen from their greed that they think they can shirk that responsibility. They hide their wealth on exploited Caribbean islands. And that needs to be punished."

"By death?" asked Frank, his attention never straying from the gunman.

"You in the news media," the Vampyr said, "are the handmaidens of the rich. America is a corrupt society that is out to despoil the world. The top one percent of the country owns ninety percent of the assets—and doesn't care if everyone else starves. So, yes, America's tax-cheating overlords deserve death."

The phone rang.

Karen was the closest. "Do you want me to answer?" she found herself saying.

"Go ahead," the gunman answered.

The guy on the other end of the line spoke in the studied, assured manner of a TV parent in the 1950s, the same sort of locution that Karen's mother adopted with her counseling patients. "This is Lieutenant McDonald. I understand we have some trouble. Could I please speak to the person who is threatening you?"

"That was quick," Frank said.

"It's for you," Karen said and held out the receiver to the person who was threatening her. "Lieutenant McDonald."

The Vampyr snatched it from her. "I'm from Vampyr, pig," he shouted into the phone. "No . . . No . . . No . . . You listen to me, or I'll kill them all. You stay away from this floor. If I so much as smell one of you coming onto this floor, I open fire. Got that?" He handed the receiver back to Karen. "Disconnect it. I no longer wish to talk to him."

Karen pulled the alligator clips from both the receiver cord and the feed line out of the phone's body.

"Now," the Vampyr said with malicious zest. "Let's ask an important question." He moved over to Skeen, who bowed his head. "Since you want to go so much. Tell me, Mr. Editor, what would you do for me if I did let you go? Hmmmmm?"

Skeen, expression swirling with hope and desperation, head jerking nervously, gazed up at the Vampyr. "I'd carry your message to the public. I'd print how the rich exploit the masses. I'd educate the people about how they're exploited."

"Would you worship me? On your knees?"

"On my knees. Whatever you say. Please."

"How nice." He moved over to Karen. "What about you?"

"I'm not playing your game," she said.

"Oh, you will." The gunman caressed her cheek and she pulled her head away.

Frank jumped to his feet. "Get your hands off her."

"I'll return to you in a moment," the Vampyr said to Karen. "On to capitalism's great reporter, Frank Vere."

Frank stayed standing and did what a great reporter does. He asked questions. "Who is Ward Mixon? He one of yours?"

"This isn't an interview," the Vampyr said with menace.

"Explosives and guns are your style. Poison is not. Why use poison on Redmon?"

"Sit down."

Frank didn't. "Why target the Billionaire Boys Club?"

"Isn't that obvious? They amass obscene wealth exploiting the working classes, who get laid off when these snakes take over a company and do their foul downsizing." He was shouting now and breathing heavily. "Didn't I tell you to sit down?"

Frank didn't budge. "Why are you wearing that makeup?"

The Vampyr's eyes widened.

"Someone did an elaborate makeup job on your face. Very convincing. Made you look horrible. The bad teeth are fake, too. The wig, at least, looks almost natural."

The gunman was about to roar his wrath at Frank when Karen sailed out of her chair.

She smacked the Vampyr's head hard with the phone receiver.

Karen stood gaping, gripping the receiver hard. Her mother, the pacifist, had taught her that violence solved nothing. This time, Karen had to disagree.

The Vampyr swayed to and fro, a tree in a small breeze. His eyes were crossed. His mouth had formed an "o." His hand still held the gun, finger on the trigger.

"Hoo," was the noise that came from his mouth. Was he introspectively asking who he was, this man willing to commit murder in the name of his wacky cause?

The finger tightened on the gun, which swept back and forth among his hostages.

"Hoo," he repeated. Was he asking who was responsible for this pain in his skull?

The trigger drew back.

"Hoo," he uttered again. Was he asking who wanted to die?

The gun stopped moving and settled on aiming at Frank.

Karen reared back to club him again with the phone receiver.

A gust of breath escaped from his mouth in a rush. He toppled over sideways and hit the floor with a muffled thump. His limbs were sprawled every which way. The gun lay by itself on the brown carpeting, a foot away from his limp hand.

Acting as one, Karen and Frank jumped on the Vampyr. Karen grabbed the weapon.

Frank began patting down the Vampyr. "Let's make sure he has no other weapons. Go through his raincoat."

The raincoat had a plaid lining and just two pockets. Karen felt a small lump in one. She stuck her hand inside.

"Car keys." She put the Tec-9 in a drawer of a storage cabinet.

"I'm getting out of here," Skeen said and bolted for the door.

"The danger's past," Frank called to the editor. He had found nothing in the gunman's jeans or work shirt. Not even a wallet.

Skeen stopped at the conference room door, then turned around. His hands and chin trembled. "How can you be sure?" he said to Frank. "What if he has others nearby?"

"Doubtful," Frank said. "We need to call the cops. First, let's find a way to tie him up." He turned to look at the fallen radical on the carpet.

"I think I broke the phone receiver," Karen said. "We better use another phone."

The Vampyr surged to his feet. With arms held in front, football lineman-style, he launched himself at Frank and knocked him out of the way. The gunman powered through the door past Skeen, who recoiled and screamed with the intensity of a coed in a slasher movie.

"Get him," Karen shouted.

Frank regained his balance and ran after the Vampyr, with Karen right behind.

Greasy locks streaming after him, the Vampyr ran down the aisle between the blocks of cubicles. When he reached an open area, where morning light blasted in from the windows, two sounds rent the processed air: a small crack and a rapid zip.

The Vampyr hollered and cartwheeled in the air. He flopped on the floor.

Frank skidded to a stop at the last partition before the open area, and Karen almost collided with him.

She scooted around Frank. "What's the matter?"

He grabbed her hand to prevent her from going forward. "Sniper round. SWAT team."

The Vampyr was down, panting. He had a red streak across his cheek. Slowly, eyes hooded beneath brow, locks dangling, he fixed the two reporters with a boiling stare.

"Why did you come here to deliver that letter?" Frank asked the Vampyr. "You sent the one to Redmon in the mail."

The Vampyr snarled at them. "You're supposed to be so smart? I'm doing this at a big magazine. Duh."

"You thought you could get publicity for your cause?" Frank said.

Touching the bloody crease the bullet had left in his cheek, the Vampyr said nothing.

"Ward Mixon?"

The Vampyr smiled with those unlovely and phony teeth, but did not answer.

The calm and rhythm of Frank's relentless questioning had calmed Karen. She asked one of her own. "Would you actually have shot us?"

"That would've been fun, wouldn't it?" the Vampyr said through the horrible teeth.

With that, he rolled onto all fours and started crawling rapidly for the fire exit.

Karen began crawling after him, but Frank grabbed her around the waist. "Christ, Frank," she shouted. "We can't let this bastard go free."

"If we're out in the open, the SWATs might shoot us. There's no telling what angles they have. He might not make it to the exit. We're better off calling 911 and telling them what he is doing. If he gets to the fire stairs, let's hope the cops can bag him when he reaches the lobby."

As Frank ducked into the nearest cubicle to call the cops, she watched the fast-crawling Vampyr's butt, with its Jejune golden stitching, sway across the carpeting. He reached the exit unscathed. Then he opened the door and disappeared into the fire stairs.

"Tell me he's not going to get away," she said.

"He might," said Frank, who had been put on hold by 911.

Chapter Five

Louis leaned against the thick fire door, lungs hot from exertion. His cheek stung from the bullet's graze. His head ached from where Karen Glick had clouted him.

He was in a short cinderblock corridor that led to the escape stairway. Monte's mail cart sat untended, since it couldn't be bumped down the fire stairs. A crowd of people was clumping downward, but they weren't looking in his direction. They'd gotten word to evacuate the building, but didn't know the threat was on the seventh floor.

He positioned Monte's mail cart sideways, so it blocked the door to the magazine's offices. He turned his back to the crowd and began tearing at the rubbery substance covering his face. As planned, it peeled free easily. He did the same to the wig, which was pasted to his close-cropped head. Then he wiggled off the upper and lower mouthpieces holding his fright teeth. The rubber face, the wig, and the mouth-pieces went down the front of his shirt. He kept the plastic coating on his fingers and thumbs, meant to stop the cops from lifting his prints.

Louis had been warned how sharp Vere was. The one he had underestimated was Glick. She was only about five-foot-four. She wrote fluff for the magazine. At the sight of the gun, she acted like your typical girl. And then somehow she had summoned the gumption to clobber him.

He scuttled along the corridor and joined the throng. They were taut-faced but not panicking. Louis pushed his way past them, drawing protests of: "Hey, keep this orderly" and "Watch out, asshole" and "Who do you think you are?"

Bursting into the lobby, Louis saw platoons of cops moving across the floor. Red lights flashed menacingly out on the street. Luckily, the law hadn't yet set up a checkpoint to screen people coming out of the stairwells.

Louis piled out onto the sidewalk with the herd. The area was alive with stern cops and frazzled office workers. He recognized a few of the staffers from *Profit*; they didn't notice him.

Edward Danton recognized Louis. He watched Louis vanish into the tension-jazzed morning, a wisp of a bad memory.

Danton pulled out the age-cracked photo of Mercedes that he carried in his pocket. As a dance student long ago at NYU, she already had a penchant for the Frederick Morgans of the world. She had preferred rich boys with confident, money-honey voices and good, crisp shirts. So that is what Danton set out to be. He had loved Mercedes even before she knew his name. Unfortunately, his father, as always, disapproved.

Returning Mercedes's picture to his pocket, Danton grimaced at the memory of asking his father for $10,000 to invest in a real estate venture outside Phoenix. An older New York University alumnus named Chris Abbott had assembled a large land tract to build homes for Northern refugees in the booming Sunbelt and was gathering investors. Edward made his pitch to his father as they sat next to the fountain in Washington Square Park, a week before Edward's NYU graduation. "James," he told his father, "you'll be investing with Edward Danton, land baron."

"Barren land is more like it," said James, an unhappily widowed English professor who preferred that his son enter academia. "And all to impress this young lady with the same name as an over-priced car."

James had denied his son's request, saying academics lived in "genteel poverty" and questioning Edward's values. Chris Abbott ended up in jail after the land tract turned out to be a half-acre toxic-waste site and his plan a big Ponzi scheme.

"Genteel poverty, my ass," Edward said. He now was rich beyond the point of gentility.

"Honey, you are one ferocious woman," Eudell said.

All Karen's friends were gathered around her: Eudell and Mike and Wendy and the Razz and the others. It was like being back in the summer house after they had won a softball game.

A lowdown Calvin Christian, bow tie askew, slunk back onto the floor and spoke to a few trusted flunkies before closeting himself in his office. His story was that he had run to alert the authorities; of course, he could only do that after safely reaching the building's lobby. People cracked jokes at Christian's expense. "Calvin is celebrating his heroism with a good Australian wine tonight," someone said. "Yellowtail."

Gene Skeen stayed out of sight, as well. After giving his statement to the cops, who had commandeered the conference room, he had chugged a Prozac and left the building, bound for the emergency care of his latest therapist (he changed frequently). Karen later learned that his story outdid Christian's: Skeen had stalwartly told the gunman to get out of the newsroom and had pledged to carry the Vampyr message to the world only in the spirit of defiant sarcasm.

Frank came out of the conference room, where the cops were taking statements, and told Karen she was next. "This cop session will interest you," he said. "You know one of them."

"Me? You're the one who knows all the cops." Then she entered the conference room.

Marcia Fink, a solid lump of no-nonsense law enforcement, sat at the head of the table, where Skeen had previously positioned himself. She had one other detective on each side. Male detectives. She was very much in charge.

Karen lit up. "Marcia. How are you? God, it's been years."

Unsmiling, Marcia Fink rose to ever so briefly shake Karen's hand, thus preventing a hug. The two men cops narrowed their eyes. One seemed to smile fleetingly.

"Good to see you, I'm sure," said Marcia, unfazed by Karen's display of girlish camaraderie. She spoke with the same slow, wise-ass New York accent she had as a teenager. "Have a seat. We got a few questions." A checkout clerk at Rite Aid showed more warmth.

Chastened, Karen sat in the chair she'd occupied earlier. She noticed that the cabinet was open and the Tec-9 mercifully gone.

Marcia asked her a series of questions. The subordinate detectives recorded the session on a Sony and took notes. Again and again, Karen showed how she had clubbed the Vampyr with the phone receiver. Marcia behaved almost as if Karen were the gunman. "Ms. Glick, why did the gunman choose *this* magazine?"

In high school, they were friends. Marcia had taught Karen how to box at a Jackson Heights gym where her brothers sparred. Karen's parents didn't approve of Marcia or her father, an Archie Bunker conservative and a cop. After high school, Karen had lost track of her. Now, a dozen years on, little had changed with Marcia. Other than the wedding band on her ring finger.

Ms. Glick, was it? "Well, Detective Fink, I guess he was here to make a big, big point and get publicity. To get attention, he wore a disguise as the ugliest man this side of my senior prom date. Whom you may remember."

Benny Slatz, a neighbor who went to their school, had asked Karen to the prom. It was hellish, and college-bound Karen didn't want to see him again. Then she caught Benny, who lived across the courtyard of their apartment building at the time, watching her bedroom through binoculars. When Karen had confronted him about that, he contended he was birdwatching. At night. In Manhattan.

"And what point is that, Ms. Glick?"

"To show that indeed it was Vampyr going after the Billionaire Boys Club. Anyone could have sent the threat letter to Redmon by snail mail."

"Indeed." Marcia drew out the word. "But how can you be sure the gunman was from Vampyr? Did he flash his membership card?"

"He delivered the same black-envelope, white-inked letter that Caddy Redmon got."

After Marcia curtly dismissed her, Karen headed for the long line of staffers waiting to be fingerprinted. As she stood there, she felt a hand on her shoulder. It was Marcia, now sporting a wry expression. "Hey, Karen. Sorry if I was hard on you. I'm in cop mode today."

"Jesus, Marcia, you acted like you wanted me to confess to grand theft auto. Pardon me. I was just in old-friend mode."

"I'm a cop, you're a journalist. What can I tell you? We aren't friends with reporters."

"What's this two different worlds crap? Frank Vere is friends with lots of cops. When he was a newspaper reporter and covered police, he kept three cops out of jail. He proved them wrongly accused of corruption."

Marcia said, "Yeah, Vere should be a detective."

Some truce had been established between them. "Let me be a detective for a moment. You're married."

For an instant, Marcia held up her ring hand. "Two years. Sean Harrigan, another cop. He's up in the Bronx, working narcotics. My mother said I shouldn't be marrying an Irish guy. Like we're observant, right? My father doesn't care as long as he's a cop."

"How are your folks?"

"In Florida. It's the law. I'm not gonna ask how yours are. They didn't like me." Before Karen could issue a ritual denial, Marcia said, "Sorry about your marriage. I heard."

"Four years. To a WASP Wall Street guy. And my family makes non-observant look positively Hasidic. My father really disliked him. Tim is more Republican than my grandmother." Masses of cops were milling through the newsroom. "I didn't see you among the detectives who took my statement last night at the Met," Karen added.

"This is getting to be a habit with you, the statement business. Yeah, I only today drew the primary spot on this case. Big feather in my cap. Poppa is pleased."

Karen nodded. "Marcia, may I call you as the case develops? I'm working an investigative story on the Billionaire Boys. I need a good police source."

With a bark of a laugh, Marcia said, "No chance. I don't play that." She dug into her pocket and produced a card. "You hear anything, you call me. Okay?" Another bark of a laugh. "You still box?"

"Since I got my new editor," Karen said, "I climb into the ring on this floor every day."

"You never had a high tolerance for assholes. You almost smashed Benny Slatz's face for the Peeping Tom routine."

"My editor, like Benny, is a proctologist's delight." Karen summoned a smile for her old friend. "I'm glad you're doing well. Detective. Wow."

"And you," Marcia said. "Investigative reporter. Double wow."

"Well . . ." Karen began. Then, "Yeah, me, the investigative reporter."

As she crossed the newsroom and savored the notion, her step quickened. "Investigative reporter." When Karen reached her cubicle, she checked out Marcia's card. It contained Marcia's home number. Cops never gave out their home numbers.

Frank, busy on the phone with his multitudes of sources, was in the next cube. Such was the democratic ethos of the newsroom: only editors had offices, and these were glass-fronted, allowing the reporters to watch management scratch themselves in unappetizing places. A celebrated investigative reporter like Frank, recipient of a Pulitzer Prize, Loeb Award, and National Magazine Award, merited the same Dilbert-style treatment as Karen.

Between calls, he told Karen that they should have lunch and compare notes. Eudell had told him they'd continue their meeting at 1:30, whether Skeen resurfaced from therapy or not.

She thought about Marcia's last remark. Women seldom did investigative work. It wasn't Roberta Woodward and Carla Bernstein who broke Watergate.

Chapter Six

The Vampyr letter, actually a copy of it, lay on the table in its sinister splendor. Where could you buy black paper and white ink? Was the gunman the calligrapher? Frank had scored the copy, of course, from one of his police sources.

"It's to Simon Dengler," Frank said as he sipped his latte. They were sitting in Brew-Ha-Ha, the high-priced coffee joint a block from the office. The lunchtime crowd surged and rumbled around them. "He's next. Vampyr seems to be taking them in order of where they appear in the firm's name."

"That's how I've done it. Dengler is next on my list to interview.

Karen perused the letter, and tried to act calm about it.

Dear Billionaire Boy: By now, you understand we mean what we say. Taxes are a joke to you. You worship money and hoard it, then wipe your feet on good, honest folk who need it.

Every dollar you steal is one less dollar available to save a starving child or clean up pollution or develop solar energy. Your death is at hand. We are doing the world a favor.

"Signed Vampyr." Karen slid the paper back toward Frank. "Another reference to not paying taxes. Then it gets personal. Redmon's letter mentioned his narcissism and his womanizing. In Dengler's, there's 'wipe your feet on good honest folk.' Simon Dengler is a real mean guy, isn't he?"

"Yeah. Caddy Redmon liked to brag about his humble beginnings, but Dengler literally grew up in poverty. The 'hoarding' line in this letter is telling. The Boys are classic greedheads. But Dengler is the worst. He's a world-class skinflint. I mean, he usually doesn't tip in restaurants." Frank gestured out the Brew-Ha-Ha plateglass window to the Starbucks down the street. "Two years ago, when I was interviewing the Billionaire Boys, I went into a Starbucks with Dengler. He looked at the menu board and asked for a small coffee."

"Starbucks doesn't have a small, medium, or large. They have tall, grande, or venti."

"Right," Frank said. "That's what the snotty barista told Dengler. So Dengler ordered a tall coffee. The snotty kid behind the counter made a show of nudging the tip jar in Dengler's direction. Dengler put a penny in and the kid squawked. Dengler says, 'You just got a 'tall' tip."

"Nasty guy. How do we go about this? Where do we start?"

Frank took a bite of sandwich. "Assuming the Billionaire Boys will let you keep pursuing the story, you should get inside and learn as much as you can. I don't quite grasp why Vampyr has chosen these particular rich guys. And how Vampyr knows they avoid taxes."

"The very rich all have smart lawyers to minimize or eliminate the tax bite. But not to the degree the Boys do it. As in illegal. Could my box of documents be from Vampyr?"

"Possible. Yet how would they gain access to the documents? I imagine learning the President's missile launch codes would be easier."

"They knew how to infiltrate the Met's caterer," Karen said. "For us, as we've said, the trick is to authenticate the documents. How do we do that?"

"This morning, a handwriting expert—a good friend of mine—matched the signatures on the tax returns to those of each of the Billionaire Boys. So those are their bona fide returns. Now the challenge is to ensure that the bank statements are real."

"How do we do this? Talk about missile launch codes. The Caymans is into super-, ultra-, heavy-duty secrecy about their bank clients."

"I have a few contacts I'm working."

A few contacts. Naturally, Frank always had a few contacts. "Jesus, Frank, the only confidential source I have is my butcher. He tells me when the meat is fresh and when it isn't."

Frank chomped his sandwich. "Let's review what we know about Vampyr."

"We know jack is what we know."

Frank shook his head in disagreement. "The gunman's disguise was top-rate. Better than in the movies. That costs money."

"I guess," Karen said. "Or maybe they have a makeup artist working for Vampyr."

"The cops are checking Broadway makeup types. Also, Vampyr's intelligence work is superb. The gunman knew exactly where he was going when he walked into our newsroom. He knew we were in the conference room, where that was, what we looked like. Rose didn't tell him. Nor did Joe Blintz, who had just carded open the door when the gunman shoved past."

"Poor Joe. He feels bad."

"Vampyr is a rag-tag organization where people sleep on the floor in hovels with the law after them. But they've somehow come into money," Frank went on. "The gunman was wearing a new Burberry, which would run him around $500. The Jejune blue jeans, $200. And the car keys had a prancing horse logo—they were to a Ferrari, which can cost as much as a house. For a revolutionary, he sure likes capitalist consumer goods."

"Nothing is as hip as hypocrisy. Maybe the gunman has indulgent rich parents."

"He didn't strike me as the jaded rich type," Frank said. "More like a hardened criminal. Too much rage inside."

Karen needed to ask a difficult question. It concerned a woman.

Frank, for all his fine qualities, had one big weakness. A straight, single, solvent man in Manhattan should be in major demand. Especially one with a measure of renown. Not Frank. First, he wasn't exactly handsome. Worse, Frank, otherwise as observant as an atomic microscope, had an enormous capacity to misperceive women. Recently, he had flipped over a pretty lawyer named Amanda. They'd gone out twice. When he asked to see her the following weekend, she had said she had to go out of town but would return that Sunday night. There was a hint they might see each other then. With a bouquet, Frank had waited outside her building. When Amanda returned with the guy she'd spent the weekend with, it had been painful.

Karen asked the question. "Frank, what happened between you and Morgan's wife?"

Frank froze. Then he stood up suddenly. "I'm not talking about Mercedes." Karen never had seen Frank angry.

They trudged back to work in silence. In front of the Templar Media Building, an array of cameras and reporters awaited them. Frank and Karen knew many of the people. Unlike in movies, the reporters here weren't a crazed, screaming mob. Separately, Frank and Karen answered a series of polite questions.

At the end, a famous network TV blonde named Cassie Milton sidled up to Karen and said, "You are such a gutsy woman."

Karen didn't know high-level TV types like Cassie very well. "I was probably foolish."

Cassie gave Karen the winning smile that kept viewers from switching channels between diaper ads.

"You're my hero. And God, so is Frank Vere. I'm in awe of his body of work—the bad guys he has sent to jail, the good guys he has gotten justice for."

"Why don't you ask him out? He's between girlfriends."

Cassie's smile faded.

Frank had already gone inside. When Karen entered the newsroom, she steered for the conference room, bracing for another bout with Gene Skeen.

As Karen entered the conference room, she saw Frank and Eudell. No Gene Skeen.

"Gene is going to take some time off," Eudell announced. "You're back to me."

Karen let out a small cheer. "Great news."

Oddly, Frank and Eudell looked as if they had both received terminal diagnoses.

"What's the matter?" Karen asked.

"I've talked this over with Bill," Eudell said. "You and you alone are on the Billionaire Boys Club story."

"What? What about Frank? We have to track down those bank statements to the Caymans to ensure they are real. Then we bang the Boys for tax fraud."

Eudell leaned over the table toward her. "Wrong, honey. Frank is to have nothing—and let me stress that, *nothing*—to do with this story."

"What are you talking about?"

Eudell produced a large, glossy photo from an envelope next to her. "Taken two years ago. By someone connected to the Billionaire Boys. If we'd printed a story by Frank about them, they'd have had a good libel case against us."

The photo showed Frank kissing a woman, passionately. His arms were around her. Her left hand was ruffling his hair. She was slender, pretty, and tall, about five-nine.

"That woman," Eudell said, "is Mercedes Morgan. It was taken when Frank was investigating the RDS&M buyout firm. It raises questions about his objectivity."

Karen turned to Frank. He met her eyes, then lowered his gaze to his lap.

"Now," Eudell said to Karen, "if you can nail the Billionaire Boys on tax fraud, fine. If not, we have a personality piece on how they are coping with this tragedy, where one of their partners was murdered."

"But without Frank . . ." Karen spread her hands for him. "Frank, maybe you can give me those contacts you had who can authenticate the Caymans bank documents."

"They'll only talk to me," Frank said, barely above a whisper.

"What the hell happened between you and Morgan's wife?"

He hung his head. "No, I didn't sleep with her, although the picture suggests that. I don't understand her relationship with her husband. When I was reporting the story, she called and asked to meet me, to tell me the good side of her husband's firm. The charity work, that kind of stuff. But she ended up telling me all her frustrations. She is a deeply unhappy woman. Her son means the world to her. Her husband? I'm not sure. Outside the bar, we sort of . . . fell into this kiss. Then she ran away." He got up and walked out.

"Eudell," Karen said, "I'm going to dig until I get to the bottom of the Billionaire Boys' tax evasion."

"Honey, I love you," Eudell said and patted her arm. "But you're good at the nice little personality pieces. You are no investigative reporter. You are not Frank Vere."

Stung, Karen stepped back. "Eudell, you watch me."

Chapter Seven

The leveraged buyout firm of Redmon, Dengler, Strongville & Morgan occupied a mansion built on the Upper East Side in 1895 by Ignatius Ludlum, the robber baron who ran Ludlum Iron Works with the compassion of Vlad the Impaler. Folk songs had been written about the vicious beatings his goons had meted out to union organizers. Ludlum felt his efforts were justified and ennobling because they helped build—as he put it, in a letter to one of his illegitimate children—"the God-given blessing of the American system that has shone its grace on me."

A like-minded Frederick Morgan had studied the lore about Ignatius Ludlum. About his will, his cunning, his courage. Morgan ignored the old tycoon's eccentricities late in life.

The elderly Ludlum liked to stroll down Fifth Avenue holding animated debates with imaginary union organizers. He had a mural commissioned for

Ludlum House's Great Hall, depicting his goons' most bloody anti-union head-cracking session, the infamous Stomcox Massacre. At one point, he supposedly turned to witchcraft and paid for curses to fall upon labor leader Eugene V. Debs. This may have backfired. He had died suddenly and mysteriously in 1925, a year before Debs; someone supposedly had hacked Ludlum's heart out of his chest. According to legend, Ludlum's ghost still walked the halls of his mansion as he searched for his missing heart and argued the perils of unionism.

Frederick Morgan, who had engineered the purchase of Ludlum House for RDS&M, never told others about the bizarre side of the old rascal's reputation. He preferred regaling people with how his great-grandfather, J.P. Morgan, had financed Ludlum Iron Works and made it an industrial powerhouse. In their prime, J.P. and Ignatius had enjoyed each other's company, spending hours together shooting birds, playing golf, and swapping filthy jokes.

Ludlum House featured twenty-five rooms, a series of spooky gables, leaded glass windows and an entry canopy designed by Louis Tiffany, carved oak wainscoting, and frilly plasterwork. Security cameras and motion sensors were ever-present and well hidden. Frederick Morgan had festooned Ludlum House with paintings of J.P. in his scowling, mustached glory and of Ignatius with his display of sideburns. The only old art Morgan didn't want in the place was the Stomcox Massacre mural, which Strongville blocked him from selling to a Russian oligarch.

Seated at the vast desk where J.P. once had controlled much of the world's economic fate, Frederick Morgan was talking on the phone with his social secretary. "And did Mrs. Morgan like the flowers?" This was the anniversary of their first date.

"Yes, sir. They're in the conservatory. She adored them." Miranda, the social secretary, had reminded him of the anniversary, one of those occasions that he used to remember himself before he got so busy and could afford to hire others to take care of little things.

"I called her, but she didn't return—"

"Mrs. Morgan was busy with the contractor all day, sir."

"I guess." The odd part about being rich was how people would spare nothing to please you and lie with abandon. "I'm glad. Tell her I will be late. We have a partners' meeting."

"You may recall she is at Lincoln Center tonight for the gala. She took Bert."

Thanks to her husband's largesse, Mercedes sat on the board of Lincoln Center. She was a particular patron of the Juilliard School's dance program at Lincoln Center, which had rejected her for admission a quarter-century ago.

"With Caddy's death," Morgan said, "we have a lot to discuss. We have to—"

Miranda choked at the mention of Caddy. " "I understand, sir," she managed to say.

Morgan hung up and sat there trying to compose himself for the meeting. Today, Morgan had to struggle to project his usual smoothness and charm. He tried thinking of the statue he had commissioned of J.P. Morgan.

A soft upper-class English accent came over the intercom. "The others are assembled, sir." Morgan insisted his secretaries be British and work late. Fiona was as British as Sunday treacle and she never slept, judging by the owl-like circles beneath her eyes.

Morgan went out his ornately carved office door. His two bodyguards, Al and George Jr., fell in behind him. "I don't know how long we'll be, guys," he told them. Like a good patrician should, Morgan believed in seeming concerned about the help, even if he really wasn't.

A janitor was wheeling a barrel with a mop in it. "You want I should clean up your office, Mr. M.?" He wore a photo I.D. RDS&M's security vetted even the lowliest employee.

"Sure, Pasha. But clear it with Fiona first. She gets territorial."

"I cleaned Mr. Redmon's office good."

Morgan hesitated at the mention of Caddy's empty office. Then he and his entourage crossed the Great Hall, past the gruesome mural of the Stomcox Massacre. George Jr. threw open the huge baronial doors to the conference room of what had become the nation's premier leveraged buyout firm. Redmon, Dengler, Strongville & Morgan amassed billions from large investors like pension plans and insurers, then bought a controlling interest in promising companies (known in buyout parlance as "targets") that they made more valuable. Later, with the stock up, they sold it and reaped a fortune that would make Ludlum's ghost weep with envy.

The bodyguard closed the massive doors behind him and sealed them inside. Pretending all was well, Morgan asked, "I hope I didn't keep you waiting, you scamps."

By turns jocular and courtly, Morgan was first among equals at RDS&M. He led the discussions on what companies to buy, spearheaded the strategy, and kept the big investors happy, especially when a target company whined to the press about being pressured. The Billionaire Boys Club preferred that a company agree to be bought out. If it unwisely resisted, the buyout firm attacked with all the subtlety of the Wehrmacht entering France. The Boys offered a target's shareholders princely sums to surrender their stock to RDS&M and thus present management with a humiliating fait accompli.

"That's fine, Frederick," Simon Dengler said. "Maybe we can dock your pay." Dengler figured out the elaborate financial structures of deals—how much to bid for a company, where the capital would come from, which Byzantine tax tactics to employ to lessen the bite on RDS&M and its investors.

"Let's move this along," Butch Strongville growled. "I want to mourn Caddy, but in my own way—out of here." Strongville did the hard-headed final negotiations with target companies, using a combination of eyeball-to-eyeball intimidation, fist-under-nose threats, and bellowed demands to push through RDS&M's unswerving agenda. Those on the other side usually caved under his onslaught.

One vacant chair sat off by the side, belonging to Caddy Redmon. Morgan had planned on assuming

Redmon's duties anyway, expecting Caddy was going to the Senate. When RDS&M targeted a company, the chief executive officer got a Redmon PowerPoint presentation aimed at making him think he had been granted eternal life at God's right hand.

The Billionaire Boys usually promised a CEO he would be left in place after the takeover, and that a future of lush bonuses and stratospheric salary increases were guaranteed to him. But what actually lay ahead for the CEO, once the deal went down, was a brace of security guards escorting him from the premises. Amazingly, this history never prevented the latest target CEO from believing RDS&M's promises. CEOs always believed they were special. Strongville, who enjoyed firing people, made sure to be on hand to do the dishonors and once personally dragged a blustering CEO out by the scruff of his neck.

"We've got a lot to discuss, Butch," Morgan said as he took his seat in a high-backed chair that would have made Henry VIII proud. "Before we start—is it your turn to sing the national anthem, Butch?—seems we have a visitor. We only see the occasional itinerant preacher or encyclopedia salesman in these parts. State your business, stranger."

Standing before the long partners' table with the humble pose of a penitent seeking a blessing, Jacob Cooke, their new P.R. man, smiled obsequiously. "Thank you for seeing me, Mr. Morgan. This is an honor. I'm Jacob—"

"He knows who you are, schmuck," Dengler said.

"Simon," Morgan said, "never lose your winning ways." He turned to Cooke. "I was teasing you. I know you. You have a special place in my prayers. Give us what you've got."

"Well, sir," Cooke began, "we can be sure Frank Vere won't be involved in this story."

"Thanks to the picture my guy took of Vere lip-locking Mercedes," Strongville said.

"Which was an unwanted advance from Vere that she broke free of," Morgan said with asperity, his sense of humor shorting out.

"Of course. Didn't mean to offend, Frederick." Strongville's tight smile showed anything but contrition. "I know we're all tightly wrapped after Caddy."

Morgan simmered down and gestured for Cooke to continue. Sometimes, the Wall Street frat-boy practice of needling each other went too far.

Cooke delivered another sheepish grin. "You gentleman can, I assure you, anticipate a very positive article in *Profit*. Karen Glick only writes puff pieces. The magazine wouldn't dare write anything bad. The tragic death of Mr. Redmon will help build public sympathy for you."

He had better hope so. P.R. firms got fired by clients more often than New York restaurants failed. Cooke Associates's chief job would be to handle spin control for each of the Billionaire Boys' corporate takeover campaigns. Working previously for RDS&M's chief rival, Naylor & Cross, the Cooke outfit had been wickedly good at this. A kindly target-company patriarch who had built a good business and cared for his employees became, after Cooke got through, a senile dinosaur satisfied with sub-par growth and a bloated, inefficient workforce.

"Why do we need a puff piece on us?" Dengler asked. "I can see paying you for putting a good public spin on our takeovers. But I don't want some reporter following me around and writing down what I eat for breakfast."

"You're too cheap to eat breakfast," Strongville said. "Yeah, that last CEO I fired held a news conference and burst into tears." Strongville shook a cigarette free from the pack he held in his big hands. "What a weenie."

"You showed decisive leadership, sir," said Cooke, whose toadying talents qualified him for permanent residence on a lily pad. "Anyway, Karen Glick also is one of those held hostage by that nut who delivered the threat letter to Mr. Dengler. She will be very sympathetic to us."

"No smoking," an outraged Dengler said, as if Strongville were peeing on the floor.

Strongville blew a plume of smoke at Dengler. "I'm simply testing the products of our latest target company. Call this due diligence."

"Very good, that will be all," Morgan said, dismissing the P.R. man. He flinched as Strongville's smoke plume wafted his way.

As Cooke headed toward the doors, Strongville called out, "Hey, P.R. guy, did Caddy screw this Glick chick?"

"Uh, I wouldn't know. She recently separated from her husband."

"Is she good looking?" Strongville asked.

Cooke tried to look thoughtful. "Not bad. About five-four. Dark hair. She does have a smart mouth."

"Five-four," Strongville said. "Good. We don't like tall women around here. Poor Frederick. Mercedes towers over him."

Morgan kept his anger in check this time. "Maybe by an inch. Butch, you can't stop talking about Mercedes, can you? She never talks about you."

Once Cooke left, Morgan summoned Ashlea via intercom.

The firm's top investment analyst, Ashlea Kress, took her spot in front of the Boys' table and started laying out the financial particulars of their pending takeover of Pulmon Tobacco, the nation's third-largest cigarette peddler. Blond, with a headband and a single strand of pearls, Ashlea was a registered trademark of Darien, Connecticut. Her assistants flashed various financial charts onto a screen, and she recited her observations about the colored bar and pie graphics with vowels as round as a lawn-tennis ball.

"How much longer will this go on, Ashley?" Strongville asked as he tapped his ash onto the burnished floor. He never had understood that her name was pronounced "Ash-lee-ah." Or perhaps he had.

Ashlea wasn't about to correct him. "We have a good bit to go, sir, to grasp the full entirety of our proposal."

"Why don't we save this money crap till last?" Strongville said. "We have to discuss the Vampyr stuff. That's first priority."

Morgan leaned forward and pressed his fingertips against the polished tabletop like a pianist on a keyboard. "Ashlea, please wait outside until we're ready."

After Ashlea and her minions had filed out,

Strongville said, "Now for the important part. How do we divide Redmon's stake?"

"If you'd bothered to read our partnership agreement," Dengler said, "you'd know that half of Redmon's interest in the firm goes to his various trusts and ex-wives and children. They can't cash it out for ten years. The other half is divided among the three of us."

"Meaning Frederick and I get even more once Vampyr bumps you off," Strongville said.

"Why don't you have another cigarette?" Dengler said. "Maybe the nicotine will get you before Vampyr does."

"Children, children," Morgan said. "Vampyr is not getting anybody. We're going to curtail our public appearances. The whole world knew Caddy's itinerary. He was running for the Senate. We can be much more careful. No one will know where we are."

"So I gotta do the low crawl for the rest of my life?" Strongville said. "Screw that."

Dengler nodded at Strongville. "I like to move about this city in my own way. Unlike you FOPs, who won't walk a block when someone can drive them, I take the subway."

Morgan hit the button on the intercom. "Fiona, please have Herman join us."

The big doors opened to admit Herman Heinrich, the Boys' new director of security. The linebacker-large Heinrich lumbered into the room and said in a monotone: "We are currently at this time engaged in pursuit of the appropriate suspect individuals. When we find them, they will be dealt with. No cops." Then Heinrich turned and clumped out.

"Where did you get him?" Dengler asked Morgan. "We pay him in bananas?"

"He's ex-CIA," Morgan said. "He can do the bare-knuckled stuff the cops can't."

"Looks like he drags his knuckles on the ground," Strongville said. He and Dengler joined in mutual laughter.

Morgan didn't laugh. "Herman advises that we don't attend Caddy's funeral."

"What are we paying bodyguards for?" Dengler said.

Strongville took out another cigarette. "These Vampyr pricks know things about us."

Ashlea's presentation dragged on for two hours, as Strongville probed for weaknesses in the financial plan she and Dengler had constructed. "I've gotta negotiate this son-of-a-bitch, and it better hold up," he roared.

"No, Butch, we want it to fall apart," Dengler shot back.

"Are you two vying for the Miss Congeniality Award here?" Morgan said.

"Why don't you tell how J.P. Morgan would have done it, Frederick?" Strongville said.

RDS&M had bid $10 billion for Pulmon Tobacco. Some $4 billion of that, or forty percent, came from cash that investors had given the Billionaire Boys as part of their latest buyout fund. The rest was in debt, also known as leverage—basically, bank loans and junk bonds. The more leverage the deal contained, the better for the Boys and their investors. If after a few years someone came along and paid $20 billion for Pulmon, $6 billion of which would go to pay off the debt, RDS&M's gross return would be a sweet $14 billion, or 3.5 times its cash outlay.

While they prepared to leave, Strongville said, "I want to go down and check out Pulmon's tobacco operations in North Carolina."

"We've already taken care of that," Ashlea said.

"Ashley, is your headband too tight? I said I want to go down there."

Gratefully, Morgan at last got to his car for the short drive to his home on Park Avenue.

He rested his head against the back seat's handcrafted leather and closed his eyes. George Jr. climbed into the front seat beside the driver, and Al sat next to Morgan. The car climbed the ramp from the underground garage to the street, where two armed Ludlum House security men stood watch. A few minutes later, Morgan stepped out into the underground garage of his apartment building. The two bodyguards went up the private elevator with him.

They bid him goodnight and he went into his palatial co-op. He stopped to admire the Monet water lily painting he had just acquired for the cathedral-sized foyer.

Slumping, Morgan passed the stripped walls. Mercedes was undertaking yet another renovation, tossing out the plaster covering that evoked the fall of Rome. That wall treatment had lasted a mere three months. Some kind of hand-painted fabric would be next.

"I'll bring your supper to the study," Mia told him.

"Is Mrs. Morgan in bed?" he asked the servant.

"About an hour ago, sir." Mia slyly cast her eyes about. "She had a couple of stiff brandies after she got back from Lincoln Center."

So Morgan's wife would be sleeping very deeply. He wanted to talk to her, if only to be reassured. Did she really adore those flowers? Why had she kissed Frank Vere?

Chapter Eight

Thomas Wolfe was wrong: You can go home again. You might not want to, but sometimes you need to. Gran's townhouse sat on a quiet Upper West Side street, a block removed from the Broadway hoopla. It glowed with the understated elegance of antique lamps.

When Karen was searching for a new apartment, Gran first had suggested that Karen move in with her. That wouldn't have been too bad. The only problem: Karen's parents already lived with Gran.

Karen's mother hugged her ferociously. "What you've been through, dear. Oh, oh, oh, oh. They poisoned that man, then came the gunman."

"You're going to crush her, Emma," her father said from his chair, where he hadn't put down his newspaper. Maury Glick, unlike his wife, didn't believe in touchy-feely. He believed in the inevitability of history. Unfortunately for him, the state that had withered away belonged to Marxists, not capitalists. Maury, a perpetual student at the New School, was writing a dissertation about how socialism was only taking a breather. The decades-long delay in getting his doctorate was the fault, he said, of the fascists who controlled the New School.

Karen extricated herself from Emma and kissed Maury's cheek. "Don't worry, Pop. Nobody's going to hurt me."

"Hey, knock on wood when you say a thing like that," her grandmother declared as she walked into the parlor carrying a cordless phone. "Don't tempt fate."

"Since when did you get superstitious?" Maury asked.

"Since when did you stop wanting free housing?" Gran retorted.

Muttering to himself, Maury settled back into his paper.

"Yes, she's here, but she doesn't want to talk to you," Gran said into the phone, then stabbed the button to disconnect the call.

"Who was that?" Emma asked.

"Karen's no-good husband," Gran said. "He'd better not come around here. If he does, he'll end up in the morgue with my shoe up his ass."

"Gran, for God's sake!" Karen exclaimed. Everyone had called her after the gunman episode, except Tim.

Gran headed back for the hallway, where the phone was berthed. "Tim Bratton, huh? More like Tin Tomb Rat."

"Enough with the anagrams, Gran," Karen called after her.

"Your husband," Maury said with contempt. "The golden boy. He would've fit in in the Third Reich. Hitler wanted everyone to be blond and perfect."

"Then who would've been the best friend?" Karen said. "Hey, Pop. Tim is a lot of things. A Nazi isn't one of them."

Emma plunked her peasant-skirted self in her customary perch on the settee. She patted the cushion for Karen to sit beside her. "I was never too clear on my anagram," said Emma, who took a gloomy view of the world. Emma Sami had kept her maiden name. "Miasma Me?"

Maury Glick rattled his paper. No one ever forgot Gran's anagram, especially an unkind one. "Mine was Karmic Ugly. Nice," he said.

"Gran made Karen Glick into Regal Knick," Karen said. "That was when I'd go to the Knicks games at the Garden with Marcia Fink and her brothers."

Emma smoothed her skirt. "She was an awful girl. So tough."

The name on Karen's birth certificate was Sunshine Sami-Glick. She had told everyone at school that her first name was Karen. Upon reaching adulthood, she had changed her name legally, opting for the Glick surname because it was easier for reservation takers to spell. She still kept an early picture of her as a baby being held by her parents, who looked like Woodstock citizens, complete with long hair and tie-dyed T-shirts.

"Emma," said Maury, now a graying, bald-headed psychedelic relic, "ask our capitalist tool daughter if she is going to the animal rights demonstration with us." He never had been too pleased that she worked for a business magazine.

Since her breakup from Tim, who used to get into shouting matches with her father over politics, Emma and Maury had begun to invite Karen to their many protests.

"There's a convention of cosmetics companies at the Javits Center later this week," Emma told Karen. "Do you know what they put these poor rabbits through to test makeup?"

"Why do rabbits need makeup?" Karen said. "They're already cute."

"That does it," her father said, and adjourned with his reading to the bathroom, which he referred to as his private study.

"I need to talk to you, Pop," Karen said to his retreating back.

"He's very worried about you," Emma said.

"Ma, I'm fine. Nothing has happened to me," Karen said, shading the truth.

"Traumas like this can be very debilitating," said her mother, who counseled rape and domestic abuse victims. "You probably should see someone and talk about what occurred. It's like a scarring you can't see."

Karen reluctantly followed her mother to the kitchen for some heated-up leftovers. Vegetarian leftovers. Emma wouldn't so much as kill a bug. Karen listened politely to Ma's chatter about the latest Republican outrages in Washington. With the lentils smushed around on the plate with the steamed broccoli, to give the appearance of consumption, Karen went to find her father. He was back in his chair, now perusing a student protest newspaper.

"Some kids on campus these days may finally be ready to follow in our footsteps and rise up to challenge the establishment," he said.

"Yeah, the students are revolting, Pop," Karen said. "I want to talk to you about radical politics. You stay in touch with those types."

"Still too few of them in this corrupt age," Maury said.

"I've been doing research this afternoon on Vampyr. Nobody seems to know much. Do you know anyone in radical, underground groups who could hook me up with them?"

Maury scrunched up the newspaper. "What? Are you out of your mind? These people are bad news. Stay clear of them."

"Can you keep a secret?"

"Who am I going to tell?" her father said.

"I'll take that as a yes. I'm very close to getting the goods on the Billionaire Boys Club. I can show that they've been cheating on their taxes. Not a little bit. To the tune of billions." Her father's funny expression troubled Karen. "You know who they are?"

"Those jackals, sure. They lay off thousands upon thousands of workers when they take over companies. They love to move factories out of the country to avoid union wage scales, and locate jobs in the Third World where they can really exploit people." Maury tossed the paper onto the floor. "What I can't believe is that your magazine, a cheerleader for Corporate America, is going to challenge these icons of capitalism."

"Frank Vere has been doing this for years. We like capitalism, but not crooked capitalism." Her father thought all capitalism was crooked. "Let me have a chance at it, Pop."

Maury bowed his head. "Sunshine, you're my daughter. If anything ever should happen to you, I couldn't . . ."

"Please, Pop. Nothing will happen."

Unexpectedly for a non-touchy-feely guy, her father grasped her hands. "Karen, I'd prefer you write the glowing portraits of smug, pampered CEOs."

She gripped his hands back, harder. "Listen, I'm thirty-three years old. My marriage is shot, and I feel nobody loves me. I can't keep doing these nice-girl articles. I need to break this story, Pop. I really do. But I've got nowhere to start. Please help me."

Maury disengaged his hands. "Someone loves you." He picked up a pen and a pad of yellow Post-Its. "I'm going to give you several names of kids I have met who may or may not be involved with radical, anti-global groups. They listen to my stories about the SDS in the 1960s and early 1970s. I tell them I firebombed the ROTC building."

Actually, his Molotov cocktail had exploded in midair a second after he had hurled it. He had to be treated for first-degree burns. The ROTC building stayed untouched. "Thanks."

* * *

When Karen reached Broadway, she pulled out her cell phone and called first her home machine, then her work voice mail. Nobody had called. More importantly, Tim hadn't called.

Why had he called Gran's and not her apartment or office? And why hadn't he called earlier? And why did Karen care anyhow? She tried to answer the last question and couldn't.

What was it about him? Tim had blond, strong-chinned good looks, courtesy of a bloodline that twisted back through generations of Philadelphia gentility. All his forbearers were handsome rascals with a knack for commerce.

One ancestor, Phineas Bratton, had been William Penn's first commissioner of sanitation, which involved a self-drawn cart, a large broom, and streets where many horses had passed. Phineas made a fortune in fertilizer. Another ancestor, Josiah Bratton, had signed the Declaration of Independence. But unlike a defiant John Hancock, whose large and florid signature was meant for George III to notice, Josiah's was tiny and barely legible. When the Redcoats occupied Philadelphia, they didn't know to arrest him. Josiah expanded the family fortune by servicing their needs at his bawdy houses. A third ancestor, Thatcher Bratton, created the Pennsylvania Railroad and built its famous Main Line to the west of town. Luckily for him, the railroad had to buy up many parcels of land that he conveniently owned.

Like iron filings tempted by a magnet, Karen's attraction to Tim had been immediate and forceful. His confident manner, his effortless savoir-faire, his racquet-sports-toned body—he proved irresistible. Two years ahead of Karen at Princeton, that haven for preppie WASPs who know which fork to use, Tim first talked to her at his eating club's party for his graduating class. She didn't tell him she had been watching him for a long time. That spring night, on a couch in his room during a single cut of a Sade CD playing on his stereo (it was "Smooth Operator"), he took her virginity. The couch was stained with beer and other, less noble liquids. With her head resting against his broad chest, she told him about her life and then fell asleep. Come morning when she awoke, Tim had left to go play tennis. Then he didn't call her.

Nine years later, having forged a minor reputation as a personality profile writer and having just been hired by *Profit*, she had gone to a party at an Amagansett beach house. The hosts were a crew of young Dewey Cheatham investment bankers. Someone introduced her to Tim, who was standing poolside in his khakis and boat shoes. This was in the blue hour.

"Hey, Galahad, thanks for calling me," she said.

His grin never wavered, as if his entire life were one sustained good mood. "Karen Glick. My God, you look gorgeous. How is your grandmother, the landlord? Is your mom still doing social work? And has your father finally gotten his Ph.D.?" That night, she had ended up in his satin-sheeted bed, which overlooked the silvery undulations of a moon-kissed ocean. Someone out in the night across the dunes was playing an Alanis Morissette CD. The next morning, he didn't leave to play tennis or anything else. On Monday, he called her.

So now Karen marched along Broadway, clutching her cell and debating whether to call Tim at home. Their home. Her home. Instead, Karen fished Marcia's card out of her bag. Her old friend's home number was jotted on the card. She debated with herself for an instant before calling the number.

A man answered. "Yeah?"

"Um, you must be Sean."

"Yeah? And?"

"This is Karen Glick. I'm an old friend of Marcia's. Is she there?"

She heard Sean call: "Hey, Marcia. That reporter you were talking about is on the phone. You want to take this?"

Marcia came on the line, sounding a bit too cold and brisk. "Hi. What can I do for you?"

"Well, uh, I had this idea. See, I have some leads about radical groups. Maybe I can find out stuff about Vampyr. Then you can tell me what you've developed." Silence. Karen said, "Kind of a quid pro quo deal. You know?"

"Karen, do yourself a favor. If you find out some 'stuff' "—Marcia put a snide emphasis on the word—"you had better turn it over to me. There are no deals. Nothing about a police investigation will be revealed to someone outside the department. Are we clear?"

Keep going, keep going, Karen told herself. "Can you at least tell me about the Ferrari keys? Have you been able to trace them to the car's owner?"

Marcia hung up.

"Shit." Karen hailed a cab. Some twenty minutes later, she shlumped into the pizza joint at the corner, near her new place. She already had gotten to know Carlo, the chief dough slinger. And after Ma's alleged cooking, she needed some real food. "Small pepperoni pie, Carlo."

"You okay, Karen? You seem kinda down."

"Nothing a pizza won't cure."

She turned away from the counter and wandered over to the waist-high window, which looked out onto the street. Couples strolled by, hand in hand. Then a large, scary figure with a flowing cape came purposefully along the sidewalk. He approached her. "Karen Glick?" he said.

He wore a rubber Halloween Dracula mask. His muffled voice sounded familiar.

"Who the hell are you?"

"You better stay out of my way. Or you'll be in big trouble."

"Carlo," she called out.

The masked man turned and strode off.

"Hey, come back here." Karen scrambled out onto the sidewalk.

But he had disappeared into the evening, as though he had sprouted bat wings.

Chapter Nine

For Edward Danton, visiting Vampyr's headquarters was like Anne Rice channeling Che Guevara. He didn't know whether to be scared or amused. Louis had situated his anarchist pack in old industrial space in Long Island City, across the East River from Manhattan. Through the loft's large, grimy windows, Danton had a knock-out view of the nighttime New York skyline.

Danton sat in a straight-backed wooden chair, playing with his Palm Pilot and pretending not to notice his bizarre surroundings. Clusters of young people, many of them multi-pierced, were scattered about the cold concrete floor. Some had few clothes on. Some smoked pot or crack. Some talked with a manic intensity about the injustice of capitalism. What would their parents, had they known, think of this?

Danton's own father's view of the money culture would fit in here. Danton remembered how, after he'd gone to work as a junior analyst at Dewey Cheatham, his father had suffered a heart attack. Danton had scrambled back to their old New England college town. With an I.V. stuck in his arm and his hair now white, James seemed like a gaunt Santa running low on gifts. He eyed his son's fine tailoring and French cuffs as if they were badges of shame.

Louis strode in, his cape billowing behind him. His acolytes jumped to their feet and thronged around him like animals at feeding time.

"Did you miss me?" Louis asked.

"Yesssssssss," they replied as one.

"How much?"

"A lo-o-o-o-o-o-o-o-t."

"We have to talk, Louis," Danton broke in.

Louis ignored him. "We have a big job in front of us," he said in a strident, evangelical voice. "The pig culture of America—and that's spelled with a 'k'—is going to lead to world destruction. It's a documented fact that the Ku Klux Klan rules America. There was a cross burning on the White House lawn yesterday, and the President lit it himself, but the capitalist media didn't cover the story. What a racist nation this is."

"Louis," Danton called.

"Where's my little Kyra?" Louis said. A small young woman hopped forward, and he embraced her. "Are you ready for tomorrow?" When she nodded enthusiastically, he said, "You can go back to my room."

Everyone applauded as she left for the converted office over in the corner. She might have just won a game show—a trip to the sunny shores of Aruba—instead of a night with Louis.

"Now where is my clever Henry?" Once a young, thin man raised his hand, Louis took it and said, "Are you ready to make up Mr. Danton as well as you did me today?" After hearing yes, Louis added, "Well, you can go back to my room, too."

Amid the applause, one kid shouted, "We love you, Louis."

"And I love all of you, too. Now, let me talk to Mr. Danton." The others scattered. As Louis approached him, Danton saw the garish welt on his cheek from the SWAT bullet. Louis flounced his cape out and sat facing Danton, his chin resting on one hand. "I'm your best friend. I can lend you one or several of my boys or girls for the night. Would that improve your mood?"

"My mood is fine."

Louis played with the hem of his cape. "When I got out of prison, the first thing I promised myself was to have fun. Did you have fun when you got out?"

"I got drunk. Only that once. Since then, I've been a little busy."

"I bet you thought you'd be going to one of those nice prisons," Louis said. "The kind with the Sunday brunch, the golf courses, the pay-per-view TV."

"Speaking of the Klan," Danton said, "weren't you a member of the Aryan Brotherhood in prison?" While Louis did frighten him, and had ever since their prison days, Danton knew his money gave him the upper hand and entitled him to certain impertinences. "And if you're so concerned about racism, why is everyone in your group white?"

"The mixed-up progeny of privileged, white suburbia are more open to my appeals." He shrugged. "The Brotherhood? All talk."

"You sound like a total fruit-loop. Can you pull off tomorrow's plan? Can you?"

"Wasn't my mission at the magazine outstanding?"

"Until Karen Glick clocked you with the phone receiver. You almost got caught. It's like dealing with lunatics around here. Where are the keys to my new Ferrari?"

"Don't mention that bitch's name to me." Louis grunted. "*Your* Ferrari? With us, share and share alike are ingrained."

"I happen to have a second set of keys. But you aren't going to use my car again. You weren't exactly a sharing guy in prison."

Louis's smile looked like Satan's on a bad day. "Ever wonder why your pal Chris Abbott never got any hassles from the hard-asses in prison? Because he paid protection to a certain hard-ass to look after him. Me. Ever wonder why, after your first year, you had no trouble? Because Abbott took you in. And you got his money when he died. That's protecting you now."

Standing up, Danton said, "I'm getting out of here in my people's property Ferrari. Your 'clever Henry' can make me up tomorrow."

"I'm your best friend."

Danton steered his Ferrari over the Queensboro Bridge toward Manhattan. Once he had finally gotten released from prison and collected Abbott's money, he had figured that surrounding himself with creature comforts would bring him some small measure of happiness. That hope proved to be in vain. But he still kept trying.

When he bought the Ferrari Enzo, one of only 400 made in 2002, he figured the sports car would thrill him. And indeed, with its Formula One styling, gull-wing doors, 660-horsepower engine, and six-speed gearbox, the Enzo fulfilled a basic male fantasy of sex appeal, power, and speed. If he had any friends, he would have loved to boast (subtly, to be sure) of its $675,000 price tag. Yet he had no friends. And the car gave him no pleasure.

Careful to avoid the careening taxis swarming around him, driven by people loonier than the Vampyr kids, Danton vroomed the car up Park Avenue and nosed it safely into the garage beneath his co-op building. The grinning attendant recognized the car and took his keys bearing the Ferrari prancing horse logo and wished him a very good evening. The operator in the mahogany-paneled elevator also wished him such an evening. Danton stepped into his vast and cheerlessly empty apartment. It had a couple of tables, a few chairs, a bed, and—his other concession to luxury outside of the Ferrari—an elaborate home entertainment system where he watched movies by himself. He watched *Dangerous Liaisons* endlessly.

He plodded onto the patio and stared across the wide avenue. Below was a median strip planted with a riot of colorful flowers designed to please the eye even under streetlamps. Above, a jetliner rumbled west, bound for California. He didn't need to use the gorgeous telescope that stood next to the balustrade.

He could tell that the curtains were drawn over the many windows of Morgan's apartment, which was directly across Park Avenue.

Danton had spent hours peering through the telescope at Morgan, drifting through his handsome halls, swathed in smugness. Morgan's son, Bert, was a good-looking boy who radiated his father's self-assurance. What kind of child would Danton and Mercedes have had?

Mercedes, now in her forties, was as bewitching as ever. When she came into view of the telescope, Danton stopped breathing. She moved with the same dancer's grace. Sometimes, he had to quit watching her. It was like a potent drug. Too much would kill him. He watched her move, he watched her talk, he watched her cry.

The single tear that Danton always shed, when spying on Mercedes's home, zigged down his cheek. He wiped it away and went to his bedroom. Ali, his lone servant, had turned down the bed. The white cotton curtains swayed with the nighttime wind. But sleep was elusive.

In the strange hours after midnight, Edward Danton's father let himself into the apartment. He eased his old frame into the chair beside his son's bed.

"Your big plan is coming to pass, eh?" His father sounded far from approving.

"Yes, James," his son said groggily. "I'm sure you read in the papers what happened to Redmon. That pond scum deserved what he got."

"I suppose you believe that his tirade before he collapsed was some sort of poetic justice?" James adjusted the knit tie beneath his white beard.

Edward hoisted himself up on an elbow. "That would be a big yes. The police will have a tough time matching the poison I put in his wine. The stuff is called maleficum. This was a popular potion in the Middle Ages among court plotters. It disinhibits you, like a dozen stiff cocktails. It worked on Redmon exactly as I wanted. And the bastard realized how he had shamed himself, right before he keeled over. Perfect."

James displayed the same lack of empathy he'd shown years back when they sat in Washington Square. "Perfect? You don't seem like a man who is celebrating. But then, you're such a loner, you have no one to celebrate with."

Edward sat up in bed, his sleepiness vanished. "You're not my shrink, James."

"My son is a murderer and I'm supposed to notify my alumni newsletter about how proud I am of you?"

"You're lucky I talk to you at all about my plans."

"Oh, then I'll wait until you are captured. What an alumni news item that would make. Let's see. Smith's son is a biochemist working on a cancer cure. Jones's son has written a Pulitzer Prize–winning novel. And my son is a model prisoner."

"Let me remind you of a few facts. The Billionaire Boys Club made me their fall guy and had me sent to prison. Then they heaped on the gun-threat charge to make sure I'd stay in for a long time. With the help of all the lies, Morgan stole Mercedes from me. And let me add that my defense cleaned you out financially and took a toll on your health."

"Who cares about money? My son was on trial. And my health problems are in the past." His father leaned forward. "What bothers me is how this obsession, this hatred, runs your life." He gestured to take in the Park Avenue apartment. "You are fortunate. You are wealthy. Why not enjoy yourself? Why not forget these nasty people?"

"James, did you enjoy yourself after Mom died? No. You were in permanent mourning."

Stroking his beard, James said, "I'm a teacher. I'm vexed that you have learned nothing."

"What am I supposed to learn? That people are shits? Big news."

"Why do you think these four men have been so successful?"

"They're devious, sneaky, and ruthless. That's how."

James grimaced. "Wrong. When you know the answer, you'll understand what you have missed." He got up to go.

"Christ, what's with the riddles? When they're all dead, I'll be with Mercedes again," he shouted after his father. "How's that for an answer?"

James halted at the bedroom door. "Why do you believe she will come back to you?"

"I know Mercedes."

"Whom you haven't talked to in almost two decades. If you did get her back, could you go through life keeping secret that you were behind her husband's death?"

"Sure," Edward said. "Has Morgan told Mercedes what really happened with me? No. He has lied his phony head off. Told her it was my fault."

"And what if, during your campaign against them, someone other than the Billionaire Boys dies? You almost fed poison to that reporter at the Met dinner."

"I stopped her before she had any of that soup. I'm not a bad man, James. I'm entitled to get even with them for what they did to me."

But his father had gone. And the white cotton curtains fluttered in the night breeze like forlorn ghosts.

"I'm not a bad man," Edward Danton repeated to himself.

Chapter Ten

Ludlum House sat in spooky majesty off Fifth Avenue, an awe-inspiring artifact from the Gilded Age. Two uniformed men with hard eyes stood out front. Cameras protruded from the old façade, standing sentinel, too. A tasteful brass plaque was to the right of the impressive front door; it proclaimed that this belonged to Redmon, Dengler, Strongville & Morgan—and if you didn't like it, you could kiss their assets.

Karen, bleary-eyed, plodded along the street toward Ludlum House, coffee cup in hand. Her sleep had been substandard, to say the least. Even though she'd shoved the couch in front of the front door, her sense of security wasn't exactly strong. Sleep finally claimed her in the wee hours, but an early-rising Bigfoot overhead had put an end to that indulgence.

One Ludlum House guard pawed through her bag

while the other muttered into a walkie-talkie that she had arrived. A *snap* sounded from the door, which was strong enough to withstand every last member of Vampyr, not to mention Frankenstein's monster, the Wolfman, and the cast of *The Evil Dead*. The Boys didn't need to heave couches in front of their doors. The bag-pawing guard held open the door for her.

Inside lay Ludlum House's Great Hall, an expanse of old wooden walls carved in interesting ways and holding oil paintings from the Robber Baron days. In the paintings, the men wore long black coats and vests; the women dressed like Karen's mother. The Victorian chairs and tables stood on legs ending in the clawed feet of animals. Another table of guards eyed her as they might a mangy dog. Behind them was the storied mural of the Stomcox Massacre. Righteous-looking Pinkerton thugs were beating the Joe Hill out of some slimy-looking anarchists. It was a capitalist Guernica.

As Karen presented her credentials again to the table guards, she heard her name called. The table guards snapped to their feet.

Frederick Morgan was approaching her, trailed by a well-dressed entourage of men and women. One was the P.R. guy, Jacob Cooke.

Cooke opened his mouth to make introductions, but Morgan beat him to it. "Karen, I'm Frederick Morgan," he said, his cobalt-blue eyes radiating warmth. Karen knew from the Bratton family that the high WASPs had perfected the art of the sincere-seeming smile, which promised that no guests ever should feel ill at ease, even if they had every reason to.

She shook Morgan's hand with its amazingly soft skin. Morgan had a real leader's presence. He had the bland handsomeness that a well-tended gene pool spawned; his well-formed nose was used to sniffing the best air. Yet he was far from physically imposing. About five-seven, he had the superb compensating posture of one who never had to stoop for anything. Morgan displayed that Bratton-type self-assurance, as though whatever he did or said would always be right. His gray hair, which had once been Master Race blond, was perfectly parted to one side; even the storm of the century wouldn't disturb a follicle.

"Thank you for letting me continue to do this story," she said. "I realize that with Mr. Redmon's death and—"

Morgan held up a hand. As he did so, his starched cuff pulled back to reveal a cloth watchband with three muted horizontal stripes. Tim Bratton's father wore cloth watchbands and had a new one every day. "Nothing could honor Caddy more than to show the world the marvelous wealth-creation machine that is RDS&M, a machine that he helped create. And besides, you were the first at Caddy's side and gave him CPR."

"When is Mr. Redmon's funeral?" she asked.

The chief Billionaire Boy turned to an underling, who murmured some kind of code answer. "We're assuming early next week," Morgan told Karen. "The medical examiner still hasn't released his body. They are working on what kind of poison he swallowed."

"I'd like to attend the funeral."

"I'm sure you understand that the service will be a private affair," Cooke said.

Karen started to protest that she wouldn't bring a photographer and would respect whatever security dictates existed. Morgan interrupted.

"Nonsense, Jacob. Of course we'd be delighted to have Karen as our guest. The service will be held in a small coal town in western Pennsylvania." He smiled once more and shook her hand before heading off with his courtiers.

Cooke stood alone with Karen in the Great Hall. He hadn't perfected how to match his smile with eyes. "Well, we'll have to work out the details," he said, with the enthusiasm of a man agreeing to shop for baby-shower gifts with his wife. Cooke, a stuffy fellow who took himself as seriously as a papal nuncio, had a bulging double chin and a trencherman's spare tire around his waist. His job required him to eat out a lot at fine restaurants.

"Terrific. Well, in addition to interviewing the partners, I'd like to interview some of the support people. Ashlea Kress, their finance person, for instance."

"I'll make the appropriate inquiries."

"And Mrs. Morgan. She has been around for a while, unlike the other partners' wives. I'd like to get her perspective."

"I'm afraid that would be out of the question," Cooke said. "The RDS&M partners' private lives have nothing to do with their business lives."

"Oh, give us a break here, Jacob. I'm not asking about whether Frederick Morgan snores in his sleep or whether he leaves the toilet seat up. I'd like her perspective because she helps entertain people in Morgan's business dealings. Also, she was an accomplished dancer and sits on the Lincoln Center board. This is not some dumb cupcake."

"No one has ever accused Mrs. Morgan of being a 'cupcake,'" said Cooke, whose elevated culinary tastes excluded Hostess products. "You realize the sensitivity of your request. Frank Vere of your magazine sexually assaulted Mrs. Morgan two years ago."

In the photo Karen had examined, Mercedes Morgan didn't appear to be a woman fighting off an unwanted advance. "Regardless of what Frank did or didn't do, I promise not to pounce on Mrs. Morgan. Deal?"

"I'll make the appropriate inquiries."

"They're the best kind. To see how RDS&M investments are doing, I'd also like to speak with investors in their buyout pools—pension programs, mutual funds, insurance companies."

"I fail to see how that is appropriate. RDS&M is doing fabulously."

"Good. How about showing me the books to prove it?" Unlike mutual funds or other investment vehicles that the average person could invest in, a buyout firm like RDS&M did not need to disclose its finances to the public.

"Unlikely." Cooke had perhaps started to understand that Karen Glick was no cupcake.

Usually when reporting stories, Karen's strategy was to act the part of the sweet, smiley girl with the wry yet winning wit. Not now. Acting tough was the only way to get what she needed from control freaks like RDS&M and Jacob Cooke.

"Let's move, as in today," came a sharp-edged voice.

Simon Dengler was marching energetically toward the front door with two men walking abreast. He swept by Karen and Jacob Cooke.

Cooke fluttered his hand to indicate that he and Karen should catch up. He trotted after Dengler and drew even with him. "I'd like to introduce Karen Glick of *Profit* magazine," Cooke said, already getting winded. Exercise beyond lifting a fork didn't interest him.

"I know who she is," Dengler said. "She'd better be able to keep up."

Karen bounced up to the party as it shot through the front door. She kept Cooke to the other side of Dengler and his bodyguards. "I'm Karen," she said. "Where are we going?"

"I'm late," Dengler said. "We're going to the subway."

"The subway?" Karen glanced at Cooke, who already was flagging. This was like an Olympic walking contest.

"The subway is fast, efficient, and cheap," Dengler said.

Dengler was whippet-thin, a testament to this speed-walking, no doubt. His sparse hair had been combed straight back, as though to streamline his progress. Dengler's lined and dried-out face belonged to that of an elderly man, not a middle-aged one. Something had sucked the moisture out of him long ago. He had fierce, spiky eyebrows that seemed as sharp as cactus needles.

"The subway?" Karen said. She had heard he didn't

have a chauffeur, but hadn't believed it. "Will you be safe in the subway?"

Dengler stopped abruptly. Cooke trudged up to them, panting.

"That's why I pay these two," Dengler said, referring to his bodyguards. "To keep me safe. And they don't come cheap. Got it?"

The two bodyguards, lanky George Sr. and compact Mike, regarded her silently and pugnaciously. Dengler started striding toward the Lexington Avenue subway as if bearing down on the finishing line tape.

"Don't worry," Cooke told Karen between gasps. "His bodyguards are very good."

"So were Caddy Redmon's."

Danton stood by the subway stop, waiting for a call on his cell phone. He paced about urgently. He licked his lips.

Louis rounded the corner with that stupid cape draped from his broad shoulders.

"What the hell's going on?" Danton demanded. "No one has called me."

This didn't faze Louis. "Oh, no? Must be a mix up. Did you give us the correct number of your cell phone?"

"Three times, damn it. Forget the phone. Are they coming or not?"

Louis brandished his small cell phone, which was like all the others Danton had bought them. "Of course they're coming. Dengler and the two bodyguards. Also that Glick bitch and the fat P.R. guy

Cooke, who's almost having a heart attack keeping up." He tucked the cell into a pouch inside his cloak. "No one called you?"

Danton decided to drop the matter. "Everyone is in position?"

"Absolutely. It's like that bank job I told you about, the one they never solved. All my people know their tasks. We've rehearsed it again and again. No problem-o."

"Damn well better not be," Danton said. "I'm going to get into position."

"Remember. I'm your best friend."

Karen, having heard ahead of time about Dengler's walkathons, had worn pants and rubber-soled flats. She didn't have much trouble staying with him, even though she had forgotten to exercise lately. She felt the perspiration gathering down her sides and at her temples.

"So," she said to the grim-faced Dengler, who showed nary a drop of sweat. "How's the Pulmon deal going?"

Cooke had lagged badly behind. Otherwise, he would be objecting that such a question was not appropriate.

"We've made our offer," Dengler snapped. "Let's see if they're sufficiently smart to accept it."

"I heard a rumor that Naylor & Cross is interested in bidding for Pulmon."

"You people in the media make these things up just to sell newspapers."

"I work for a magazine, and I heard it from an investment banker." Actually, it was from Tim the week before, when he had called about finalizing the settlement. When she told him she was doing an RDS&M story, he told her the Naylor & Cross rumor.

"I heard you had a smart mouth," Dengler said.

"What's with this thrift business? You really think you save a lot of money by taking the subway? For a man with your assets, a car and driver are pocket change."

"I have a nice apartment on Fifth Avenue that I got in a bankruptcy auction. My home, unlike Frederick's, is modestly furnished. Just the necessities. I pay a boatload in taxes on what I earn. Since I'm paying for the subway, I might as well take advantage of my tax dollars."

Since Dengler had brought up the subject... "Taxes?" Karen said. "What percentage of your income do you pay in taxes—federal, state, and local?"

"Too much."

"How much is that?"

"None of your business." Dengler looked over his shoulder. "Hey, let's get the lead out," he shouted to Cooke, who huffed along behind, his plump cheeks as red as a thermometer.

Karen realized she had better get in the hard questions before Cooke caught up. "What about charities? Redmon gave heavily to the Metropolitan Museum of Art. Strongville, with his military background, donates to veterans' causes. And Morgan contributes to Lincoln Center. There's also that statue of J.P. Morgan he's having made, to give to Central Park. But I understand that you don't go in for charity. Why?"

"A waste of money," Dengler declared. "A bunch of smiling vultures at these charities pick your pockets then waste most of your hard-earned dollars on inflated salaries and perks for themselves. And who really benefits from some dumb dance program or an overrated picture on a wall? If someone wants to see these things, then they should pay more in ticket prices and not depend on me to subsidize them. It's all a waste of time anyway. Dance, music, art—a load of worthless garbage."

"Worthless garbage?" Karen had to laugh. "Take the Mona Lisa. That's garbage?"

"No, it's famous. It's got brand identity. But some drugged-out, boozed-up jackass who spills paint on a canvas like a three-year-old, that's garbage." Dengler slowed slightly. "Judge everything by its economic utility."

"Wow," Karen said. "What about charities that help the poor and the sick? Garbage?"

"The best step they can take is to get off their asses and quit whining. I'm sorry if some creep got AIDS by sticking his ying-yang where it doesn't belong. But that's not my problem."

They had reached the entrance to the subway. Dengler paused and motioned for Cooke to close the gap. The P.R. man steamed up, his shirt blotchy with sweat and his breath coming in ragged gusts.

"Sorry," Cooke managed.

"Yeah, you are pretty sorry," Dengler said. "Early grave for you." He signaled for them to press onward.

Mike, dark and intense, clambered down the stairs first. George Sr., lanky and loose, followed Dengler.

Karen knew that bodyguards kept to each side or front and rear of their protected person. They called such positioning the "sandwich."

"Everyone pays his—or her—own fare," Dengler called out.

With Cooke already trailing, Karen swiped her farecard through the reader and passed through the turnstile. She caught up with the sandwich and decided to take another bite. "Where exactly are we going?"

"My barber down in Chinatown," Dengler said. "He charges three bucks and is happy to get it. None of this nonsense about a tip."

They waited on the subway platform. Mike and George Sr. scanned the others nearby. With the morning rush over, the platform wasn't too crowded. There was the usual mix of New York humanity: street dudes, teenagers, mothers with strollers, delivery boys, construction workers. Everyone stared into the air.

The monster rumble of an approaching train came out of the far tunnel. The train blew into the station with a rush of air. The public address system made noises no one could understand. The train doors parted. Mike entered first.

The car was not crowded. The passengers took their places on the hard plastic benches. George Sr. and Mike had bookended Dengler by the time Karen got inside.

"Let me sit next to him," Karen said to George Sr., who seemed less uptight.

The bodyguard slid away from Dengler, allowing Karen to sit next to the financier. Cooke puffed into the car and gawked at the scene. He had no way of controlling this conversation. He sat with a large moan on the bench opposite Dengler, where he would be able to hear very little once the train started.

"Back to the Pulmon deal," Karen said as the train jerked into motion.

"Oh, no," Dengler said. "Where are the cops? We pay them to keep these low-lifes off the subway. Do you know what the tax rate is in this city?"

A disheveled beggar had come into the car and announced in a very loud voice: "Good morning, ladies and gentleman. I'm sorry to bother you."

The riders in the car suddenly became very interested in the floor or the newspaper or the inside of their eyelids. Except for Dengler, who said, almost as loudly, "If he's so sorry, then maybe he should shut the hell up."

"I am one of New York's homeless. I am hungry. Can someone please spare a nickel or a dime or a quarter, and I can get some food."

"Our tax dollars pay for soup kitchens and he says he's hungry," Dengler almost bellowed. "More like he's thirsty for a little White Lightning."

"I don't rob or mug nobody."

"I'd like to see his rap sheet with the cops," Dengler said, knowing that his bodyguards gave him license to be as vociferously politically incorrect as Rush Limbaugh.

The beggar, bent over from a life of woe, had shuffled almost to where they sat. Under his unkempt hair and beard, you couldn't see if he had ever been handsome. He wore a stained T-shirt and torn work pants stiff with filth. His old running shoes were mottled and cracked. One lacked laces. A sharp stench of old B.O. wafted from him.

"Find it in your heart," he said through stained teeth. "Any spare change?"

"Spare change, no," Dengler said. "I know where I can find a spare job."

Karen fished a dollar bill out of her bag and handed it to the slumping beggar.

Then she saw his burning eyes, which were focused, not on her dollar, but on Dengler.

She had seen those eyes before at the Met dinner. Lucifer eyes.

Chapter Eleven

"Look out!" Karen cried, crumpling the dollar in her hand. "It's Mixon."

Everyone in the car stared at her as if she were stark-raving bonkers.

The beggar drew himself erect.

Karen pointed at him. "He's the waiter who poisoned Redmon."

Then many things happened very quickly.

A small woman seated next to Mike produced a can of Mace and sprayed him in the face. The bodyguard howled in agony, his hands clamped on his eyes. Mike twisted and flailed and fell to the floor.

A lightly built young man next to George Sr. tried to do the same. But George Sr. grasped his slender wrist in time and pointed the spray can at the ceiling. The young man moved to grab George Sr.'s throat with his free left hand. George Sr., much larger, caught the young man's left wrist, too. Then the young man charged George Sr. head first, trying to crush his nose.

Dengler jerked his head from side to side in alarm and confusion.

The beggar clamped on to Dengler's arm. Mike flailed on the floor, helpless. Another man, who was sitting next to a saucer-eyed Cooke, jumped up. As big as a bodyguard, he rushed over and secured Dengler's other arm. He was standing right in front of Karen. A cape hung from his wide shoulders. Karen recognized the cape—from the night before, outside Carlo's pizza parlor when the guy wore a Dracula mask.

The caped man and the beggar hauled a stunned Dengler to his feet. In his shock, Dengler could manage only a small gurgling noise.

The guy with the cape had a ski cap pulled down almost to his eyes. His jaw was strong and his cheeks had a day or two of stubble. He had a long wound on his cheek, partially healed—from a bullet. His mouth was set in a determined line.

Karen hadn't boxed since her teenage days in the Jackson Heights gym, where Marcia and her brothers had given her pointers.

She got up herself and slammed a fist into the caped man's stubbly cheek. His head rocked to the side. His hands involuntarily released Dengler's arm. He stumbled a few steps.

"Get a hold of him, Louis," the beggar shouted.

Karen's fist was a bonfire of pain. She must have connected with Louis's jawbone.

The small woman hopped over Mike as he squirmed

on the floor. She darted around the beggar and made to secure Dengler's arm. Fright had paralyzed Dengler.

But George Sr. had succeeded in getting rid of his assailant by bodily heaving him into the air, where the young man collided with a pole. Then George Sr. pulled a sleek and mean pistol from under his suit jacket.

Recovering, Louis yelled, "Pig's got a gun."

Outside the subway car's windows, a new station flashed into view. The train began to slow and everyone swayed with the deceleration.

The young man's dropped Mace can rolled down the aisle, hitting a few shoes belonging to the fear-frozen riders. Cooke was hyperventilating, and not from exercise.

"Abort," the beggar bellowed.

"Let go of him," George Sr. commanded, his arms outstretched, holding the gun in firing position. "Now."

"Abort, Kyra," the beggar repeated. He released Dengler's arm and the woman did, also.

The train rocked to a halt.

"Henry," the beggar shouted. "Get up. Abort."

The young man, who had been lying dazed by the pole, lurched to his feet.

The subway car doors slid open and the whole pack of brigands ran out onto the platform. Henry, in pain, ran with a stuttering motion. Louis, cape billowing behind him, ran while holding his cheek.

"Stop them," Karen called. But no one wanted to get involved. She cradled her aching right hand under her left armpit.

George Sr. stepped in front of the ashen-faced Dengler, meaning to shield him from any other assault. He swept his gun around the car. The passengers cringed. None, though, launched into a second attack on Dengler.

Mike had risen to his elbows and knees. His hands still covered his eyes. "Oh, my Christ," he wailed.

In what may have been a few minutes or a few hours later, a posse of burly cops thundered into the subway car. Dazed, her hand aflame, Karen let herself be guided off the train to a wooden bench on the platform. She massaged the back of her hand and her fingers.

Dengler sat a few seats down from her. George Sr. stood vigilantly beside him. His gun was back out of sight. There was no sign of Mike. The platform had become a police convention.

Nearby, she heard a beefy cop, whose extreme youth made him a more likely junior high hall monitor, tell an older cop with three stripes on his sleeve: "Witnesses say they had a van waiting outside and left the scene at a high rate of speed. No makes yet on the plates."

The cop with three stripes rumbled a question at the younger officer, one that Karen couldn't hear.

"The beggar didn't get in the van, according to a couple of witnesses on the street, sergeant. He ran away on foot."

George Sr. took out a cell phone and delivered a crisp report of their location and explained briefly what had happened.

Dengler's shock had started to fade. He motioned for George Sr. to hand him the phone. "Hey, how much are we paying Mike?" He listened for a few seconds. "Well, I don't care. He screwed up. Lose him."

When Detective Esposito finally released Karen from answering the same series of questions posed fifty different ways—Marcia wasn't on duty—Karen emerged from the precinct to find Frank waiting. He hugged her. After what she had been through, that felt good indeed.

"Eudell let me come," he said.

"Thanks for coming," she said.

They went outside into the lilting air of a June afternoon, with the sun benevolently shining on the asphalt and tar of a New York street.

"I've gathered a few scraps of information," Frank said as they waited at an intersection. A bicycle messenger speeding the wrong way on a one-way street almost clipped them. Who needed Vampyr when you had bicycle messengers?

"Uh, are you allowed to talk to me about the RDS&M story?"

"No. We didn't talk about it. We're talking about this weekend out in the Hamptons. We're talking about the Yankees' pitching rotation. We're talking about my ridiculous love life."

Karen shook her head. "Well, okay," she said reluctantly. But she had to admit to herself that, given her lack of sources, she really was as eager for scraps as a baby bird in the nest with its little mouth wide open.

"About the Ferrari keys," Frank said.

Bring it on, mother bird, Karen thought. "The keys."

"My police sources say they can't track the owner.

He ordered the car from a Ferrari dealership up in Westchester County and paid cash. He used the name of a guy who had committed suicide in Buffalo. Somehow, the buyer got a duplicate of the dead guy's driver's license. Warden Moxley's the dead guy's name. The car now is registered to the dead guy's address in Buffalo."

Karen had difficulty understanding how this scrap was worth much more than a segment of worm. "Well, how does the mystery Ferrari owner do stuff like get the car inspected? You need that sticker on your windshield."

"The owner bribed a gas station attendant."

"I'll bite," Karen said. "What does this scrap of information tell us?"

"The Ferrari dealer and the gas station attendant gave descriptions that pretty much match that of Mixon."

"So if I see someone driving past in a Ferrari with a Buffalo Bills bumper sticker, I should call the cops?"

"Well, this Ferrari is distinctive. It's a 2002 Enzo, a limited edition."

"I can't tell the difference between a Ferrari and a Ford."

They had reached Brew-Ha-Ha. They exchanged glances, then went in for an afternoon caffeine fix.

While they waited, Frank said, "That's not all. The cops have almost certainly identified the Vampyr types who were in that subway car."

"Now here's some news. Tell."

"What I have is sketchy. Their leader is this Louis, not Mixon, even though Mixon was calling the shots today. Louis is Louis Roman, an ex-con. I'm not sure what he was in for yet. The woman with the Mace is Kyra Selden, age 21. Her father is a prominent doctor outside of Boston. She had lifelong involvement with drugs and shoplifting and other wholesome hobbies. Kyra had some promise: She was a pretty decent computer hacker who had managed to change her high school D's to A's with a few keystrokes. Henry is Henry Warren, age 23, who has done costumes and makeup for Broadway shows. He's likely the guy who made up Louis to look so hideous. His daddy is a big corporate executive with Coca-Cola in Atlanta. Henry spent part of his teen years in a psych ward. His parents thought he'd be all right once he got into the theater. The cops thus far have zip on Mixon. It's like he dropped from the sky. When he was with the caterer, he had rented a small apartment. I haven't been able to find the address yet. The cops can't find fingerprints on him there or from the dinners he catered."

"They sound like nice people."

"The bombing in that club for soldiers, outside Fort Drum, is the latest for Vampyr. Twelve soldiers died."

"Frank," Karen said, "if I come across them, what should I do?"

"Run like hell."

As before, Karen was welcomed back to the office by the embraces of her friends.

"This shit is getting freaky," Wendy said. "I'm worried about you."

"Shit freaky, shit freaky," said the parrot on her shoulder.

"You need a weekend out at the house, badly, badly," Mike Riley said. Every weekend out at their Hampton Bays summer house was a good excuse for a party. Mike's philosophy held that excessive eating and drinking cured all ills.

"Make sure that I get drunk this weekend," Karen said. She very much needed a weekend at the summer house with her pals. None of them, to her knowledge, had bombed anything. Now, getting bombed, that was a different story.

"Guaranteed, you'll be drunk as a monkey," Mike said.

After giving Eudell an extensive rundown on what had happened—minus Frank's contribution—Karen settled into her cubicle and thumbed through her notebook. She marveled at the quotes from her speed walk to the subway with Dengler. Unlike her parents, Karen believed in the free enterprise system. But a character like Dengler gave capitalism a bad name. He was like Ayn Rand on steroids.

Her mother called. "I saw on the news. This is dangerous, what you're doing. Your father is going crazy with worry."

"I'm okay. They're not after me."

"Are you sure? Your grandmother wants to talk to you."

Gran came on the line. "I hope they're paying you well to trail these horse's patoots," she said. "Combat pay, maybe."

"They're not paying me a lot, Gran."

"I did an anagram on Simon Dengler," Gran said. "Demon Slinger."

"Well, he's not a nice man."

"Yeah, Butch Strongville is Vergil Blotchnuts. Fred Morgan is Damn Forger."

"He prefers Frederick."

"I can't make a good anagram with Frederick."

After getting rid of her family, Karen checked her e-mail. It was the usual stuff, a lot of it spam. By taking a $100 course in investing, she could become a millionaire by New Year's. Maybe she should forward this choice opportunity to Tim.

Another message promised her as many dates with accomplished, attractive men as she could stand. Right. This reminded her about the joys of singlehood. Before her blessed union with Tim, she had tried a dating service once. Her swain, specially chosen to match her interests and desires, turned out to have all the sex appeal of a codfish. During their one and only date, she learned that he collected old comic books and had a fascinating riff on the inner lives of the Fantastic Four. Also, a hyena-like laugh that erupted with no warning.

Then there was an e-mail trying to enlist her for a psychic's reading of her future, provided she forked over $50. This one claimed the psychic, Madame Bilko, had forecasted everything from the winner of *American Idol* to the demise of Enron. Karen always had wondered why she never had read this headline: "Psychic Wins Lottery."

Then, as she scrolled down her directory, a more intriguing e-mail appeared. The subject was "Louis Roman, Vampyr leader." The sender was listed as "Boxerbelle."

Boxerbelle? A female boxer? Marcia?

Karen opened the e-mail. It contained no message, but did have an attachment. She clicked on that. It was an Adobe file of what appeared to be an FBI report. She began reading avidly about Louis Roman.

Although written in a dull bureaucrat-ese, the report contained a few fascinating scraps. Judging by his date of birth, Louis Roman was thirty-eight years old. Born in Newark to an unwed teenager who went on to a life of heroin addiction and prostitution, Roman had committed several early crimes that the record didn't list because, as juvenile offenses, they had been expunged. (Karen assumed that some trace of them must still exist on a database somewhere, for the FBI to say this.) Anyway, by age eighteen he was an enforcer for New Jersey's dreaded Malapropini crime family. The law suspected him of several Mob hits but never could prove them. He beat an indictment for loan sharking amid rumors of jury tampering. Grand theft auto landed him in Rahway Prison for a couple of years before a sage lawyer got him sprung. Later, he was convicted of running a counterfeiting ring and landed in Iffewon Federal Penitentiary, a maximum-security facility for hardcases.

Released from Iffewon, Roman went back to the Malapropinis, but after a while took a different career path. He turned up as the new chief of the radical group Vampyr. Its founder, an earnest fellow who preached world brotherhood, disappeared and was feared dead. Louis Roman turned out to have a mesmerizing power over the disturbed and impressionable youth attracted to this anti-globalization cause. Vampyr moved from the occasional rowdy demonstration outside an International Monetary Fund meeting to actual bombings of banks, chemical plants, and military sites. They had been accused of links to Al Quaeda, but the FBI dropped that idea because Vampyr had no Muslims in it, and was as exclusively white as the most posh country club. Louis Roman had several aliases: Lou Leadpipe, Luigi Rotten, and Josef Stalin. He had signed in as Stalin at the Templar Media lobby with the company's ever-vigilant security force. An enclosed police photo of him matched the guy she'd hit: a man with a strong jaw who radiated menace. He seemed ready to assault the camera.

Karen felt oddly cheered that Marcia Fink might actually be trying to help her. Boxerbelle?

Around nine, Karen took the bus home. No one suspicious was aboard, although no one had looked suspicious on the subway with Dengler. Tonight, she saw no one with Lucifer eyes.

She felt hugely hungry, and realized she hadn't eaten a bite the entire day. While another pizza from Carlo's struck a gastronomic chord, she ruled that out: Louis knew she went there. Karen decided on more healthy fare for her dinner. She got takeout Chinese with extra MSG.

After she polished off the meal at her kitchen table, she toyed with the notion of calling Tim. Aside from that one call at Gran's, why hadn't he phoned her? Karen picked up her phone and called . . . home.

"You're easy on the eyes but hard on the heart, darling," she muttered as she hit the speed dial for her former number.

"You've reached Tim," his recorded voice said. "Please leave a number." He had changed the greeting. It used to be her voice saying: "You've reached Karen and Tim's." She slammed the phone down. It hurt her hand, still tender from hitting Louis.

Before she could return the cordless receiver to the cradle, the phone rang. Tim?

It wasn't, proving that she was no Madame Bilko.

A by-now familiar male voice came on the line, this time not muffled by a Dracula mask. "You fucking bitch. You sucker punched me twice. I told you to stay away. I'm through with holding back on you. You're gonna get yours. Do you hear me, bitch?"

"Hey, Louis," she retorted, "what's the matter with you? What are you doing this for anyway? What are you trying to prove? How did you get my number?" Well, her new listing was under "K. Glick." Maybe she needed an alias like Josef Stalin.

Louis disconnected.

Karen knew that the cops could trace calls. But had Louis been on long enough?

She hit star 69.

There was a long succession of rings with no machine kicking in.

Then someone answered. She heard breathing.

Karen sucked in a draft of air. "Hello," she said.

"Who this?" asked a man with a Latino accent.

"Karen. Put Louis on."

"No Louis here, lady. This a pay phone."

"A pay phone?"

"Yeah, Thirty-third and Third. I be passing by."

Louis had called her half a block from her apartment. He was in her neighborhood. He could be right outside her door.

Chapter Twelve

As dusk spread shadows over Ludlum House's burnished wood floor, Frederick Morgan sat in front of Pulmon Tobacco financial documents, which were fanned out on the desk in front of him like a cold hand of cards. Back in Wall Street's grand old days, J.P. Morgan had perused similar deal documents on this desk, and with them formed an empire. But tonight Frederick Morgan couldn't concentrate. The numbers before him seemed unreadable, mere blobs of ink.

Fiona appeared at his door with her single strand of pearls and single-minded efficiency. As always, she looked tired. "The others await you, sir," she said, just this side of cranky. Sometimes, Fiona acted as though she was in charge of RDS&M.

"Do they?" Morgan heaved himself to his feet. He brushed past her. George Jr. and Al fell in step with them. Morgan didn't feel like being chatty to the help tonight. They crossed the Great Hall, with the Stomcox Massacre mural looking over them in bloody glory.

His bodyguards sealed the doors behind him, and Morgan was alone with his partners. They sat very silently. The lone sound came when Morgan seated himself, scraping his large chair along the floor.

Strongville said, "What the hell are we going to do with these bastards? They know our every move. Christ, first the Met. Now they tracked Simon like a damn deer. They had people placed on the exact subway car he got on. In the army, we called that a Class A ambush."

"You and your army," Dengler muttered to the tabletop.

"What did you say?"

"Why don't you do a Rambo on Vampyr, Butch?" Dengler said. "Mow them down."

"If I get my chance," Strongville shot back, "you won't see me cowering and quivering like a damsel in distress." He patted beneath the armpit of his suit jacket. "Anybody who gets in my way will meet my friends Smith and Wesson."

"That's very edifying, Butch," Morgan said. "Now you're Dirty Harry. Listen, Herman Heinrich is after them and will keep us safe meanwhile. So long as we stay out of sight."

"The best bodyguard we've got is that chick reporter, Glick," Strongville said. He lit up a cigarette. Everyone was too tired to object.

Morgan stood up. "Well, if that will be all, I am going out to dinner."

"Out to dinner?" Dengler said. "What's all this about staying out of sight?"

"May I remind you," Morgan said, "that Mercedes and I are taking Digby Graves to Chez Boo tonight." Graves was the chairman of Pulmon Tobacco. "Unlike the Met dinner, ours has not been advertised. And we are taking intense security precautions."

"You want to put Mercedes in the line of fire?" Strongville said, concerned.

"We'll be perfectly safe," said Morgan, hoping he was right. "Perfectly."

Warren, the interior decorator, had a vision. "What this room needs is some dash," he said as he drifted through the conservatory. His right arm clasped his left shoulder, and his left arm waved theatrically.

"Dash?" said Mercedes, who followed him from room to room, her expression a mixture of amusement and exasperation.

"Yes, darling. I'm thinking late-nineteenth-century Hitchcock chairs, some built-in cabinetry—only old lumber, of course—and a great deal of silverware. My heavens, you have no silver. I used to think we needed balance in our rooms. Now I'm into chaos."

"Silver is chaos?" Mercedes thought of her mother hand-polishing the silverware once a month at the kitchen table. The family never used it and seldom displayed it. Perennially short on money, they should have sold it. But the silver had to shine in its dark cupboard.

"Yes, the cabinetry must have a coat of intentionally

bad paint. I call this accelerated aging. This highlights the authenticity element, you see."

"Aging happens fast enough already, if you ask me," Mercedes said. She extended her hand to Warren, which meant the session had concluded. "Thanks for your insights."

Warren unclasped his shoulder and took her hand, which he bent over to kiss. "Darling, this has been my pleasure, as always." He swooped out.

Miranda, the social secretary, appeared. "Mrs. Chapin is waiting in the drawing room," she reminded Mercedes. Miranda, a voluptuous young woman with innocent eyes, was better than any digital organizer.

Mercedes thanked her. "Could you see that my clothes are laid out for tonight? Mia knows what I'm wearing." When Miranda left, Mercedes slid the letter out of her pants pocket and examined it. It was addressed to her in scrawled handwriting. The postmark was from Manhattan. There was no return address other than this single inscription: "E. Danton."

She hadn't opened it yet. The letter had arrived two months before.

Frederick reminded himself to behave nonchalantly as he entered the foyer, with George Jr. and Al accompanying him. They seldom came into his home. He told the bodyguards to wait. "Only a sec, guys.'

Mia hustled down the hallway, with its ingloriously stripped walls, to welcome him. "Do you want to change, sir?"

"No, Mia." Morgan treated her to a smile. "I'm running a little late. We have to get to the restaurant. Is Mrs. Morgan ready?"

"She's coming in a moment. Mrs. Chapin left only recently."

Mia enjoyed giving Morgan the house scuttlebutt. Mercedes might not have told her husband about Kay-Kay's visit. And since there'd been a Kay-Kay visit, Mercedes would have at least two strong cocktails aboard now. Mercedes had been drinking more lately. On the other hand, with her cool elegance, it never showed.

Morgan marched down the long, bare-walled hall to his son's room. Bert was gripping his videogame controller and furiously fighting a hatchet-wielding, fire-breathing madman. The hero figure had a gun so enormous that Butch Strongville would salivate in envy.

"Are you winning?" Morgan asked his son.

Bert was immersed in *Destruction 101*—the latest hot game, which no other kids had yet. His ever-solicitous mother had ensured that he got the game before it appeared in stores; the game maker's chief executive sat on the Lincoln Center board with her. Bert hit pause and the action on the screen froze. Bert turned to his father and gave a small, impish smile. "Sure."

At fourteen, Bert had friends whose reactions to grownups fluctuated between contempt and boredom. Bert, however, had inherited charm from his parents. He acted unfailingly pleasant to his father. But he seldom gave Morgan more than a single word.

"How did you do on that math test?" Mia had told Morgan about the test.

"Fine," Bert said.

"Your mother and I are going out to dinner. You eat yet?"

"Yes."

"Well, that's good," Morgan said. "How was your tae kwon do lesson today?"

"Skipped it."

Two words? "Well, perhaps you can get a black belt in Nintendo."

Bert didn't respond. The unspoken tension between them hung in the air like a dark and rumbling cloud.

As Morgan left, the hero's massive gun sliced the monster in two at its midsection. Blood and guts splattered everywhere. "Ha," Bert said.

Head bowed, Morgan went into his study and glumly checked his e-mails. With Mercedes, Bert was a little chatterbox. He doted on his mother. And she doted on him. When Bert was younger, he would light up at his father's return from work, those few instances when it was before Bert's bedtime. "Daddy, Daddy, Daddy," he'd cry. Morgan used to carry Bert around on his shoulders. Now, he couldn't carry on a conversation with the kid.

Miranda appeared at his door to tell him that Mrs. Morgan awaited him in the foyer. Why did Mercedes need to send an emissary? Earnest Miranda was his wife's personal vassal. She was efficient, loyal, and a little dim. When Caddy had taken up with her and predicably cast her aside, Miranda was shocked and heartbroken. Morgan straightened his tie and examined the shine on his handcrafted Italian shoes. He followed Miranda to the foyer, smile firmly in place.

Mercedes, standing near the Monet and rivaling its delicate beauty, cooked up a smile for her husband, although it wasn't her best. They both were good at smiling on cue. She wore a pale blue silk chiffon dress that clung to her tall, lithe frame. Its floral pattern echoed Monet's lilies. She asked politely how Simon was holding up after the incident, and Morgan assured her that Dengler was fine.

On the elevator down, with Al and George Jr. flanking them, Mercedes asked, "What is Digby Graves like?"

"He's a good ol' boy, hail fellow well met. There are a few rough edges. Being a tobacco executive isn't easy these days. Someone always is suing, claiming they didn't know cigarettes gave you cancer, despite the Surgeon General's warning that has been on every pack since 1964. Pulmon and the other companies get picketed a lot. Someone once threw blood on Digby."

"Why do you want to buy a tobacco company? Cigarettes do cause cancer."

"Well, darling, the profit margins still are large. Smoking isn't growing in this country, but it sure is overseas. Pulmon has a good foothold in China, where demand is robust."

"Oh," Mercedes said, her usual response to a patronizing lecture from her husband.

As they got into the car in the underground garage, Morgan noticed a second car full of men swinging behind them.

"Extra security," Al said with his normal humorlessness, which did nothing to allay fears.

They soon pulled up to Chez Boo's unmarked side

entrance. Several large men in suits formed a cordon as Frederick and Mercedes traversed that questionable space called the public sidewalk. When they moved up a flight of stairs and passed the kitchen, Al said to Morgan in a voice that Mercedes couldn't hear, "We have someone watching food preparation, sir."

The elegantly appointed dining room was filled with the chic, sleek, and unique—media luminaries, corporate satraps, FOP aristocrats, and various richies in from the suburbs, murmuring politely under the soft, moonlike glow of Chez Boo's famous sconces. Morgan's usual table was near the front, where he could better see and be seen. Tonight, though, security dictated that his table be at the back in a corner. En route to the table as they emerged from a rear door, he paused to shake only a few hands. Mercedes smiled and kissed.

Graves already had arrived. He got to his feet, belly jiggling, jowls flushed with hard, hell-bent living. Under his bushy gray moustache, his grinning teeth had a brown film over them from inhaling, over the years, several hundred cubic miles of smoke. "Come on over here, you magnificent bastard," he boomed at Morgan.

The other diners' eyelids fluttered at the loud and gauche bonhomie.

Graves pumped Morgan's hand and clapped his back while laughing heartily at nothing in particular. Morgan, only five-seven, appreciated it that Graves stood a full inch less.

"Good to see you, Digby," Morgan said with unflappable cultivation. "I suspect you'll like this restaurant."

"Aw, shit, man. I been coming to Chez Boo since Hector was a pup. And he's a big dog now. Every trip to New York, I hit this joint." Lowering his tone so only Morgan and Mercedes could hear, he added, "I always slip old Jean a box of primo Cuban cigars." Jean owned Chez Boo. "And I mean to tell ya, they're from Fidel's personal humidor." He winked at Morgan.

In his career, Morgan had heard countless chief executives claim that they had a special line to Fidel Castro's personal cigar collection. And that was despite the fact that the dictator had given up smoking years before—and was a Communist.

Graves turned to Mercedes, the tallest member of their party. "Hell, this is the little lady I been hearing about." She threw the switch on her best smile, an excellent array of white enamel. "You are the prettiest thing I've seen in a long time." She offered a polite handshake. He took her hand with both his. "Holy Jesus, Frederick, how did a little skunk like you land a gorgeous creature from heaven like this one?"

"Lucky, I guess. Short people have some reason to live, right? Shall we be seated?"

As they moved to the table, Graves noticed Al and George Jr. taking up positions to each side. Several other bodyguards stood nearby.

"I hear tell you boys been having a peck of trouble," Graves said.

"Nothing we can't handle," Morgan said. "Nothing that will negatively impact our deal."

"Good. I like to sleep at night myself. And I'd hate to think that you boys are so busy running for cover that you can't make this deal happen."

A busboy appeared to fill their water glasses. No one noticed his slightly trembling hand gripping the water pitcher, or the sheen of sweat on his forehead, or his nervous eyes. He scuttled past the bodyguards and disappeared through the kitchen door, primed for his next move.

Mercedes knew the drill at business dinners. As the wife, she had to look beautiful, behave charmingly, and shut up when the men began talking seriously—which typically happened very quickly. After they ordered wine and food, she pretended to listen politely while Graves brayed some story about taking an influential and refined senator quail hunting.

"And the senator needed to take a piss, see, and asked where the facilities might be," Graves went on. "Shit fire, man, we was in the middle of the damn boondocks. I told the senator to haul it on out and hose down a tree. The quail wouldn't mind it none."

"That's a great story, Digby," Morgan said after feigning a laugh.

Graves turned to Mercedes and placed a hand on her bare forearm, which he massaged in a borderline inappropriate way. "Little darling, you were a dancer."

Hesitating, then deciding to put up with this manhandling for now, Mercedes imitated her son's responding to Frederick. "Yes."

With an enthusiastic nod, Graves removed his hand. "Tell you a little secret. I saw you do *Chaconne* back when old Balanchine was around. He did killer choreography. And you"—he pointed at Mercedes—"knocked 'em dead with your *pas de deux*. You did it with Baryshnikov, and you floated through the air. Too bad you didn't do more ballet."

Stunned that he knew about dance, let alone her career in it, Mercedes said, "Why, thank you, Digby. George was very nice to let me perform. And Misha had this wonderful spirit. No, I'm too tall for classical ballet. That was my nickname, Too Tall."

"Hell, I saw you a bunch of times when you was with Twyla Tharp. You never could predict what that little gal Tharp would set a dance to—jazz, Shaker rhythms, David Bowie tunes, you name it. Whatever, you always stood out. And not just from the height."

Delighted, Mercedes found herself smiling genuinely. "I loved working for Twyla. She was tough, made impossible demands, but the result was worthwhile. She said I had 'a purity and directness.' That's when she wasn't telling me to get off my sorry butt and move right." Mercedes laughed at the memory.

"You were a star, darling."

"I wanted to be a galaxy, Digby." And now she was Frederick Morgan's wife. "Well, no one stays a dancer after forty." How easily he had won her over. She could see why, despite his boorish manner, Graves headed a major corporation.

"What? And here I pegged you for twenty-five if you was a day."

During their conversation about dance, the sommelier had come with the wine, which Morgan tested and ordered poured. "A toast," he said, "to our mutual fortune."

Graves chugged down half his glass. "Hmmmm. What is this swill?"

"Haut-Brion," Morgan said. "Simon recommended it. He's our wine expert. But he buys it by the case to get a price break."

"Hell, I've seen this place's wine list. The prices are high enough to make me crap my drawers. You're paying tonight, right?" Graves slugged down the rest.

"Of course," Morgan said, having steered the conversation away from his wife's petty concerns. "What's this I hear about Naylor & Cross being interested in you?"

Graves reached for the bottle before a hovering waiter could snatch it. "Well, Frederick, them folks done paid me a courtesy call. They might be interested and they might not. We've kept this out of the media."

"Discretion should be the watchword. No media."

"No media?" Graves leaned across the table. "Then why do you have that magazine reporter doing a story on y'all?"

"Anything on our deal, Karen Glick will put in after it is done. She's under control."

"I hate those liberal media people. Always twisting the news. They treat tobacco companies like Satan Incorporated. Hell, folks want to smoke, they'll smoke."

Morgan popped on a fake smile. "Digby, you wouldn't want to start a bidding war to buy Pulmon, now would you? That could get nasty."

"Not nasty for my shareholders if I get the right price for our stock. Helen Naylor and Tommy Cross might just provide that there. We live with a free market here, my friend." The toughness that had gotten Graves to the top was on display.

Graves's sharp, almost belligerent reply, attracted the bodyguards' attention.

"Digby, we have an agreement."

Graves raised his voice. "Then why is Butch Strongville coming down to inspect our operations? Ashlea Kress and her bunch already done that for you. I know what Strongville really wants. He wants to check out how to lay off my people as soon as y'all take over. We already run a tight ship. We don't need us no layoffs."

"Naylor & Cross routinely lays off workers when they take over a company, too. They call Helen Naylor 'the face that launched a thousand pink slips.' "

"What concerns me more," Grave railed, "is one layoff in particular. Mine. I like being the CEO."

Mercedes, watching in silence, could see why. Chief executive officers were paid gargantuan sums, enjoyed bonanzas of stock options that let them buy valuable shares for very little, received lavish perks like corporate jets and pro football skyboxes, and occupied a status in society akin to a crown prince. For those with fabulously inflated egos such as Graves, being CEO was oxygen. The loss of it was unthinkable.

"We have committed to giving you a nice three-year employment contract."

"But y'all have a bad-ass history of breaking it once you collect enough shares to control the company.

That damn Strongville likes to throw a CEO personally out the door."

Morgan tried to be conciliatory. "Digby, Digby, Digby, we've terminated some CEOs we kept on, that's true. But they were performing badly and, as we saw matters, had broken the contract. We don't expect that from you, and value your ongoing leadership."

"Don't yank my twine," Graves barked. "A bunch of them boys you tossed out the very day you got the keys."

Everyone in the restaurant was watching now.

Their sights on Graves, Al and George Jr. shifted their weight in case they needed to stop him from taking a poke at Morgan.

They didn't see the busboy closing in on the table. Until it was too late.

Chapter Thirteen

The busboy ran at the table, a large bowl in his hands. At the very last instant, Mercedes saw him.

"Look out!" she shouted.

The bodyguards took too long to react. Al swiveled his head. George Jr. got out half an obscenity. The other bodyguards, farther away, were a still life.

"Your turn," the busboy cried.

He tossed the contents of the bowl onto Graves—a pound of ashes. The filth hit Graves square in his fleshy face.

Al tackled the busboy first. The busboy offered no resistance. George Jr. stood over them with his weapon out. Women screamed. Men shouted. Several diners ran from their tables.

Mercedes made to dust off Graves's clothes, but he rudely pushed her hands away. His face, shirt, and suit jacket were coated in gray ash.

Mercedes sat back. To her, Graves looked like Wile

E. Coyote after the defective Acme bomb had exploded in his face.

"You killed my father," the busboy was hollering.

Angry and mortified, Graves got to his feet and crossed over to where Al had the busboy pinned. "You crazy fucker," Graves bellowed at the busboy.

"You sold him lung cancer." The busboy strained his neck over Al's shoulder to face the approaching Graves.

"I'll see you never be a father." Graves made to kick the busboy between the legs. One of the other bodyguards, though, grabbed the tobacco chief executive and pulled him back.

Unable to assault the busboy, Graves spat at him. The spittle hit Al's head instead.

Morgan, who had initially been too shocked to move, got up and scrambled to Graves's side. "Digby, let my men take care of him. We'll call the police."

Graves wiped the ashes from his eyes and smeared his cheeks. "And you want to own a tobacco company, Frederick?"

Karen wasn't sure what to do. If she called the cops, one or maybe two officers would respond. Would they canvass the neighborhood for Louis, or just take her report and leave?

On the other hand, if he posed a genuine threat to her, not calling the cops made no sense.

At the pizza parlor, Louis had simply warned her to stay away. Now he seemed actually primed to harm her.

She fished out Marcia's card and called her home

number. There were several rings. Just about the time the machine usually kicked in, Marcia answered.

"Yeah?" she said, hardly welcoming. Did she have caller I.D.?

"Marcia, it's Karen." Karen waited for a response. None. "Glick."

"I know who you are."

"Thanks for the FBI file you sent me."

"What file?"

"Have it your way," Karen said. "Listen, I need your advice." She described what had occurred with Louis. "What do I do?"

"Do? Shove a couch in front of your door."

"I've already done that." She tried not to sound scared.

"You got a fire escape outside your window?"

"Sure. But my window has pretty good bars. No one could get through them."

Marcia's matter-of-fact cop manner was hardly soothing. "He doesn't have to get through your window bars. He can shoot you from out on the fire escape."

"Shoot me? Jesus." Karen became instantly aware of how brightly lit her little apartment was. "He'd shoot me?"

"Nothing worse than a homicidal nut with a grudge. He'll do whatever he wants."

Karen exhaled raggedly. "You're making my night here, Marcia. How am I supposed to live my life if this nut is out to get me?"

"Well," Marcia said nonchalantly, "I could send some uniforms around, but that won't do any good.

They won't see him because he's the kind of guy who can hide damn good. And the uniforms won't scare him away."

Marcia put her hand on the phone and talked to someone else indistinguishably. Then she came back. "Listen, I gotta go."

"Wait one minute here, Marcia. What the hell should I do?"

Marcia gave one of her bursts of laughter. "Watch your step and bide your time. Sooner or later, we'll catch this skel and his pals. And remember, his main target is not you. That would be Simon Dengler. He's the guy who really should be watching his fanny."

"That's comforting as hell, Marcia, but—"

Marcia hung up. Karen listened to the dial tone for a few moments before slamming down the receiver.

She raced around the apartment turning off all lights. Her heart thumped audibly in her chest. In the luxury building where she had lived with Tim, a doorman screened everyone entering the lobby. Security staff roamed through the building, alert for problems. Cameras in the hallway could detect someone trying to jimmy open an apartment door. Intercoms throughout their apartment could let you summon help instantly.

Not that she yearned to return to her old Tim-infested co-op, mind you.

Karen had nothing on premises to protect herself. Not a baseball bat. Not a can of Mace. Not even a good kitchen carving knife; she had brought along minimal cutlery.

Sitting on her sofa in the darkness, Karen listened to

her heartbeat. Outside the window, the scaffolding of the fire escape loomed. The night breathed in and out.

Bump, bump, bump, bump, bump. That wasn't her heart.

Karen shrieked.

Bump, bump, bump. The noise was only Bigfoot upstairs.

First passing her hands over her face, Karen decided that she might as well go to bed. While very tired, she wasn't sure if she would be able to sleep. At least her bed lay off to the side from the window. Provided that she lay near the wall, no one could see her well enough from the fire escape to get off a good shot. Or so she told herself.

Karen slid beneath the sheets and moved to where the bed met the wall. She was on her back, which allowed her a view of the window. Her heart kept tripping loudly. Not a chance she'd be able to fall asleep. Not a . . .

She dreamed she was strolling through a field with Frederick Morgan. He displayed his confident and composed self. She had been asking him questions, although their content was unclear. "You could have been married to me," Morgan said. "Were you ever a dancer?"

Karen replied that she was many things, yet never a dancer. He took her hand. She wanted to shake it free. She turned to tell him that she shouldn't be holding hands with a married man. Then she saw she was walking with Tim.

Clang, clang, clang, clang, clang.

The metallic sound jerked Karen awake. She sat straight up in bed.

Someone was outside. On the fire escape. Moving fast.

Karen stood up on the bed and flattened herself against the wall. She clapped a hand to her mouth to muffle the panicky sound of her breathing.

The clanging stopped right outside her window. A blur of shadow fell across her floor. Then came a low muttering. There were two people out there.

A flashlight beam played along her floor. It moved across the sofa to the bookcase to the still-unpacked boxes to the tiny galley kitchen.

Karen tried to merge with the wall. If they angled the flashlight right, they could find her.

Then she heard a clumping across her ceiling. A harsh female voice shouted out from above: "Who the hell are you? What are you doing?"

Next came a clanging as the two intruders climbed down the fire escape.

"I'll call the cops," Bigfoot railed at them.

Well, maybe Karen had a security system after all.

"And don't come back," Bigfoot shouted.

Please, Karen echoed to herself, don't come back.

Danton was peering through his telescope into the Morgans' lives. He observed Mercedes and Frederick leave. She looked dazzling; Danton knew they were off to meet the tobacco executive. The entire evening, Danton surveyed their co-op from his balcony. He saw nothing except for their son, playing a videogame, and their maid, trying on Mercedes's clothes.

Then, too early to have returned from dinner out,

Mercedes suddenly appeared in the drawing room. Danton must have missed her entering the apartment. She held an envelope. Danton somehow knew it was his. With her finger, she ripped the letter open. Slowly, she removed the single sheet of paper and read it. And she rushed away.

Danton felt himself grow faint. Tonight, he shed two tears. She had waited this long to open his letter? "Mercedes," he whispered.

"Spying on the neighbors?"

Whipping his head around from the telescope's eyepiece, Danton found Louis standing at the wide doors to the inside. Louis with his cape and his sadist's smirk.

"What are you doing here?" Danton tried to summon up menace. He had seen that smirk many times. The first was as a new inmate at Iffewon. A smirking Louis Roman had backed Danton into a corner and demanded his money.

"Is she naked? Lemme sneak a peak."

Danton moved to re-assert his position. He aimed an index finger at Louis, as if it were a weapon. "You aren't supposed to be here."

"You didn't expect I'd find out where you live, right? Vampyr knows all, my friend."

"Oh, for Christ's own sake. How did you get in here?"

Louis flung up a hand in mock carefree style. "I'm a professional criminal."

"After today's screw-up, you . . . What do you want?"

Louis nodded and showed his teeth. "Today's

screw-up? You mean when you blurted out our names on the subway—mine, Kyra's, Henry's? Not that you're entirely to blame. That sneaky bitch reporter hit me again when I wasn't looking."

"What? Are you going to complain to the rules committee?"

You could see every tooth as Louis snapped out his reply. "I'm gonna kill her, shithead."

A mere two feet separated them, sufficient for Louis to easily grab Danton and heave him over the balcony.

"The name isn't shithead," Danton seethed at the man. "I'm the one who gives you the money, understand? I've hired you for an assignment, understand? Karen Glick will remain unharmed, understand?"

A sapling-thin fellow suddenly appeared beside them, as if magic had materialized him. "You got a problem, boss?" Ali asked.

Louis took in Danton's servant, then stepped back. Despite his slender frame, Ali radiated a lethal nature that Louis, with his thug radar, detected at once.

"Remember. I'm your best friend," the Vampyr leader said to Danton. "Boss."

The next morning early, before going to work, a sleep-deprived Karen phoned Gran and told her about the situation. Within a half-hour, four burly guys showed up at Karen's apartment door and helped her pack clothes and toiletries in a series of laundry bags. The Billionaire Boys' documents filled an entire bag; it was the heaviest. She knew two of the men. In her bathroom, she changed into the overalls they had brought her. The group of them carried her stuff outside to a waiting van. The pain in her hitting hand had begun to fade a little bit. With her hair pulled up under a large baseball cap, Karen scanned the block but saw no one out of the ordinary.

Riding in the back of the van with two of the guys, Karen sat hunched over as they crossed the Triboro Bridge to the Bronx. To ensure no one had tailed them, they wound through several quiet Bronx neighborhoods and then came back to Manhattan via the Willis Avenue Bridge, a small span that even at rush hour moved well. They parked the van outside another of Gran's tenement buildings, this one in Morningside Heights. With dispatch, they trooped Karen's belongings down to the basement.

"You folks are so nice to do this for me," she told Joey, the head guy, as they hoisted the bags down the stairs.

"Anytime, Karen," Joey said.

Gran, in a navy Chanel suit, was waiting outside the door of Karen's temporary apartment, which was next to the boiler room. "Okay, you lugs, put the bundles inside and get back to work. You're behind schedule."

Karen's new home was little more than a closet. It had a bed, a sink, a shower, and a toilet. The floor was concrete and the walls cinderblock.

"There's a small bug problem," Gran said.

"The bugs are small?"

"No, they're from out of a science fiction movie. But you're not here for long."

"I hope. Thanks, Gran. You haven't told my parents?"

"I'd rather not put up with Emma's worried wailing day and night. Out of self-preservation, I'm keeping my trap shut." She snatched her granddaughter's baseball cap off her head. "Are you trying for the Mickey Mantle look? Oh, speaking of your mother, a word of warning: She thinks she has a boy for you."

"A boy? As in someone too young to drink or vote?"

"As in a replacement for your scum-sucking husband, smarty pants. I'm sure he'll be like your parents—a self-righteous, left-wing do-gooder. In other words, no sex appeal."

"Something to look forward to."

Gran handed her a set of keys. "You should be safe here. Make sure no one puts a tail on you when you leave work."

"You're pretty good at this cloak-and-dagger business."

Gran sniffed. "I learned more from being a Communist than Marxist dialectic." In her youth, Gran had been a member of the Communist Party. Her daughter, Emma, had been brought up as a "Red diaper baby," schooled in party thought, which is how Emma came by her left-wing sympathies. Gran had been arrested, been wiretapped, been followed. To this day, she bragged, she could tell an FBI agent by his shifty eyes. Her later switch to the Republican Party had been too dramatic for Emma to comprehend.

"I'll watch my back," Karen said.

"Don't trust a soul," Gran said. "Don't tell Eudell or Frank or Wendy or any of your friends where you are. There's no phone in here, so you can't be tracked down that way. Use your cell to make calls. At night, stay inside, keep off the street."

A roach the size of an M-1 tank skittered along the floor. "I'll be fine."

"Your father told me a little bit about your story. They're tax cheats, right?"

Karen grimaced. "I told him to not talk about this. I shouldn't be blabbing about it."

"Not to your own grandmother?"

Sighing then smiling, Karen said, "Well, don't tell anyone."

Gran's answer was like Maury's: "Who am I going to tell? J. Edgar Hoover?"

"Basically, I'm trying to prove they're hiding income—and I mean billions—in an offshore account that the IRS doesn't know about and can't touch. I guess a lot of wealthy people do this, but they've gone way overboard. I simply have to prove that account records I have from their bank in the Caymans are genuine. Not easy."

As Karen gave her the gist of the story, Gran's old eyes widened, forcing the wrinkles in her forehead to compress. "A bank in the Caymans, you say? Which one?"

"First Caymans Bank and Trust," Karen said. "I have the records here in one of these bags. Have you heard of it?"

Nodding sagely, Gran said, "Maybe, maybe, maybe." Then she clasped the strap of her Hermes handbag. "Well, I gotta go. I'm needed in the office to kick some butts. Get out of that getup, willya? You look like a jackass."

After Gran left, Karen doffed her overalls and took a shower. Instead of a steady stream of water, she got a fine mist. It would have to do. Then she got into some real clothes rescued from the bags. There was no sense hanging things up because she had no closet.

Wearing a big, droopy-brimmed hat that obscured her eyes, Karen rode the Broadway Local to Midtown. She furtively examined the other passengers on the subway car. Nobody seemed suspicious, but then nobody did on the train trip with Dengler, either. That old electricity buzzed up and down her spine. She got off at 50th Street and threaded into the crowd, which could contain anyone. She whipped her head around to see if anyone was tracking her.

A secret of the Templar Media building, one of the giant cereal boxes lining Sixth Avenue, was that it could be reached through a labyrinth of underground passages. She entered the lobby of an adjacent building and, checking behind her, trundled down the stairs to the subterranean walkway. No one was on the stairs behind her. Karen called Templar Media security on her cell as she approached her building. She came up into the Templar building in a small corridor off its lobby, where the service elevator stopped.

A security guard met her and took her up the elevator to her floor, where another security man awaited. The company believed that it had stepped up security by turning to the same brainiacs who had allowed in the gun-toting Louis.

With their rubbery girths and dazed demeanors, the Templar security team was as intimidating as the Pillsbury Doughboy. Karen instructed Rose that she wasn't really in.

"Man trouble?" the kindly receptionist said. Rose had her own sense of humor.

"Yeah, the one who came here with the gun in his hand. He may be asking for me."

"If he comes, you're not here," Rose said. "Me neither. I head for the stairs, like Calvin Christian."

Karen spent the day finishing her story about Redmon's murder and Dengler's almost-kidnapping. She had a problem with the FBI file because she couldn't authenticate it. A bored-sounding functionary at the bureau said he would neither confirm nor deny its authenticity.

Early afternoon, Eudell sidled up to her desk. "Frank checked with the FBI," the editor said. "The file on Vampyr is real. You can use it."

"Uh, I thought Frank wasn't supposed to be helping me on this story."

"Well, this one doesn't concern Frederick Morgan directly." She cast a baleful eye toward the managing editor's office. "But don't tell Calvin Christian that Frank helped out."

After filing her story, she sneaked out of the building in the same fashion as she had come to work. No one seemed to be following her. Back in Morningside Heights, she decided she deserved a pizza. She brought the pie back to her little warren, where a couple of cocky roaches hungrily observed her devouring every last morsel. That night, she slept well for a change. With the lights off, the tiny room was like a sensory deprivation tank. Friday morning, she packed a backpack with weekend duds and retraced her steps to work, feeling more confident. She passed much of the day fielding queries from the copy desk and the fact checkers.

The toughest questioning came from her friend Lynn Landers, the magazine's lawyer, who tried to keep stories as libel-proof as possible. "How can we prove that Redmon was a womanizer?" Lynn asked.

"I've got papers from his three divorces," Karen said. "Adultry is alleged every time, with details that I didn't have space to include in the story." Those salacious details would be held for her big story; like the instance where Caddy was having a threesome beside his swimming pool in Nantucket when his then-wife arrived with their children.

Karen called Kay-Kay Chapin, the tippling socialite she'd sat next to at the Met dinner, figuring Kay-Kay could give some insight into the Billionaire Boys. Kay-Kay knew about Caddy Redmon, for sure. Kay-Kay's snotty assistant at her real estate firm said, "Mrs. Chapin is in a meeting and cannot be disturbed. Would you care to leave your name and number?"

Gatekeepers like this usually didn't pass along phone messages from the unwashed to their bosses. Still, Karen dutifully left her information.

Next, Karen tried to locate Emily Bourdain; the Met caterer's chef had known Mixon and might be of help. The catering company guy, not happy to be fielding a press call about one of his waiters who had poisoned a guest, said Emily wasn't there and refused to say how to get a hold of her. "We don't take messages," he said. "Excuse me, we're very busy here." *Click.*

Karen came up with three Bourdains in her search

of the New York metro area phone database. After identifying herself to the man who answered—"This is Karen Glick from *Profit* magazine"—he bellowed, "I don't want to buy a damn magazine subscription. Quit bothering me." The second Bourdain was an addled old lady who figured that, since a catering service was involved, Karen could provide her with better food: "The Meals on Wheels swill I get isn't fit for a dog," she said. The third Bourdain was a Barry White-voiced dude aiming to be a low-rent version of Caddy Redmon: "I don't know no Emily, but you sound cute. Want to get together?"

The police, of course, would know how to get in touch with Emily Bourdain. So would Frank Vere. Karen decided to shelve the Emily quest until the next week. She called some of the young radicals whose names her father had furnished. They all knew Maury Glick, in an amused and condescending way. She asked to interview some of them Monday and some even said yes.

At day's end, she crept out to a street corner twelve blocks distant, where Frank and the gang picked her up for the journey to the Hamptons. She had decided that her going to the garage with them to get the car was too risky. Frank's car, an ancient Ford Escort that Karen called the Ford Escargot, wheezed out of Manhattan and onto the Long Island Expressway. In its day, the battered auto had hit everything but the New York Lottery.

Karen rode shotgun. Wendy, sitting in the back, massaged her shoulders. "You'll have a great weekend," Wendy said. "No one will find you in Hampton Bays. You're safe."

"You're safe, you're safe, you're safe," said the parrot on her shoulder.

As night spread over the city with cancerous speed, Louis called for Kyra and Henry. They obediently shut the door behind them.

"What about Glick?" he asked.

"She must've left her apartment," Henry said tentatively, ever-reluctant to anger Louis.

"And why haven't you found her?"

"It's a big city?" Kyra's strategy of avoiding offense was to give answers with a questioning lilt at the end, as though she weren't quite sure she was correct.

Louis held back his urge to pound both of their faces to mush. "I'll give you two some help. She usually spends weekends at her friend Mike Riley's summer house."

"Hasn't Danton put Glick off limits?" Henry asked meekly.

"Danton is not the head of Vampyr," Louis said. "All you need to understand is that this Glick bitch hit me twice when I wasn't looking. I should trash her myself, but . . ." He gave a barbaric smile. "When you do it to her," he told them, "make sure no one else is around. We don't need witnesses."

"I hate her," Kyra said. "She hit you, Louis."

"She deserves it," Henry said.

"When you're done with her," Louis said, "bring me back a keepsake. Her finger."

"Ears are easier to cut off," Henry said.

Louis succeeded in tamping down his anger. "I said a finger. Finger means finger."

Kyra, seeing Louis was very near another Krakatoa eruption, hauled Henry away. "We'll give you the finger. Not a problem."

Louis, enfolded in his cape, scowled. "No more problems allowed."

Chapter Fourteen

Mike Riley had won the Hampton Bays summer house a couple of years before in a poker game. He called the place the Busted Flush, but no one else in the gang picked that up—the name's association with plumbing problems somehow didn't resonate with fun times. And the house was made for fun times. It sat on a quarter-acre lot about a mile from the beach. There were several trees on the property, from which Mike had strung hammocks where you could swing during a lazy afternoon or snuggle under the stars at night. Mike called the hammocks "a spiritual investment."

The house was a saltbox built in 1980, with a large fireplace, a skylight, and a wing someone had added around 1990. So it contained numerous bedrooms for house members and their guests. The kitchen had mostly up-to-date appliances, although Frank the cook objected to the no-name stove whose oven didn't always maintain the constant temperatures he required for his exotic desserts. The dining room had a long table, perfect for their famously raucous dinner parties, and an adjoining deck had a gas grill that the male barbecue wizards—who wouldn't deign to prepare food during the week—fought to control.

The house was in a quiet, suburban neighborhood of similarly modest middle-class homes. Stoner, the next-door neighbor, worked as a handyman. A former biker who now only occasionally rode his Harley, Stoner had a fierce beard, a jovial manner, and a sideline growing pot in his backyard. Several times during the workweek when Mike's house had sat deserted, a shotgun-brandishing Stoner had warded off vandals and thieves.

The other neighbors were quiet working types who also lived year-round in Hampton Bays: a plumber, an electrician, a gift store owner. Karen referred to Hampton Bays as the Un-Hampton—a ghetto for working stiffs who served the plutocrats weekending at their sumptuous palaces in tonier towns nearby, such as Quogue, Amagansett, and Southampton.

After a raucous dinner at an Italian red sauce joint out on Montauk Highway, they returned late and happy to the house. Everyone piled into bed. This summer, Karen had Wendy as a roommate. Thankfully, the parrot spent the night in the living room, where he kept his remarks to himself and snoozed peacefully. The previous two summers, Karen had had a room with a queen-sized bed that she shared with Tim. Now, the Razz and his new girlfriend, a performance artist named Sheila, had that room. Dazzling Sheila had said nothing the entire evening and had picked at a salad during dinner.

"Are you okay?" Wendy asked. "The divorce and the murder and the violence and the threats and all that shit. This can't be easy." Wendy was a real sweetheart, forever concerned with others' feelings.

"I'm fine. Go to sleep." The drinking had dulled the ache in her hitting hand.

But Karen lay awake, mulling over those very issues.

Parked in a van near the summer house, Henry lowered the binoculars. "She's in the corner room. They just turned the lights off. Everyone should be asleep soon. Since they don't lock the house, this should be easy."

"But we don't know the interior of the house?" Kyra observed. "We can't get to her inside without knowing where we're going?"

"If they're all sleeping, it won't matter."

"Louis said to take her when no one else is around?"

"When else should we do this? She's always with those other people in the day."

"Someone could wake up?"

"We'll do them, too."

"That will be awfully messy? We can wait for an opportunity?"

Henry never liked to admit that Kyra could be right.

The next day, with its gorgeous sun, was perfect for the beach. Karen sat reading under a wide umbrella, her one-piece suit doing a poor job disguising the winter pudge she'd lacked the time or energy to diet away. The boys kept missing the Frisbee they were tossing around because they were too intent on ogling silent Sheila in her tiny bikini.

That was when Karen and Lynn decided to take Lynn's car and go shopping in Southampton. As they drew near the village, a Rolls-Royce passed them.

Karen got a glimpse of the passenger. "It's Mercedes Morgan."

The Rolls pulled into a parking spot in Southampton's ungodly chi-chi shopping district, which made Rodeo Drive look like a slum.

Karen, in her proleterian T-shirt and shorts, hopped onto the sidewalk. One of Mercedes Morgan's bodyguards was holding the car door open for her. It was Ron, the older fellow who had been guarding Caddy Redmon. Karen hustled in their direction.

"Mrs. Morgan," she called.

Someone jumped in Karen's way, full of menace. Jimmy, the other Redmon bodyguard, blocked her like a metal stanchion. Rubber lips set in a scowl, he grabbed Karen's shoulder to stop her from taking one more step.

"Hey, hands off, Jimmy," Karen said. "We don't know each other that well."

Mercedes, taking a gazelle-like step out of the Rolls, eyed Karen from beneath her wide hat brim. She wore a short pastel sundress and had sleekly long legs and fine-boned shoulders.

"There you go again, Jimmy," said Ron with seen-it-all avuncular steadiness. "That's Karen Glick. She tried to save Mr. Redmon's life."

Jimmy released Karen but stayed between her and Mercedes.

"This is Karen Glick?" Mercedes came up beside Jimmy and extended her hand to Karen. "I want to thank you for putting yourself on the line, both for Caddy and Simon. You are one brave lady."

Karen shook her hand. "I wanted to say hello, Mrs. Morgan. I believe I'll see you at Caddy's funeral."

Mercedes gave a faint smile. "Well, I insist you fly out with us." She turned to Ron. "We'll include Ms. Glick on the RDS&M plane going to Caddy's funeral." She said to Karen, "It's a very nice Gulfstream. Quite comfortable. We're going to western Pennsylvania or some such place for the service. I'm sure we'll have time to chat."

"I like Gulfstreams," Karen said, never having been on this or any other executive jet. Cooke didn't seem to want her on the RDS&M plane. She had figured she would fly out commercially. She usually got a screaming infant on one side and a fat snoring guy on the other.

Mercedes favored Karen with a smile that was an orthodontist's nirvana. "Our people will be in touch." Then she floated into an exquisitely twee shop, her bodyguards in tow.

Lynn suggested that they go to a candle store down the street. Her fiancé, Gary, would return from his European trip the next week and she wanted to have a romantic reunion. The two friends strolled past the elegant storefronts, browsing in the windows at the pricey merchandise.

Karen noticed a small park beside the candle shop with benches and lovely plantings. It was shady and no one was using it. "Tell you what," Karen said. "I want to take in this lovely little park. I'll join you in a minute." Really, she wanted to think about how and what to ask Mercedes once she could interview her alone—and wanted to do it before the lingering image of the magnificent woman faded.

Karen wandered into the small park and stood before a fine stand of roses.

She didn't notice the van lurch to a stop on the street outside the park's entrance. Nor did she see the doors swing open and the two dark-clad figures emerge.

But she also didn't catch how they froze at the sight of two cops moving along the sidewalk. Nor how they scurried back into the van and zoomed off.

That night, as usual, the gang had a big party. Guests tumbled in the front door. Margaritas were poured. The men slapped tire-tread-thick steaks on the grill. The woman fussed with the salad. Frank prepared several souffles. The Razz popped wine corks. Everyone laughed and joked, except for Sheila. Wearing a tiny skirt and a midriff-baring haltertop, she didn't have to speak to draw attention to herself.

Afterward, Karen collapsed into a hammock. Frank dumped himself beside her. The voices and laughter from the house died down as people went to bed. Karen and Frank swung gently to and from, watching the stars through the leaves above. A chaste, brother-sister distance separated them.

"I could have been Tim Bratton's trophy wife," Karen said. "That's what he wanted from me. But I don't have the looks for it. People have always said I was 'cute.' Not 'gorgeous,' like Mercedes. I can't be a Mercedes."

"She's an accomplished woman in her own right," Frank said sleepily.

"Mercedes *was* an accomplished woman. Now she's a trophy wife."

"You were meant to be a reporter, not anyone's trophy except your own." He lurched out of the hammock.

"That's sweet," Karen said.

Karen swayed by herself for a while. The solitude was nice. A teasing wind tossed the trees around. The crickets serenaded her. Out in the deep night, a dog barked. She vaguely was aware of the van pulling up across the street.

Swinging her legs onto the lawn, Karen took in the night surrounding her. It was so peaceful. She could stay here forever and a day. Slowly, she walked barefoot through the silky grass. Karen clasped her bare arms to her chest. It was getting cooler. The wind thrashed the tree boughs, whose leaves rustled and whispered something she couldn't understand.

"I drank too much," she said to the night.

Metal creaked as the van's doors opened.

Then another vehicle swung into view, its headlights bathing the asphalt. The car stopped in front of the house. The driver's side door opened noiselessly.

Christ, it was Tim's BMW.

Her husband spotted her at once. He wore boat shoes, khakis, and a polo shirt. He stood there with his blondness and called to her. She couldn't move. He crossed the lawn to her and came within six inches. She stepped back.

"I heard about everything that's happened," he said.

"Yeah, it's only been all over the news all week long. Thanks for calling."

"I did call."

"To my grandmother's house."

"I figured you'd be there," Tim said in that maddeningly reasonable tone that he used to explain why two plus two equaled five. "You always go to her house when things go wrong."

"What do you want, Tim?"

Tim examined his boat shoes, trying for school-boy adorable. "This isn't about the divorce. This is about the Billionaire Boys Club."

"What about them?"

"Well, it turns out that Dewey Cheatham is getting work on the Pulmon Tobacco deal from RDS&M. I want to be sure that you're not going to write a story that will complicate our deal. Since you're my wife, that would really reflect badly on me."

"Your wife, huh? So that's what you were calling about. Nothing to do with consoling me for the trauma I'd been through. How nice." She tilted her head back and closed her eyes before bringing it level and shaking it. "Tim, have I ever written a story that's not a puff piece?"

"You never know. Frank Vere almost did a negative story on them a couple of years ago. It could be resurrected under your byline. Don't crack my rice bowl, Karen."

"Jesus, your rice bowl. You wouldn't touch rice unless it was Florentine risotto."

She turned to go, but he put a hand on her arm. "I'm serious, Karen."

Karen shook her arm free. If it was about himself, he was serious. If about her, it was a joke. "Please." Karen headed for the front door, then looked back. He hadn't moved. Perhaps because he had mentioned Frank's aborted story on RDS&M, she thought of something Frank had said about them. "Tell me why the Billionaire Boys left Dewey Cheatham."

"Oh, hell. That was back in the 1980s, long before I came along. I was a kid then."

"But you hear things. Tell."

Tim held up his hands. "There was some unpleasantness. I don't know the details. Long forgotten. Hey, the old guard has retired from Dewey Cheatham and RDS&M's contemporaries are in charge. Our firm is tight now with the Billionaire Boys."

"What kind of unpleasantness? I've read every story that has been done about RDS&M. I never read of any 'unpleasantness.'"

"Who knows? The old Dewey Cheatham partners from those days are mostly dead. Life goes on. What can I say?"

"Say goodnight, Tim."

"Damn," Tim said. He tromped back to his BMW and peeled rubber as he sped away.

Karen watched him. Then she saw a bulky figure charge out of the darkness toward the parked van. Loud threats followed. The van's motor fired up and it drove off.

The bulky figure lumbered onto their lawn. It was Stoner, the next-door neighbor. And he was carrying a shotgun.

"My God, Stoner, what's the matter?" She eyed the shotgun uneasily.

"A couple of assholes was sitting in that van. I know they're up to no good. I seen them here last night. Nobody's gonna rip off any of our houses with old Stoner around."

"Good," Karen said with great weariness. She went inside.

A mile away, Henry and Kyra argued about what to do next. They decided that, despite Louis's orders, they would have to move on Karen Glick even if others were around. She always was with people.

Chapter Fifteen

"Crack his rice bowl. I mean, can you believe him?" Her head hurting, Karen was hunched over her bagel and coffee the next morning, out on the deck, with her pals clustered around. Several copies of *The New York Times* were scattered on tabletops.

"You go, girl," Wendy said.

"I did go. All we need to do is sign the divorce papers."

"I wish Stoner wouldn't wave that shotgun around," Lynn said.

Frank had a worried look. "I noticed that van parked outside last night and Friday night, too," he said. "Didn't you say the Vampyr bunch escaped from the subway station in a van?"

"You're weirding me out here, Frank," Karen said. "Anyone got aspirin?"

Karen's cell phone, which she carried deep in her shorts pocket, trilled. She grimaced.

Putting two aspirins beside Karen, Mimi said, "If it's Tim, I've got more of these."

As Karen flipped open her phone, Wendy asked where the Razz and Sheila were.

"Karen Glick," she said, her delivery slurred as she swallowed the pills with coffee.

"Still in bed," Lynn said. "They didn't get much sleep. With the noise they made, neither did I."

A man on the other end of Karen's phone said, "Hold, please, for Mrs. Chapin."

"Ah, young love," Mike said.

"Well," Wendy said, "at least Sheila is finally turning chatty."

Because the chatting was too high-decibel, Karen got up from the picnic table and headed for an unpopulated part of the deck.

Kay-Kay Chapin's voice, laden with old money and world-weariness, filled Karen's ear. "Sorry I couldn't get back to you Friday, or whenever it was."

"Not a problem. I wanted to interview you for my—"

"I assume you're in the Hamptons," Kay-Kay interrupted. "Everyone is. I'll pick you up and we can talk. I'm going back to New York. Steven Spielberg insists I show him personally the townhouse he's buying. What a bore. Where are you?"

Karen had been looking forward to relaxing in the hammock most of the day, reading a trashy novel. She gave the address in Hampton Bays.

"Hampton Bays?" Kay-Kay said. "Where the hell is that? Tell Mel."

After she gave directions to Mel, Karen padded back onto the deck. The Razz and Sheila had emerged from their bower of bliss, with Sheila wearing an even tinier garment than on Saturday—this time a white thong bikini that displayed her bare derriere, Rio style. The men were agog; the women were aghast.

Trying to ignore the tableau, Karen told everyone why she would be leaving early. "Does anyone have any nice clothes? People like Kay-Kay dress up to go out for an ice cream cone."

"I've got plenty of clothes," Sheila said.

"You're kidding," Karen said.

Kay-Kay arrived in a vintage Citroen. Stoner, who had been watering his cash crop situated clandestinely in his backyard, sensed the presence of an automobile never seen in Hampton Bays, and came onto his front lawn to gawk. Karen had settled for wearing jeans and the blouse she had worn to work Friday; the blouse wasn't too wrinkled and Karen hoped it could pass for some sort of tousled chic. She had no choice but to carry her battered old Kenneth Cole handbag, which looked as if it had endured several military campaigns.

She waved goodbye to the gang. Kay-Kay's driver, Felix, a very large Jamaican-accented guy in a leather jacket, tossed her stuff in the empty trunk. Kay-Kay, who could afford to keep clothes all over the globe, didn't do weekend luggage.

Kay-Kay was nice enough not to seem to notice Karen's less-than-glam attire. Her eyes hidden behind Dior sunglasses, Kay-Kay wore a Tom Ford Napa jacket, a cotton camisole, wide-flare trousers, and crocodile sandals. One of the handsomest young men

Karen had seen this side of a multiplex screen sat in a small jump seat opposite her. He had on a tight designer T-shirt. Karen put on her own, much cheaper, sunglasses, so no one could tell what she was watching. Kay-Kay welcomed Karen onto the broad backseat next to her.

Kay-Kay stroked the handsome man's magnificently muscled forearm, which had just the right amount of hair. "Mel, fix Karen a Bloody. She looks like she needs one. Lord knows I do."

In a jiffy, Mel handed the women tall Bloody Marys, with mutant-large celery stalks protruding from them. "Careful not to spill," he said to Karen.

"I never spill a drop," Kay-Kay said, and took a long pull from hers.

"What can you tell me about Frederick Morgan?" Karen asked. She contemplated the drink. Hair of the dog? Considering her booze intake this weekend, more like hair of the fish. She sipped the Bloody Mary. It had enough alcohol to fuel a St. Patrick's Day celebration. She took another sip.

"I won't be quoted by name unless I give permission, right?"

Karen nodded and got out her pad and pen. For background interviews like this, a tape recorder would freak out the subject, so she kept that in her disreputable-looking bag.

"Mercedes settled for Frederick. A shame, really. I didn't know her then. Back in the late 1980s, when she was dancing for Twyla, Mercedes fell in love with a young Wall Street fellow. She calls him Eddie. He was at Dewey Cheatham with Frederick and the rest of them. Eddie somehow got in trouble with the law. He went to prison for a long time. Mercedes tells me how brokenhearted she was. I'm not sure why she wouldn't wait for Eddie. You can't ask those things. Anyway, Frederick swept in and won her."

Karen remembered what Frank had told her of his encounter with Mercedes, which had led to the fateful kiss. "Even though Mercedes settled, is this a happy marriage?"

"Is this a happy marriage?" Kay-Kay swallowed a gargantuan amount of Bloody Mary. "Frederick adores her, as you might a fine painting. The same goes for their son, Bert, whom she dotes on. But Frederick doesn't know how to give genuine affection. He's far, far too busy."

Karen had a sudden memory of Tim last night, talking about his rice bowl. "Why did she settle for Frederick?"

"Why did you settle for your husband, that Tim of the Philadelphia Brattons?"

"You've looked into me?" Karen took another hit of the potent red concoction. "Partly rebellion, I guess. My parents are very politically correct, very moralistic, very tolerant of all kinds of people—unless the people happen to be wealthy, conservative Republicans. But that aside, Tim was exciting, as well. For a while." They were leaving Hampton Bays behind. Felix drove very fast and very well. "He turned me on. Later on, as I wised up, I had to leave."

"I respect social climbing—in the abstract. Mercedes grew up poor in a rural Texas town. She knew only two things about herself: She was pretty, and she could dance. Her mother poured her all into pushing Mercedes as a dancer. When Mercedes could see that her dancing days were numbered—you can only do it for so long—she glommed on to Frederick. At least Frederick doesn't cat around like Caddy did." Kay-Kay drained her glass and handed it to Mel.

"Caddy never could get enough women, I hear." Karen hadn't finished half her first drink yet. "I wonder if that would have come out on the Senate campaign trail?"

"In New York, it would've gotten him ten thousand extra votes." Kay-Kay caressed Mel's forearm. "I won't go to his funeral. I hate funerals. You have to wear black. I look bad in black."

"About the night at the Met," Karen said. She noticed that they had zoomed onto the Long Island Expressway, traveling comet-fast in the outer lane. "Mixon had befriended the chef, an Emily Bourdain. I'm trying to find her, with no luck."

"Oh, yeah? Mel, call Eric Pogue at home." Kay-Kay took a fresh drink and clinked glasses with Karen. "He's the museum director. He'll find out." She pointed to Karen's half-consumed Bloody Mary. "Hey, you're falling behind."

"Well, I had my share last night, and I'm kind of working here, so . . ."

"Oscar Wilde, one of my heroes, said it best: 'Work is the curse of the drinking classes.'"

While Mel was dialing Pogue's number on the car phone, their car got a jolt. Felix the driver cursed. Then came another jolt.

"What the hell's going on, Felix?" Kay-Kay de-

manded. She had spilled some of her drink on her pants. And to her, spilling a drink was a sacrilege

Karen looked through the rear window. A large, dark van was to their left and slightly behind. It swerved and knocked into the Citroen's back-left corner.

"Is that bastard crazy?" Mel shouted.

Felix wheeled the Citroen onto the shoulder and came to a stop. The van slid around them and parked diagonally in front of their car, to block a quick forward escape.

"Christ, I think that's the same van from last night!" Karen exclaimed.

The van's doors opened. Two black-clad figures hopped out and marched toward them. The man carried a machete. The woman wielded a knife. Karen recognized them at once.

"Christ, they're the ones from Vampyr."

As calmly as if he were stopping at a gas station, Felix swung open his own door and hopped out onto the highway shoulder. Cars arrowed past, ignorant of what was going down. Kyra and Henry raised their blades.

Felix yanked out a large pistol from underneath his leather jacket.

Kyra and Henry stopped, as though their batteries had gone dead. Their sallow faces, so menacing before, now grew slack. Their blade hands dropped.

Then Felix drew the gun into a two-handed shooter's grip and fired. Once. Twice. The van's two rear tires deflated instantly, dropping its rear. Next, Felix turned the gun on the two Vampyrs. Kyra and

Henry bolted from the shoulder and ran madly across a field.

"It's you they're out to get?" Kay-Kay asked.

"Uh, yeah."

Kay-Kay plucked a small cylinder out of her bag and pressed it into Karen's hand. "Use this. Pepper spray. Hit them in the face. It's as good as Mace."

Because Kay-Kay didn't want to go through the hassle of filing a police report, Karen called Marcia on the cell. No one home. She left a message about what had happened.

Bidding Kay-Kay, Felix, and Mel farewell in the garage beneath Kay-Kay's Fifth Avenue redoubt, Karen stole up to the street and hailed a cab. She dumped her belongings in her new cubbyhole—fortunately, no cockroaches greeted her when she hit the lights—and crept over to the subway, bound for the address she'd gotten from Kay-Kay. This was a glorious June day, full of buttery sunshine, so Emily Bourdain might not be in. But Karen figured the direct approach would work best, rather than calling first. Emily might be too wary on the phone.

Emily Bourdain lived in an old walk-up on a quiet, tree-lined Greenwich Village street that could have been in Paris. Karen climbed the front stoop and buzzed the apartment for Childs, which was Emily's husband's last name. No answer. She buzzed again. Nothing.

A couple with a small boy approached and climbed the stairs. The woman had short, smartly cut brown hair and a mouth that seemed used to smiling, although it hadn't in a while.

"Emily Bourdain?" Karen ventured.

The woman's eyes narrowed. "Who are you?"

"I'm Karen Glick from *Profit* magazine. I'd like to—"

"You people cost her a job," snarled the husband. The kid, carried on his shoulders, started to wail like a demon in torment. "Get lost."

"I was there the night Redmon died," Karen said, knowing she needed to talk fast. "Of course you had nothing to do with that. I need to talk about your friend Ward Mixon."

Chef Emily eyed her with interest. "You were the one who did CPR on Redmon. And I read you also punched out some of those Vampyr bastards."

"The media has caused us nothing but trouble," her husband broke in.

Emily shook Karen's hand. "Phil, please take Tommy upstairs. He needs his bath."

Karen and Emily walked to the little bistro on the corner, with Emily hunched over as if she lugged all humanity's sorrows. "I apologize for my husband. Money is a little tight."

Thinking of Kay-Kay, Karen said, "I know someone who can reverse that."

"Everyone blames me because I put Ward on the head table that night. He asked for it. He was my friend. I trusted him. Krapp and the others working the dinner—thanks to me, no one got paid a stipend for the evening. My husband blames the news coverage."

They took seats at an outdoor table and ordered

cappuccinos from the waitress, who knew Emily. Karen asked Emily to talk about Mixon. "Did he seem like the violent type?"

"Ward had the sweetest disposition. He baby-sat Tommy lots. Are you hungry?" As a chef, Emily had a sixth sense for when people hadn't consumed more than a bagel that day. Karen followed Emily to the kitchen, where the cook greeted her with a hug. Behaving as if she owned the place, Emily took down an omelet pan.

"Ward had elaborate credentials that the cops discovered were fake." Emily chopped scallions and cheese as she talked. "He supposedly had worked on the West Coast as a waiter. He did have a sarcastic side. He made a lot of references about when the revolution would come. I thought he was joking. That night at the Met . . . Redmon was late and holding up the dinner. Ward said we should kill him after we humiliate him. Another joke, I thought."

"But he didn't behave any differently that night than any other?"

With one deft hand, Emily cracked open three eggs into the omelet pan. "He was the same as ever. But after he poisoned Redmon—I didn't realize at the time what was going on—he ran off and he hit poor Krapp and I was there. And he . . ." Emily bit her lip and mixed the cheese and scallions in with the eggs. She turned on the burner.

Karen waited.

"He told me Tommy was a monster," Emily said. "And then he kissed me. And then he ran away." She swirled the pan's contents over the hissing flame.

"And to think I let him baby-sit my little boy. I feel sick about it."

Karen could appreciate how chilling that must feel. "Did you ever see his home?"

Emily expertly flipped the omelet. "It's near here. I have a key."

Karen nervously stood across the street from Mixon's old apartment. No one on the street seemed to be paying any attention to her. But she had also believed that, wrongly, out in the Hamptons. Mixon had lived in a nondescript cubical building that developers in the 1950s and 1960s had considered modern. It had zero to do with the nineteenth-century elegance that flanked it: brick buildings with fine ironwork and so much character that they almost could speak. In its blandness, Mixon's apartment building was much like himself.

First feeling for Kay-Kay's pepper spray in her bag, so it would be ready for easy grabbing, Karen crossed the street and let herself in the front door. The mailbox for Mixon's apartment had no name on it. She opened the mailbox; it was empty.

She climbed the stairs to the first floor. His unit was at the end. Except for the sound of her heart, all was quiet.

The apartment's door lock required some fiddling before it opened. The deadbolt wasn't engaged, so she didn't need to use that key. She let the door bump against the wall. It was a studio apartment, about the same size as her place in Murray Hill. Dust motes floated in the afternoon sunshine. Inside was nothing more than a made bed, a kitchen chair, and a bookshelf with few books. No TV. The unit had the same charm as a Holiday Inn room in a small Midwestern burg. She walked inside, her head swiveling about, alert for anyone in hiding. She turned to the bookshelves. A mere four books. All were about telescopes. "Who is this guy?"

As if in reply, she heard a rapid tramping of feet on the stairs, heading upward from below. Karen ran to the open door and closed it. She threw the deadbolt.

Then came steps down the hall toward the door. They stopped in front of it. How strong was the door? Next came a harsh pounding on the door.

"Open up. I know you're in there."

She knew that voice. She had heard it offering Redmon wine at the Met dinner. She had heard it on the subway with Dengler. She cautiously flipped open the peephole in the door.

Those Lucifer eyes stared back at her. Then she heard his key in the door.

Chapter Sixteen

He undid the lower lock and pushed. But then he discovered that the deadbolt had been thrown, too. The door stood firm. He shuffled his feet.

Karen heard him slide a key into the deadbolt lock.

Her bag sat beside the door near her feet, and she rummaged through it in near-panic. Where had she put the pepper spray? She thought she had positioned it for quick access. It must have fallen to the bottom, amid the combs and receipts and Kleenex and tape recorder. She couldn't find her cell, either.

"Don't come in here," she shouted at the door. "I've got a weapon."

Where was the damn spray? She looked frantically around the apartment for a phone.

There. On the tiny night table by the bed. She vaulted over to it and snatched the receiver. No dial tone. "Shit," she said.

Then Karen noticed that his key hadn't snapped

open the deadbolt. She ventured gingerly over to the door and peeked once more out the peephole.

Those Lucifer eyes were still staring at her.

"What do you want?" she said, working to keep the shakiness out of her voice.

"I don't want to hurt you," he said through the door.

Karen spread her hands on the door and braced herself against it. Maybe she could prevent him from entering. Likely not. He was a guy and bigger than her.

"Oh, really? Then why did you send Kyra and Henry after me in the Hamptons? They ran our car off the road. Thank God my friend's driver had a gun."

He didn't speak for a good five seconds. The tension seemed to melt through the door. "What happened?"

"What happened? You mean you don't know?" In a voice she couldn't keep the tremors from, she related what had occurred the previous night and earlier on the LIE. "This is news to you? And I figured you for the boss of the operation."

"You have to understand," he said, sounding reasonable, almost like her mother sounded counseling a troubled social-work client. "I'm not out to hurt you."

"Tell that to Henry and Kyra. These are seriously deranged persons."

"What," he asked, "are you doing here?"

"Trying to find out who the hell you are. What does it look like?" She got an idea. With one hand still braced against the door, Karen bent down and retrieved her small tape recorder from her bag. She clicked it on.

"I'm Vampyr, that's who."

"Oh, yeah. Louis Roman was the head of that fine group, last I checked. Where does that leave you in the hierarchy?"

He paused again. "We don't believe in hierarchies. That is for the capitalist world. Everyone in Vampyr is equal."

"Bullshit. On the subway, you were giving orders." When he made no reply, she pressed on with: "What do you have against the Billionaire Boys Club?"

"You've read our letters to them. They despoil the environment. They trample on workers' rights. And they don't pay taxes."

"How do you know they don't pay taxes?"

"We know many, many things," he said.

"Okay, Mixon, or whatever your name is. Did you send me all those tax and bank documents on the Billionaire Boys?"

He paused again. "What documents?"

Minutes clicked by. She flipped open the peephole once more. No Lucifer eyes. Nothing.

Karen leaned against the door, trying to decide what to do. Then she heard more steps from the hallway.

A new voice: "Are you in there?"

It was Marcia Fink.

Karen twisted the knob to free the deadbolt and pulled open the door.

Marcia stood in the hall, wearing a Yankees baseball cap, an Army windbreaker, and a visible shoulder holster. "What are you up to?"

"I'm looking for a new apartment, since Vampyr isn't making my regular one feel too homey. What's it to you?" Karen craned her neck out into the hall. "I was talking to Mixon a moment ago. Where'd he go?"

"I didn't see anybody." Marcia brushed past her into the apartment. "If he ever lived here, you could have fooled me." Marcia pointed at her. "Did you sleep with that shirt on?"

So much for tousled chic. But Karen caught a whiff of their old girlhood bantering in Marcia's snide comment. She pointed at Marcia's baseball cap. "Since when are you a Yankees fan?" The Fink family, like everyone else in Queens, was legally required to root for the home-borough, constant underdog Mets. "Do your brothers know about this?"

"I'm undercover today. Manhattan only has Yankees fans. Gotta blend, right?" Marcia crossed over to the window and looked at the sunny street below. "Nice day not to be indoors."

"How did you know I was here?"

"Good old-fashioned gumshoe police work. After I got your message on my machine, I contacted Mrs. Chapin, who said you were going to see Emily Bourdain. Ms. Bourdain said you were here. I came cuz I'm worried about you. That's what old friends do."

"Old friends?" Karen recalled the fruitless attempts she'd made to connect with Marcia through the years. "It isn't like you exactly tried to keep up. You'd think I had a disease."

"I can't take snotty Ivy League kids. What were you doing going to Princeton?"

"Finding the wrong husband. Hey, I went to Princeton because it's prepped-out to the max. My parents hated the idea. They wanted me to go to Bard or Antioch." Karen joined her by the window. "And I didn't turn into a snotty Ivy League kid."

Marcia shrugged. "No, you turned into a reporter. Cops shouldn't be talking to reporters." She gestured at the small tape recorder Karen held. "Did you get Mixon's voice on tape?"

"What if I did?"

"We don't have a recording of his voice. It'd help in identifying him."

Now came Karen's turn to shrug. "What could you tell me in return?"

"I told you we don't—"

Karen slid the recorder into her pocket and strolled toward her bag. "Too bad."

As she stooped for her bag on the floor, she heard Marcia say: "Mixon wore a good wig and fake mustache when he was playing waiter. He's had his fingertips coated in plastic, we suspect, so he left no prints, just like Louis Roman the mad gunman. Mixon never slept in this apartment. It was a ruse to fool the catering company and Bourdain that he was a regular guy."

Karen turned around and faced Marcia. "Is he Vampyr's leader?"

"Nobody knows. By the way, the Suffolk County cops found that van on the LIE with the tires shot out. It was registered to one Warden Moxley." Marcia held out her hand. "The tape?"

"Ward Mixon, Warden Moxley. I guess there's a connection. But since the real Moxley is dead, you can't trace the vehicle ownership to Vampyr."

"So you know about Moxley. One of Frank Vere's cop sources told him, I'll bet."

"About our sharing relationship, Marcia. Or should I say, Boxerbelle? If I give you stuff in the future, you'll give me stuff back?"

"Boxer who?" Marcia gave her barking laugh. "You were a pushy kid, too. I'll take it under consideration. A word of warning for you."

Karen removed the tape cassette and handed it to the detective. "What?"

"Do not call my home when my husband is there." She noticed that Karen was massaging her right hand. "What's the matter with your hand?"

"It aches from when I hit that Vampyr guy in the subway. But that's mostly gone."

"Have you forgotten what you learned back at the gym?" Marcia went into a boxer's stance. "Keep your fist tight. Go for the gut when you can—it's an easier target and stops them cold." She shuffled around the floor. "And keep moving."

Karen laughed and hoisted her dukes. They circled each other, laughing and jabbing without connecting. Karen remembered how much fun they'd had.

"My mother went nuts that time I came home with a bloody nose."

"You should've slammed Benny Slatz for looking into your bedroom with his binoculars. Benny the nighttime bird-watcher."

Karen remembered what Marcia had said when first told of Benny's voyeurism: "He's spotted the small-breasted pimple popper."

"Look on the bright side," Marcia said. "You don't have pimples anymore."

"Mixon seemed to like looking at distant, heavenly

objects." Karen pointed to his book collection on telescopes.

Marcia stopped and dropped her fists. "Next time you see Mixon—*pow.*" She punched the air quickly.

"I don't get it. Mixon said just now he wasn't out to hurt me."

"And you believe him after what happened on Long Island?"

Danton sat in his Ferrari on the deserted street. The sun was easing down toward the Manhattan skyline. On the LIE ramp a few blocks distant, cars crept along like molecules, homeward bound from the Hamptons.

At last, Louis appeared, sauntering in his Jejune jeans down the steps from his building. His cape hung from his broad shoulders. He grinned oddly. Henry stood behind him. The shadows couldn't conceal the bruises on Henry's face. Was this Louis's punishment?

Louis leaned down and rested his thick forearms on Danton's driver-side door. "Why don't you want to come up? We're not good enough for you?"

"Why did you send Henry and Kyra after Karen Glick?"

"Who says I did?"

"I do. And you abandoned the van? What if the cops can trace it back to us?"

"I don't have a clue what you're talking about." Louis placed his face perilously close to Danton's. "What van?"

"Where is the van, Louis?"

"You let me worry about that." His words were like stones dropped from a great height.

"I'm paying the damn—Owwwwww!"

Louis had captured his little finger and had bent it back. "Forget Karen Glick."

Danton said through gritted teeth, "I told you I don't want her . . ."

"I'm your best friend. Time for you to go back to Park Avenue."

A pre-dawn chill flowed off the East River. Mist drifted about the old Brooklyn Heights block, shimmering and spectral in the dull glow of the streetlamps. This was when living beings should be snug and safe in bed.

Karen clasped the thin jacket around her shoulders. She wished she had brought something more substantial. But wasn't this supposed to be summer?

"So what you're doing here," she asked her companion, "isn't this a crime?"

Darby, her face mostly obscured by her sweatshirt hood, gave a naughty grin, the kind found on a ten-year-old heading into the darkness with an armful of water balloons. But Darby, twenty-three, carried bumper stickers. "If the cops catch us, it's a $250 fine."

"Have you ever been caught?"

"Yeah, once. I tapped my trust fund for the money."

Karen had put up with a few tirades from Tim about trust-fund leftists. Tim had no problem being a trust-fund rightist.

"Your dad is a great old dude," Darby said. "Did you know he fire-bombed the campus ROTC building?"

"He was a real firebrand." Karen hadn't the heart to

tell how Maury had only firebombed his throwing hand.

The vandal and the reporter drifted along the street of quaint brownstones at an hour no one was up. In the early-morning gloom, they were hunting for sport utility vehicles.

Growing up in a family of leftists, Karen was used to the impromptu sermon. And here came Darby's: "These SUVs are monsters. They get twelve miles to the gallon. That's obscene. And when they smash into small cars—the ones with halfway decent gas mileage—these SUVs are like a death sentence for the small cars. I mean, what do people need to drive a truck for?" On the subway out to Brooklyn, Darby had boasted that she only rode mass transit or her bicycle.

"Aha," Darby cried. There, next to the curb, sat a Toyota Land Cruiser. "Look at the size of this damn tank." She peeled the backing off a sticker and pressed it against the Toyota's bumper. It read: "Buy a Gas-Guzzling SUV. Destroy the Environment."

As they bustled away from the crime scene, Karen asked her main question: "On the phone you said you'd had some exposure to Vampyr. What was that?"

Darby tripped on the uneven sidewalk. She recovered before she went down or Karen could grab her. "I'm fine. Vampyr?"

"Yes, you said you knew about Vampyr."

Pulling her hood forward to further hide her face, Darcy said, "Yeah, well, I was in college. Protesting globalization and all that. And, well, they made a lot of sense. They spoke truth to power. They had a really sweet and intellectual leader named Barry Puffin. The worst we ever did, though, was drown out speakers or tie up traffic by lying in the road. My dad has good lawyers, and I never spent much time in jail. Then Louis showed up."

"Louis Roman?"

"A real scary guy. He'd been in prison. A lot of the kids took to worshipping him. He'd bang everyone in sight—boys, girls, whoever you got. Poor Barry didn't know what to do. Louis led raids on SUVs in dealer lots, and he'd torch them all. I didn't go for that, and I wasn't going to go to bed with this sleaze. Barry objected to the car lot arsons, and Louis decked him. This was in front of everybody. A couple days later, Barry disappeared. Louis was in charge. I left."

They walked a block saying nothing, past two SUVs. "Do you keep in touch with anyone in Vampyr right now?" Karen asked.

"I hear they have a place out in Queens, maybe Long Island City or Astoria. It's near the East River. That's all I know. I don't want to talk about this anymore."

They wafted along for two more blocks, the silence as thick as the mist.

Karen made a brief appearance in the office. She scoured through her e-mails and called to confirm her appointments throughout the day with her father's young radical pals.

Monte rolled his mail cart up to her desk. "Special for you, Karen. Uh-huh."

The envelope contained instructions about showing up at Teterboro airport the next morning to board the

RDS&M jet to Caddy Redmon's funeral in western Pennsylvania.

The phone rang and she picked it up, expecting one of her leftie kids. It was Jacob Cooke, the P.R. guy. "I read your story about Caddy's death over the weekend," he said. "We were most disappointed."

"Why is that, Jacob?" You never could tell how people would react to a story. As a young reporter, Karen had once written about a heroic man who had dragged several people from a motel fire. Since he was supposed to be in Montreal at the time, and since one of those he saved was his girlfriend, his wife didn't appreciate reading the story. The wife had called Karen and screamed at her for ruining a fine marriage.

Cooke was brimful with righteous indignation. "You wrote about Caddy as a lecher," he said. "You defame his memory."

"So you're saying I can't go to the funeral?" When he said nothing, she said, "Fine. Then I'm showing up for the plane ride tomorrow." Karen put down the phone. She felt her adrenaline surging. She quickly dialed Kay-Kay's number. As usual, Kay-Kay was "in a meeting." Karen left word that Kay-Kay, as a Met board member, should help poor, out-of-work Chef Emily by getting her reinstated with the caterer.

With that, she set forth for her appointments with young radicals. She took her secret route and emerged onto a Midtown sidewalk amid the morning bustle.

That was when she passed one young radical with whom she had no appointment. He almost missed Karen. With the city deep into summer short-skirt season, Matthew was busy studying the passing women on the street. Stroking the soul patch that festered like a weed below his lower lip, he was intent on a leggy blonde when Karen blocked his view. Hot damn, with Henry and Kyra in disgrace, here was his chance to shine.

He followed Karen and got onto his cell phone. He had no trouble reaching Louis.

"Karen Glick has been acquired in Midtown," Matthew said. "It looks like she's headed for the subway."

"Stay with her," Louis said. "We'll be right behind you."

A half-hour later, Karen emerged from the subway into the bohemian quarter of the East Village. Across the street from her, in an otherwise vacant lot behind a rusty chain-link fence, rose a two-story-tall sculpture made of discarded auto parts, girders, road signs, and industrial pipe. Everyone around her was incredibly young and hip. They all wore black, just like Vampyr.

The fortune teller's shop lay on a gritty block amid nail parlors, check cashing outlets, and cheesy lawyers' offices ("Unjustly convicted? We will spring you."). The year before, Karen had written a colorful story about palm readers, astrologers, mystics, and pet psychics. This was no exposé, but merely a consumer's manual about these guides to the unseen world.

One mentalist had told Karen that someone was out to get her. Karen, who hadn't given her name, asked who this nemesis might be. The mentalist replied that the person's initials were K.G. Thus Karen had learned that she was her own worst enemy.

She thought about Madame Bilko, the psychic who had sent her spam. Surely, Maury Glick, who disdained all superstition, wouldn't be consorting with such riff-raff as a fortune teller. Would he?

The sign out front simply said: "Tarot Readings." The door jingled when she walked inside. Shouldn't the reader be able to sense her arrival without the bells? A young woman with unwashed brown hair and a Nirvana T-shirt sat in an overstuffed armchair and read the *Village Voice*. Sunshine washed in from the broad window that looked onto the street. Cardboard placards were mounted on every wall, with spiritual sayings written in a fine hand. One read: "Invisible life is cavorting around us, if we had but eyes to see. Listen to the wind, the rain, the beat of the stars, at once ancient and fresh."

"I called before," Karen said. "You know Maury Glick." The young woman looked at her blankly. "I'm the reporter, Karen, his daughter."

The reader didn't get up or smile or extend a hand. She put down the paper. "Have a seat." She indicated an uncomfortable-looking, plastic-mold chair, the kind they put out for parent-teacher nights.

"So you're Pat?" Karen said, taking her place. She checked inside her bag to be sure this time that she could find the pepper spray. Pat seemed harmless, yet Karen had this odd feeling about her. It must be the unwashed hair; Karen hated unwashed hair. And she hadn't been too fond of Nirvana, either.

"No names," Pat said. "You want a reading?"

"That's not necessary. I only need a few minutes."

"It'll be $40, in cash." Pat began laying out a deck of bright-backed cards on the table.

Figuring she didn't have a choice, Karen nodded. "What the heck."

"Payment up front."

Snide remarks about putting the fortune in fortune teller leapt to mind. Instead, Karen pulled her wallet out of her bag and peeled off two $20 bills.

In tarot, Karen knew, there were seventy-eight cards divided into groups. How they fell from the reader's seemingly random dealing gave the keys to destiny, at least for the next three to six months. A short enough time to require you to come back for a new reading.

Pat began turning over cards. "I see a lot of negativity. I have the Hanged Man card. I have the Death card. I have the Devil card. Great danger lies ahead of you."

Of course, Pat could simply have read the newspaper about how Karen's recent activities. She knew Karen's name.

"My father says you might know about Vampyr."

Pat kept her head over the cards. "I fear for you."

"What do you know about Vampyr, Pat?"

"I only know what I see in the cards."

Karen slumped in her seat and tilted her head back in frustration. Then she got another look at the sayings on the wall placards. The elegant handwriting seemed very familiar. "You wrote the threat letters to the Billionaire Boys, didn't you?" Karen said, sitting straight up in her hard chair. "On the black paper, with the white ink. It was you."

That made Pat lift her gaze from the cards. She had a pleading look on her face. "I don't understand what you're talking about."

"Come on, Pat. Don't blow smoke at me. You can't miss the calligraphy."

Pat held a hand above her cards, as if receiving warmth from them. "Isn't it obvious to you?" she said with the intensity of a street-corner prophet. "They are everywhere, they know everything, they will stop at nothing."

"So is Louis Roman really the boss of this bunch of sickoids, or what?"

"Listen, a very rich man is giving Louis and the rest of them a lot of money. Money buys power. Money buys people's souls. They can do whatever they want."

A rich man? That would explain the Ferrari keys. Not to mention Louis's Jejune jeans. "Are you in touch with them?"

"I did some work for them. That's all. Please don't make trouble for me by going to the police. Louis will find out if you do."

"I don't want to get you in any trouble. But you should voluntarily go to the cops—"

"You should leave."

Karen rose, gripping her bag. "Let me leave my card in case—"

Pat pointed to a doorway across the room. "Go out the back. I have a premonition."

Placing her card down among the tarot cards, Karen said, "Premonition?"

"Do it!" Pat shouted.

With a shake of her head, Karen left. She went out the back way.

Pat placed her elbows on her knees and her hands over her eyes. A few moments later, the bells over her door jingled.

Louis, in his cape, bathed in his shockingly red aura, stood over her. Several Vampyrs clustered behind him. Their auras were almost as crimson. "Where is she, Pat?" Louis asked, in a snake-like, seductive manner.

But Pat couldn't meet his eyes and couldn't speak. She lowered her hands from her face and stared at her knees.

"You've already written the letters we'll use for the rest of the Billionaire Boys. We don't need you to write anymore." Louis plucked Karen's card from the table. "What did you tell her?"

Sometimes, you need desperately to lie. Other times, when nothing will do, you cannot think how to lie.

Chapter Seventeen

Ever since they left Manhattan, Mercedes had had a feeling that something bad was going to happen. Clad in a black Gaultier suit, she stepped out of the car onto the tarmac of Teterboro Airport, an exclusive landing area for corporate jets that sat amid the flat, featureless terrain of New York's western suburbia.

She and her husband had bickered over whether Bert should go to the funeral, and she had won. She didn't see why her son should be a target. As the Chez Boo incident showed, some loon could breach even the best security. There was a strong argument, as well, that none of them should go to this funeral. The entire world knew that RDS&M would attend Caddy Redmon's funeral en masse. Frederick, off to the side conferring with Ashlea Kress, believed he had nothing (yet) to fear: He and Butch hadn't received their threat letters.

Butch Strongville came swaggering up to Mercedes.

He wore that confident, macho grin and seemed as eager for her appreciation as a tail-thwapping Irish setter.

"Are we safe, Butch?" Mercedes said.

Strongville laughed at the little lady's distress. "You bet. Our people have personally cleared everyone in this airport today. We have cops stationed outside the airport who are ensuring that no one locks onto our plane with a Stinger."

"Excuse me? Isn't that a drink?" Mercedes had begun to regard life as Kay-Kay did.

"Shoulder-mounted, surface-to-air missile. The most dangerous time is when we take off and land. At cruising altitude, we're out of range. Back in my army days, when an earlier version was coming into the inventory, I used them with great effect. But that won't happen today. We've given generously to the local politicians. Their cops won't let anyone acquire us as a target. Same goes for when we land in western Pennsylvania. Besides, Frederick and I—"

"I know. You haven't received your letters from Vampyr yet."

The dove-white Gulfstream lifted into the air without a care. Morgan's tensed back muscles relaxed. None of Butch's Stinger missiles came streaking toward them. The pilot's calm voice came over the intercom, saying they would soon clear the cloud cover and that they might encounter a little bumpiness. There was none.

"No sweat-erino," Strongville said. "Hell, you should have been with us when we took off during the fall of Saigon. The NVA were firing all they had at us. We were in a Chinook and that damn bucket could haul ass."

The three partners were huddled in the front of the long, luxurious passenger compartment in beautiful, ergonomic, German-designed chairs.

"I still don't like having that reporter on the plane," Dengler said. Karen was sitting at the rear, safe-guarded by Cooke.

Morgan glanced over at his wife, who was asking the steward for a glass of champagne. A little early. But he didn't reproach Mercedes, ever. She wasn't the reproaching kind. Mercedes bowed her head over a piece of paper. It seemed to be a letter.

"Is it true that they're getting Julio Iglesias in for the funeral ceremony to sing "To All the Girls I've Loved Before"?" Dengler asked.

Morgan glanced down the cabin. Miranda was sitting near his wife. The social secretary appeared to be quietly sobbing. "I guess I'd better deliver the eulogy," he said.

"Is this some kind of religious service?" Strongville asked. He lit up a cigarette.

"Yes, Catholic," Morgan said. "His mother made the arrangements. We tried, but . . ."

Dengler hooted. "Catholic? I wonder if they'll send around the collection plate."

"What are you going to put in the plate, Simon?" Strongville said. "A penny or a nickel?"

Waving away more cigarette smoke, Dengler said, "Zero. The collection plate, hah. God had the power to create the world, the beasts of the field, the stars in the sky, and mankind in seven days. But you see, He's got this little problem with money."

Strongville pointed out the oval window. "Hot damn. We have a fighter escort. Two F-15s." He squinted at them. "Pennsylvania Air National Guard."

"The Pennsylvania governor is a friend of RDS&M," Morgan informed them

Morgan noticed that his wife still was reading that letter, reading it as intently as if it contained the secrets of life and death.

In her career as a reporter, Karen had learned that the rich and powerful love media attention so long as it is on their terms—praising them for their courage, their brains, their looks. Otherwise, they view the media as pests.

"I'm sure they wouldn't mind if I went up to talk to them," Karen told Cooke. "Why else am I on this flight?"

"Consider yourself lucky to have gotten this far," Cooke said. "They don't want to be disturbed in their time of grief by the media."

Karen gestured toward the Billionaire Boys, who seemed to be having a jolly chat. "They don't seem too grief-stricken to me." Damn Forger, Demon Slinger, and Vergil Blotchnuts displayed an easy, if edgily macho, camaraderie. It was easy to see how they worked as a team.

Mercedes, on the other hand, hardly radiated happiness. She was absorbed in a single sheet of paper, which she read over and over and over again. Her social secretary, Miranda, the one Caddy Redmon had loved and left, had at last stopped crying. Miranda stared out the window at the fighter planes.

They landed at a small airport outside Pittsburgh. As they climbed down the ramp to the ground, the Air Guard jets passed overhead and waggled their wings in salute.

A line of black automobiles awaited them. Karen wedged into the last car, next to Fiona, Morgan's oh-so British secretary, who seemed to have missed several weeks of sleep.

State police cruisers and motorcycles accompanied them to the church, where a group of reporters had been cordoned off. When the motorcade stopped with its flashing lights, and bodyguards and state troopers whisked the Billionaire Boys inside, Karen saw Cassie Milton in the press pack. Pennsylvania's governor had devoted almost as much manpower to corralling the press as he had to security.

"What are you doing way out here?" Karen asked the TV correspondent.

"I could ask you the same question. I need to talk to Jacob Cooke," Cassie said. "He hasn't been returning my calls."

"What are you working on about the Billionaire Boys?"

"I could ask you the same question. Can you get him for me?"

Karen rejoined a scowling Cooke, who only grunted

when she mentioned Cassie, and they sat at the back of the church. Morgan gave a touching eulogy. No women spoke.

When the mass had concluded, Karen watched the people from the front pews head past. She recognized several ex-wives from their photos. They were uniformly attractive, their faces and bodies gifts of nature, or in the case of his earliest wives, of surgery.

A number of women were crying, most notably Miranda. None of the wives cried. Nor did his good-looking gaggle of children, who ranged in age from five to twenty.

Karen, with Cooke as close as an unwanted suitor, next went to a country club, whose ballroom sported three bars, an ice sculpture of a swan, and enough Swedish meatballs to sink a Viking longboat. Karen said, "They always throw you a great party the one time they know you can't make it."

Cooke took Karen by the elbow. "You want some food?" He always did.

"Trying to quit." He trailed her to a side hallway and stood post. This was an old trick she had learned as a teenager. When she got into the restroom, she discovered another door. It didn't get any better.

Everyone in the country club's ballroom was waiting for the immediate family and the RDS&M partners to return from the cemetery. Karen noticed the first Mrs. Redmon, a lacquered, middle-aged beauty named Brigid, near one of the bars. She and her two college-aged sons held stiff drinks. Karen introduced herself.

Brigid was eight sheets to the wind in a 100-year storm. "Was he boffing you?"

Karen blanched. "Uh, no. I was the one who gave him CPR."

"Izzat a sexually transmitted disease?"

"Actually . . ."

The tallest boy stepped in front of Brigid. "Mother no longer wishes to speak to you."

"Caddy was a shit," Brigid said. "Like a dog in heat." Her sons led her away.

Mulling this over, Karen floated by a couple of Redmon's other ex-wives, who were snarling at each other—and she decided not to even try talking to them.

"Well," said a sultry 35-ish redhead with prominent cleavage, "I'm entitled because I was Mrs. Redmon, too."

"Well," said a pretty 40-ish brunette with amazing eyes, "you were Mrs. Redmon Three. I was Mrs. Redmon Two."

Well, Karen was about to go for her own stiff drink and some gut-bomb meatballs, when she saw John Sands. Tim's uncle. President of the Union League. Blood bluer than the summer sky. And chief investment officer for Philadelphia Mutual Insurance Company of America.

"Uncle John," she said.

The old fellow's face, hanging in bulldog folds, brightened. "Karen, darling." He kissed her cheek. "What a delight."

At stuffy Bratton family gatherings, he and Karen

had always had great gabfests. He was the one Bratton relative Karen liked. He often traveled to New York for the theater. He adored the opera. In warm weather, he wore a seersucker suit. He enjoyed having fun, which the rest of the Bratton clan had outlawed centuries before.

"I'm doing a story on the Billionaire Boys Club," she said.

"My nephew is an ass for letting you go. You're following RDS&M? Why haven't you called me before?"

"I'd love to, Uncle John, but I had no idea you—"

"Philadelphia Mutual is invested in RDS&M buyout funds," he said. "Has been for years. Ever since these boys broke off from Dewey Cheatham in the 1980s. We first encountered them there. Crackerjack group, those lads."

Karen's eyes widened. "You don't say? Why did the Billionaire Boys leave Dewey Cheatham? I heard they had some sort of tiff with the older partners."

Uncle John nodded. "They sure did. I never got the complete details, but it concerned a young man who worked for them on deals. I forget his name."

"Eddie? Edward?"

"I believe. Something like that. Anyway, he got involved in an insider trading scandal. He found out about deals that Frederick Morgan and his friends were contemplating, then bought the stock of the target company. When the buyout was announced, the target company's stock surged, of course. This fellow cashed out. Only slightly against the law, unfortunately for him."

"So this reflected badly on the Billionaire Boys, I guess."

With a chuckle, Uncle John said, "Worse than that. I heard that there were accusations that they were hip-deep in the scheme—and got caught. Somehow, they quietly left Dewey Cheatham. And this Eddie or Edward ended up the fall guy. He went to prison."

"I've done an extensive search from the 1980s and found no such news stories about that. No insider trading scandals at Dewey Cheatham, nada, zilch, zippo."

"The Dewey Cheatham partners managed to keep this under wraps." Uncle John turned his head. "Looks like the cemetery contingent has returned. Can I buy you a drink?"

Uncle John always said this when there was an open bar. Karen caught sight of Jacob Cooke across the room, as he whipped his gaze around, searching for his quarry. "I think I'll go outside and get some air. But . . . have you heard that RDS&M cheats on its taxes?"

"No. Still, at my age, nothing is a surprise."

Karen wandered along the outside of the clubhouse. The coal barons of the 1800s, the Billionaire Boys of their day, had built the place. Its decor had no trace of black to remind anyone of coal. Just whites and pastels.

There was a commotion as she rounded the corner. A circus of state police cruiser roof strobes flashed crazily at the clubhouse's front portico. The Billionaire Boys and their group from the private burial at the cemetery were heading into the front door. A team of RDS&M bodyguards surrounded them.

A man in a groundskeeper's green coveralls

brushed past Karen, moving as fast as a shark, aimed at the funeral party. He had no hair. She caught the spark of his eyes.

She knew him and those Lucifer eyes.

"Hey," she shouted at Mixon or Eddie or whatever his name was.

The man in the green coveralls kept churning toward the cemetery arrivals.

"Hey," Karen called after him again. She started running, not easy in two-inch heels on soft turf. Mixon picked up the pace. A large number of dignitaries and other toadies emerged from the clubhouse to greet the Billionaire Boys. Several crossed in front of Karen. Damn. She'd lost sight of Mixon.

Dark funeral suits and dresses swirled around Karen like moths.

George Sr. loomed before her.

"Listen, George, Mixon is here," Karen blurted. "He ran into this crowd."

The bodyguard's face scrunched in annoyance, George Sr. said, "Who would that be now, miss?"

Karen, bobbing her head about to find Mixon, said, "The guy who poisoned Caddy Redmon, for God's sake. He's right here."

With a skeptical squint, George Sr. signaled to one of the largest men Karen had seen outside of the National Football League. The large man lumbered over and slowly introduced himself as Herman Heinrich, head of RDS&M security. He had been on the Boys' plane, but sitting mostly out of sight up front in the cockpit. She repeated what she had said.

"You claim to have gained a visual sighting of the threat individual?"

"You better believe it, Herman. Somebody do something."

What Heinrich did was walk away.

Left outside was Butch Strongville, huddling with a silver-templed man who either ran General Motors or General Electric. Karen, usually good with names and faces, didn't care now. She stomped up to them. Bob, one of Strongville's bodyguards, intercepted her.

"Butch," she called, peeking around Bob, "I gotta talk to you."

Strongville and the GM/GE poo-bah glanced at her for a withering second, then resumed their important conversation.

"Butch, life and death, pal."

Bill, the other bodyguard who had been listening to his walkie-talkie, cut in. "Sir, we have a visual on one of the persons on the Vampyr list. He was inside the clubhouse."

Strongville pulled a massive pistol out from under his suit jacket. "They arrested him?"

Karen flinched at this cannon, which Butch had pointed at the ground, very near her left foot. Her Joan and David grosgrain pumps wouldn't appreciate getting blown to bits. She shifted her foot to the right.

"No, sir. He bolted out the back. They've given chase. The description is he's wearing green coveralls."

"That would be him," Karen said.

Chapter Eighteen

The motorcade zoomed through the gates of the airport and jolted to a halt beside the Gulfstream. Doors popped open and they hustled, amid a cluster of security men, toward the airplane. At the foot of the boarding ramp, they waited for a moment while the flustered crew, whom no one had told about the early departure, made the cabin and the plane itself ready. The wind moving across the tarmac blew their well-cut hair.

"Everybody on the plane now," Strongville thundered when the pilot gave the high sign.

Strongville followed Karen up the ramp to the cabin. Was he checking out her butt?

Heinrich appeared at the front of the cabin and announced another delay. "Tower clearance has not been effectuated. The arrival of the Air Guard escort is in an uncertain mode, and this must be rendered go status before our flight receives clearance."

"Who needs those Air Guard morons?" Dengler said. "Let's get going."

Mercedes swung her chair around from Miranda's. "Let's all have a drink."

As he ran down the culvert, Danton could hear shouts. He couldn't be sure where they came from, but they didn't seem to be ahead of him. He sprinted through the concrete-lined ditch, his shoes wet from the rivulet that meandered underfoot. He jumped over stones and trash and other debris, hoping not to lose his balance.

Where the culvert bent slightly to the right, he slowed, then stopped. And he listened. No shouts. No sounds of state troopers dashing through the brush in the surrounding woods. And thank God, no dogs. Panting like a greyhound after a big race, Danton pulled the cell phone out of his country club coveralls and hit his speed dial.

Damn. He only got voice mail. "Where the hell are you?" he seethed into the phone.

Getting the coveralls with the country club's insignia had not been hard. He had feared that security would halt him when he tried to enter the clubhouse with the cemetery group. If only Karen Glick hadn't spotted him.

Up close, Frederick Morgan and Simon Dengler were interestingly older versions of the young blades Danton had known back at Dewey Cheatham. Morgan was a well-preserved specimen, with that soft skin; Dengler looked dried-out. Seeing them up close was better than in news photos, or through the telescope. And Mercedes . . . Danton had stood there gawking at her as she moved inside the clubhouse, regal, lovely, Morgan's wife. That was when one of the RDS&M bodyguards had challenged Danton. He had run away faster than a Baghdad thief.

Now he resumed his fleeing. Winded from the exertion, he could only trot. Up ahead, the culvert ended in a concrete apron that fed into a large stream. Danton pulled himself out of the culvert and clambered up the brush-thick bank to where the road should be.

Yes. There it was. A two-lane blacktop with not a car in sight. Danton hovered in the trees near the deserted picnic area. Where was Ali?

Danton was too busy watching the road to hear the state trooper moving behind him with a deer slayer's stealth.

"Don't move," the trooper said.

Danton whirled around in horror.

"I said: 'Don't move,' you dumb shit," the trooper barked. He had hauled out a black, .50-caliber Berretta. He reached for the radio on his belt.

Dengler announced he would uncork the wine himself. "We're starting with a Chateau Petrus," he announced to the benighted others. "I bargained them down to half what they were asking. See, I found that some of their bottles were counterfeit." He arched his spiky eyebrows. "The wine merchants were so embarrassed they cut the price for me. This is a twenty-year-old vintage. The base of the cork, inside the bottle but visible, should be dark with absorption. Some of the corks I inspected were white as a soda cracker."

"That is so brilliant," said Ashlea, a wiz at both finance and sucking up.

"In other words, the corks were new," Dengler pressed on, thinking everyone would be impressed by his cleverness. "Then we shone a light in the bottles. Some had no sediment. A fine old bottle will have sediment."

Strongville pulled Karen into the plush chair beside him. "Fiona and Dana can pour. Let's talk about tomorrow." Fiona's eyes narrowed. "You're flying with me to Pulmon headquarters in North Carolina."

"In this Gulfstream?" Karen stared at his hand on her wrist until he released it.

"No. In a MiG-25 fighter. Soviet Air Force. Takeoff, 1300 hours tomorrow afternoon at Teterboro. That's one P.M., civilian time. We'll send a car for you."

"For security reasons, I'll arrange a pick-up point that's not the Templar building." She held up her glass as a gorgon-faced Fiona poured wine into it.

"It'll be a very short trip. We can be back in New York by nightfall." Strongville nodded at Fiona as she filled his glass. Then he clinked his against Karen's and said in a lower, laughable attempt at a seductive voice, "Unless, of course, you'd like us to overnight down in North Carolina. I love Southern cooking."

Karen hadn't heard that Vergil Blotchnuts here was the swordsman that Caddy Redmon was. But Strongville had run through several wives. "I have to be back in town tomorrow night, Butch. But thanks."

This was sort of true. Tuesdays, she often went over to Gran's and pretended to eat her mother's cooking, which surely fell short of the best Southern cooking, or even—Karen glanced over at Fiona—the worst British cooking. Gran always ordered in food, but Karen didn't dare.

"I like you. You got cajones. Fire. Mercedes likes you, so hell. She's a woman and a half, all right, that Mercedes."

To move the conversation into a safer area, she asked Strongville, "So I hear you're the flight specialist of RDS&M, right?"

Strongville, seeing Dengler swirling his wine around, did the same. "I own five aircraft: three prop-driven, a helicopter—surplus Huey, which I know well from Vietnam—and now the MiG that I bought last year. I'm qualified on them all."

Strongville launched into stories of his military days, complete with expressions like "lock and load" and "roger that." "See, our gooks couldn't fight, but the North Vietnamese could kick ass."

After a while of this, Morgan crossed the cabin and stood beside Karen's chair. "Butch, stop monopolizing Karen. You get her all to yourself tomorrow." He lifted his wineglass to her. "Come sit with me for a minute."

"I want to show you the statue I'm doing for my beloved ancestor," Morgan said as he took his seat. Karen noticed the chief Billionaire Boy's cloth watchband today was black. He called over to Fiona. "The binder, please?"

Fiona finished her wine and, with a scowl, carried a leather binder over to her boss, who thanked her cordially. "Central Park needs a statue of J.P. Morgan," Morgan said. "Think of what he accomplished. The railroads never would have worked well enough together to build this country. He consolidated them so they could run on each others' tracks; they all started out with different gauges. He formed U.S. Steel and General Electric. Plus that miraculous company of old Ignatius Ludlum's. J.P. personally bailed the United States out of three financial panics. And he gave one of mankind's greatest art collections to the Met." He paused. "I was personally gratified that Caddy sat on the Met's board."

"You're paying for the statue yourself?" Karen said.

"That I am." Morgan opened the binder, which had likenesses of a grumpy J.P. Morgan. "It is finished. Master craftsmen in Italy have put on the finishing touches and are shipping it to us. From the foundry, in Pietrasanta, it will be flown here any day now—the great J.P. Morgan, whose bronze statue will for centuries inspire people in Central Park."

Not to mention the pigeons. Karen nodded and sipped more wine. God, this was good.

The pilot announced over the intercom that they were cleared for takeoff. The National Guard planes were overhead, waiting for them.

Mercedes piped up with: "Frederick, quit boring Karen with your statue. I want her to come sit by me."

"Whatever you wish," said Morgan to his wife, with a salesman's smile.

A definite frost existed between them. But according to Kay-Kay Chapin, Frederick Morgan "adored" his wife. Karen, who came from a family where little stayed hidden, didn't understand.

* * *

Karen crossed over to a free chair beside Mercedes. Fiona, who could drink the Billionaire Boys out of house and chateau, was leaning toward the ashen Miranda. "You bloody cow, 'e's not worth it. So you got a leg over with him. I've 'ad better men than 'im."

"You and Caddy . . ." Miranda began, shocked to hear Redmon had not been hers alone.

"Cor, 'e was good for a few mattress bounces, then bugger all," Fiona said.

Her upper uppercrust accent was a memory washed away by several glasses.

This was like *My Fair Lady* in reverse.

"Be quiet, both of you," Mercedes said, as though to children. "I want to talk to Karen."

The plane was gathering speed down the runway. The engine shriek was barely audible. The three surviving Billionaire Boys had seated themselves together and were talking. The Gulfstream rose swiftly and smoothly into the sky like an answered prayer.

Mercedes regaled Karen with tales of her dancing days. "My mother was a dance mother. She was constantly coaxing and pushing me. When I got into NYU's dance program, she was half-thrilled. She let me know, though, that not getting into Juilliard hurt her. I was settling. She lived through me." Mercedes peered out the oval window and watched the ground recede. The Guard jets flashed into view beside them.

"Well, now you decide on Juilliard's budget."

Mercedes nodded. "Thanks to him." She looked at her husband, who was chortling with Strongville and Dengler.

As the Billionaire Boys erupted in laughter, Karen

said, "The three of them seem to get along great together."

"It's like a fraternity. Still. They occasionally get under each other's skin. But they do miss Caddy, although they don't want to appear soft. When we got married, down on Captiva, all four left Frederick's bachelor party at dawn, wearing their tuxedos, and went water skiing. Caddy's idea."

"Wow."

"Caddy was no saint. His last wife told me, 'The way to Caddy's heart is a sharp knife through his chest.' But there are good men." Then she turned to Karen. "How is Frank?"

"Frank, as in Vere?"

"Yes. How is he?"

"Fine. He's the best reporter in the world. 'Fine' about sums it up." Karen, given Frank's history with Mercedes, wouldn't go into his disastrous love life.

"What a sweet man. A great listener. I kissed him once, you know."

Karen nodded. "I thought he kissed you."

"No, he was the kissee."

With a small breath, Karen went for the prize. "Who was Eddie?"

Mercedes gave her a strange, probing look. Then, "I want to go lie down." She unbuckled her seatbelt, gulped down her wine like medicine, and rose from the chair.

"I need to talk to you about that," Karen said.

"Maybe someday. Or maybe not. Excuse me."

* * *

"I can pay you if you leave me alone," Danton told the trooper.

"Shut your face," the trooper replied. He started speaking into the radio.

The stone, thrown with great artistry, arced perfectly overhead and hit the trooper on the top of his hat. He spun around, pointing his gun at the woods.

Ali tapped him on the shoulder. When the trooper half-turned, Ali waved. And then delivered a swift blow to the side of the trooper's neck. He crumpled to the grass.

"Will he be okay?" Danton asked. The trooper was a mean-minded thug, much like the prison guards at Iffewon, who were much the same as Louis Roman and the other animals behind bars.

"No problem, a little rehab needed," Ali said. "I parked out of view across the road. This cop, he was lurking about. He'd have heard me if I returned the call on the cell. Sorry, boss."

"Only the guilty should suffer. Let's go." Karen Glick had been the first to blow his cover at the country club. If she hadn't spotted him, then maybe the bodyguard inside wouldn't have been on the lookout for a guy in coveralls. Yes, Danton could almost see Louis's point about her. Almost, but not quite.

Louis had summoned the Vampyrs for a conclave at the center of the large concrete floor. As they crossed the floor, Matthew sidled up to Kyra. "Too bad Louis is mad at you," he said.

Kyra's facial bruises from Louis's beating would

take a while to go away. "So exactly why should you care?"

"Because maybe I can put in a good word for you," Matthew said. He eyed her.

"Don't make Henry jealous by coming on to me, okay?"

"Henry? Jealous? What about you and that other guy? Give me a shot."

"You're sweeping me off my feet," Kyra said. She plopped down next to Henry and threw her arms around him. Matthew strutted over to stand beside Louis.

Louis's thick arm came from inside his cape, and he placed it around Matthew's shoulder. "We have had hell's own time trying to run down Karen Glick. The attempts in the Hamptons were totally botched. But Matthew here is a genius. Tell us what you found, Matthew."

Beaming, Matthew said, "We've spent too much time trying to figure out how to infiltrate her office in the Templar building, or to catch her going to or from work. But I found out that she has this wealthy grandmother who lives on the Upper West Side. And that Glick's parents live with the old lady. Glick usually visits Tuesday nights."

"How do you know this?" Kyra asked, less than kindly.

"Her parents," Matthew said with teacher's pet smugness, "are these old 1960s radicals who hang out with a lot of activist young people. My friends."

"You have friends?" Henry said.

Louis took a menacing step toward Henry and

Kyra, who flinched, as if ready for new blows. The Vampyrs seated around Henry and Kyra scooted their butts away.

"We take care of Glick now," Louis roared. "Understand?"

Chapter Nineteen

The next morning, Karen recounted her adventures to Eudell. "Mixon seemed to be operating on his own. At least, there were no other Vampyrs around. I mean, can we take it on faith that, just because Morgan and Strongville haven't received any threat letters, they can breathe easy for now? Was Mixon after Dengler?"

"You have a lot of questions, and not a lot of answers," her editor said.

"I'll get answers. I know I can get Marcia to cough up more."

"I guess it's encouraging your old pal Marcia gave you some details about Mixon for a change, however minor."

"Don't forget she sent me the FBI file."

"You're sure that was Marcia who sent the FBI file?"

"Who else would it be?" Karen said, beginning to

get annoyed. "Eudell, it came from Boxerbelle. Marcia used to take me to box—"

"Honey, the task is to authenticate the Billionaire Boys' Caymans bank statements. Without that, you have a story about how the Boys are holding up under pressure from some lunatics. Nice, but not Frank Vere–level investigative work. And we don't yet know who sent you those bank documents and tax returns on the Boys."

"Stands to reason it was the Vampyr gang, right? But I con't know for a fact."

"'Don't know' is not good enough. Once the cops arrest these Vampyr nuts, every media outlet in the world will be all over this. Christian's not gonna let me keep you on the Billionaire Boys tax cheat investigation forever. If you can't prove it, you can't prove it."

"Great." Karen got up to go.

"Also, honey," Eudell said, "are you really going up in that jet fighter this afternoon with Strongville? That's suicide, girl."

With her hopes and dreams in a flaming descent, Karen didn't know what to say. In a funk, she didn't hear Mike, Wendy, and her parrot as she drifted past them. They were having a jolly conversation and called to her. Her mind was on how to get more from Marcia, or anyone.

She returned to her desk and listened to voice mails. One was from Emily Bourdain, thanking her for intervening with Kay-Kay, who had forced the Met's catering outfit to reinstate their chef at once. At least Karen had accomplished some good other than bodyguarding a bunch of billionaires. Monte rolled his mail cart by her and deposited a package in her hands—instructions about her pickup point for the ride to Teterboro. Then Frank came slumping past.

"She's as bad as Christian and Skeen," Karen told him, and described the session with Eudell. "I may not have your sources, but I do have Marcia."

Frank nodded. A pallbearer at Caddy Redmon's funeral would've looked sunnier. "Right. Well, about that FBI file on Vampyr . . ." He examined his tie.

"What about it, Frank?"

"See, um, I gave you some stuff that I, well . . . Boxerbelle isn't Detective Marcia Fink."

"Of course it is. She . . . It isn't?"

Frank couldn't meet Karen's gaze. "No. This is deep background, but I'll tell you this once. Boxerbelle is Special Agent Beatrice Boxer, one of my FBI sources. She has a special Internet account for Boxerbelle. For her friends only, not the FBI higher-ups. I asked her to send you the FBI file on Vampyr. That's why this was easy for me to authenticate."

Karen wanted to respond but couldn't.

"Eudell knows this," Frank went on. "She ordered me to be of no more help to you. Christian is leaning on her. He's so afraid the Boys will sue because of me . . ."

"Frank," Karen said with a conviction she didn't feel, "I am going to nail this story."

"I know you will," Frank said, in the kindly fashion in which friends lie to each other.

The MiG-25 jet fighter perched on the runway like a deadly bird. And a flight-suited Butch Strongville stood beside it in a pose stolen from *The Right Stuff*.

Karen, also now outfitted in a flight suit, felt that she had the wrong stuff. What, for instance, was she supposed to do with this helmet she carried?

Glancing back over her shoulder at the passenger lounge she had just left, she said, "I always wondered why they called them 'terminals.' That doesn't inspire a lot of confidence."

"Isn't she a beauty?" Strongville said, referring to the MiG, not Karen.

Karen noticed that Strongville's regular bodyguards weren't with him. "Hey, where are Bob and Bill? Not that I'm unhappy to see you guys." Jimmy scowled at her with those thick lips. Ron gave a genial smile and said nothing.

"NATO code-named the MiG-25 the Foxbat," Strongville continued in a lecturing manner, sure that he was the most important soul for miles around and the only one worth listening to. The needle-nosed aircraft had batlike wings, sort of. "This is the trainer version. There's a separate cockpit forward of the pilot's. That is, forward of me."

"So how many hours have you logged on the Batmobile here?" Karen asked.

"Getting toward one hundred," Strongville replied with a cocksure jauntiness that Han Solo would have envied. "The Russians were dying to sell this to me, but our government gave me one holy hell of a time. It was worth it."

A technician helped Karen up a small metal ladder and into her seat. They belted her in and fixed an oxygen tube to the mask that dangled from her helmet.

"Don't touch that handle," the technician said, gesturing beside her seat. "That will blow off the canopy and ignite your ejector seat."

Strongville, macho grin in place, appeared beside him. "That is, unless I tell you to eject. But I don't anticipate any enemy contact today."

After Air Marshal Vergil Blotchnuts dropped out of sight, the technician asked her, "Did you have anything to eat recently?"

"Not for hours. And I took a Dramamine." The Razz, who had flown on a U.S. Air Force fighter while doing a story once, had advised her to safeguard her stomach this way because military pilots liked to see civilian passengers get sick.

The technician pointed to a paper barf bag by her knee. "If you need it, pull off your mask and use this. Doing it in your mask is a very bad idea." He showed her how to don and remove her oxygen mask.

He lowered the hard plastic canopy and sealed it with the finality of a coffin lid. Karen examined the cockpit. It had no digital readouts, simply old-fashioned gauges. She looked behind her and saw Strongville clambering into his cockpit.

The engines started with a whine that rivaled her father's excuses for why his degree was not completed. Unlike with the Gulfstream, no noise was muffled here. Ron waved goodbye from the side, while Jimmy stood stock-still. Before she could wave back, the MiG was blasting down the runway at amusement-park speed. Karen had always begged off taking her young cousins on the Thunder Streak at Great Adventure. Why was she exactly doing this now?

In a heartbeat—about ten actually, because Karen's

heart was on fast-forward—they were aloft, with Manhattan's skyline off to the left. They appeared to be headed out to sea.

"We're going to break the sound barrier," Butch said via the earphone in her helmet. "You're not allowed to do that over land. It smashes windows and gets people's knickers in a twist. We'll be at 50,000 feet, above where commercial airliners fly."

When nothing lay below them but water and wispy clouds, Strongville told her they were approaching 750 miles per hour, the speed of sound, and to watch the gauges. Then the plane shuddered and the needles wiggled. "Mach 1, faster than thunder," he crowed in her earphones. The ride became smoother and she could see the green of the coastline to her right. A couple of times, he barrel-rolled, with the horizon doing a 360. Karen closed her eyes as he chortled.

Thank God for Dramamine. Finally, they glided in for an only moderately bumpy landing at an airfield identical to Teterboro. A technician helped a wobbly-legged Karen down the ladder. A good ol' boy with a jiggly belly and a cheek full of something foul, he asked her if she had to throw up.

"Why do they call it that?" Karen said. "Isn't it really throw *down*? I mean, check out your shoes some time. No, either way, I'm fine." Her mother would object to how vulgar she had become. But today vulgarity seemed apropos.

A motorcade and a bunch of security men, including Bob and Bill, awaited them. Also Colin, one of Ashlea Kress's assistants—a recently minted MBA who seemed to be a slightly younger clone of Tim.

Karen bet Colin also worried about his rice bowl cracking.

"What do you mean Graves canceled my appointment?" Strongville shouted at Colin. "I flew down here to see this guy. I'll kick his butt so hard his breath will smell like shoe polish."

"Mr. Graves won't let any of us inside Pulmon headquarters," Colin said. "He's busy. He's seeing Helen Naylor and Tommy Cross right now."

"What?" Strongville shouted. "What!"

After ranting for a while that Graves, Naylor, and Cross all should be shot, Strongville swung on Colin and growled, "I want to eat barbecue. You choose. And it better be damn good."

They got into cars. Karen sat in the back next to a fuming Strongville. The motorcade rumbled along a country lane. Then they bumped onto a dirt lot surrounding a tumble-down building with peeling paint. The sign read: "Put some South in your mouth."

"I'm hungry," Strongville announced. He took Karen's elbow.

She was hungry, too. And although this was mid-afternoon, another of her mother's barely edible suppers awaited in New York. "You gonna try to make me barf on our trip back?"

"I promise you a slow and even ride home," he said in a tigerlike purr.

He steered her inside to a small table with a Formica top. Colin and the security men sat at tables around them. The regulars, beefy fellows who wore John Deere caps and WWF Smackdown T-shirts and dirty work boots, examined the well-dressed, Yankee interlopers with deep-fried suspicion. An overweight waitress showing too much cleavage took their order. That was when Karen learned that she could get either sweetened or unsweetened ice tea, but that either kind used only real sugar. Diets were not big here.

So here she was dining one-on-one with Butch, albeit with plenty of others nearby. "Do you think you've lost Pulmon to Naylor & Cross?"

Strongville fired up a cigarette, which he couldn't legally do in a New York restaurant. He seemed to think this was a manly, Bogart kind of move. "That's how it'll play in the media. But this is just a negotiating ploy. Digby Graves wants to keep his job, post-deal."

Karen saw the shoulder holster beneath his jacket. "When don't you carry a gun?"

He pulled the stainless steel pistol out from under his armpit. It resembled a six-shooter from the Old West. "Smith & Wesson .357 magnum, loaded with stopping power." He aimed it at the ceiling, which was rimmed with old license plates. The other patrons gawked but didn't flinch; these good ol' boys were used to guns. "They didn't allow these when I was in the army. Too bad." He holstered the weapon.

"You talk about the military a lot. Why did you leave?"

Shaking his head, Strongville said, "I loved that life. Then I got put on a rescue operation. You might be too young to remember. The Iranians took our embassy personnel captive in Teheran, 1980. We could've pulled it off, but the Carter White House made a mess of it. At our desert assembly area in Iran, the commander was so busy soothing those pussies in the White House over the radio link that he wasn't directing the operation right. One of our aircraft collided with another. The wimps in Washington told us to abort. When I got home, I resigned and went to Wall Street, to Dewey Cheatham."

The waitress brought their food. "You looking to do some target practice with that artillery, babycakes?" she asked with a ribald laugh.

"Only if you help me," said Strongville, who looked ready to smack her copious behind. He did not have Caddy's smooth technique. When she left, chortling, he hoisted his pulled pork sandwich, its juice dribbling onto the plate, and said, "I hear you're divorced from a Dewey Cheatham guy."

"About Dewey Cheatham—"

"Hey, you're single now. We can have a nice Southern dinner here. Like they say in North Carolina: 'If it ain't fried, it ain't food.' We'd go back at our leisure tomorrow."

No doubt, Strongville used a very successful birth-control method: his personality. "My grandmother and parents expect me for dinner in New York tonight."

He gripped her forearm. "Listen, we could have a great time down here."

"Speaking of Dewey Cheatham, who was Eddie?"

Strongville returned his hand to his plate. "Eddie was nobody. Eat up."

Edward Danton must have fallen asleep. He lay on a chaise near his patio telescope. When his father called his name, Edward quickly awakened. It was late afternoon. The shadows had lengthened. James eased his old frame onto a stool.

"Don't you want a more comfortable seat?" Edward said, as he pulled himself into a sitting position.

"I'm not staying long." James pointed at the telescope. "Been spying on the Morgan family again, have we?"

Edward rubbed his eyes. "I usually don't take naps. Ali and I were traveling all night."

"I'm sure there's some logic to why you crashed the Redmon funeral. Just as I'm sure the earth is flat and George W. Bush is an avid reader of Flaubert."

Swinging his legs onto the patio to face his father, Edward said, "James, I had to see her. I was close enough to touch her. I've never dared get near her in New York. I was afraid she would recognize me. I have to appear to her at the right time."

"After the Billionaire Boys' funerals, eh? How wonderful. My son the plotter."

"James, you've never approved of anything I've done."

"What I really don't understand is why you sent that letter to Mercedes now. Shouldn't you have waited? What if she draws a connection between you and Vampyr?"

Edward got to his feet and stretched. "I want to be there at the right time when she needs me. That time is when she is scared and anxious. Now. Part of my plan."

James nodded. "That was a great job you and your sanity-challenged friends did snatching Dengler on the subway. And as for your plan to keep your home a secret from the Vampyr coven—well, that hasn't quite worked out, now has it?"

With a sigh of exasperation, Edward said, "So Louis is a sneaky type. I can outsmart him. The idea has been to pin the Billionaire Boys' deaths on Vampyr. They want to take credit for this. I need someone to keep the searchlight off me."

"Choosing Louis makes a lot of sense. Sure. He bullied you and tortured you in prison. He knows your real identity, and now where you live under your false one. You can control him. Sure. Where is he now? In hot pursuit of Karen Glick?"

Edward gripped the handrail and gazed across Park Avenue at the Morgan apartment. "I told him to stay away from her."

"And he's listening? Why involve a nice girl like her?"

"James, you don't understand. I need Karen. I use private detectives to amass dirt on the Billionaire Boys. I've fed her documents about them that should besmirch their names and stanch any sympathy for them, once they're dead. Besides, Karen is a good person who deserves this story. She's much better than a fluffy feature writer. And I feel sorry for her."

"Wouldn't it have been better to use Chris Abbott's money to start a nonprofit organization designed to aid cute, thirty-something divorcees at career dead-ends? Better than scheming to kill people."

"For God's sake!" Edward exclaimed. "You haven't been through what I've been through at Iffewon prison. And I didn't deserve that any more than Karen deserves to be hurt."

"You still don't understand why your Billionaire Boys have been successful. And why you have not."

Edward slammed a fist onto the handrail. "What those bastards did to me—" he yelled as he turned to his father.

But James had left.

Glad to be back with her late lunch still in her stomach, Karen turned the key in Gran's front-door lock. Butch, unused to rejection, had thankfully shut up on the return trip and minded his manners, which included keeping his promise to fly slowly and smoothly. Now was the blue hour on Manhattan's Upper West Side. Street lamps had flared on. She scanned the street behind her to ensure no one had followed. Well, she saw no one lurking in the shadows.

Inside, her mother immediately clasped her in a bear hug. "Oh, my baby. Those horrible people are still around." The story of Mixon's appearance at the funeral reception had hit the news in New York.

"Ma, he didn't hurt anyone." Karen kissed Emma's cheek and unwound her arms.

As Emma led her daughter to the settee, Gran drifted in and said, "That girl who became the cop, Marcia Fink, called here looking for you." She pursed her old, lined lips. "Hmmm. Marcia Fink. I remember now." Gran scribbled on the legal pad she carried. "Frick Mania. Popular with the boys, was she?"

"What does that horrible Marcia want?" Emma asked.

The sound of a toilet flushing announced that

Maury was leaving his private study. He entered, clasping his newspaper, and muttered greetings.

Karen kissed her father's forehead. "Thanks for your help, Pop," she whispered to him, so that Emma wouldn't hear.

Ma patted the place next to her on the settee. "I have a nice boy I'd like you to meet. He goes to a lot of our demonstrations. He's a student at the New School with your father."

Gran had warned Karen. "Ma, what is this? Now you're the matchmaker from *Fiddler on the Roof*?" As Emma's face fell, Karen hastily added, "No, look. I appreciate the thought. You're sweet. It's just that I'm not ready for dating and men and all that. I need to get Tim and our marriage out of my system first."

"Well," Ma began, "he's a very nice boy. Good looking. Smart. Nice manners. Thinks the right way politically."

Maury rattled his newspaper. "Emma, Jeff is not a 'boy.' He's thirty years old."

"Three years younger than me, huh? Well, as an older woman, I'm like a fine wine: I get better with age. Except someone pulled my cork." Karen could tell her mother wasn't appreciating the humor. "His name is Jeff?"

Emma nodded warily. "Yes. A nice . . . man. Jeff Davis."

"As in the president of the Confederacy? What are his views on states' rights?"

Her mother sniffed. "It's Jeffrey Davis. Not Jefferson Davis."

Gran already had worked out the anagram. "You mean, Adverse Jiffy?"

"I gave him your phone numbers, cell and work," Emma said. "I suggested that maybe you and he could get together tomorrow night."

Getting set up by your own mother is an unfailingly bad idea. Karen checked her cell. "I have one call on voice mail. Maybe it's Jeff or Marcia." Karen infinitely preferred Marcia.

"Maybe Jeff can give you some leads on Vampyr," Maury said from behind his raised newspaper. "Were any of the other kids I gave you helpful about that?" His last word dropped off, barely audible, as he realized Emma was in the room. He always had been spacey.

"What did you do, Maury?" Emma said. "Are you putting our daughter in touch with dangerous people? Talk to me."

The newspaper stayed in place for a moment as Maury tried to come up with an explanation. He slowly lowered the paper to face his furious wife. He mustered the same verbal facility that he'd displayed for years defending his doctoral thesis to the New School faculty: "I . . . I . . . I . . . I . . . I . . . I . . ."

"Pop has merely given me a few names of radical types for background on the movement, Ma," Karen said. "Don't worry." She looked between her steaming mother and her cringing father. "Listen, the most dangerous person I've run across lately is Digby Graves, the head of Pulmon Tobacco. Talk about a mass murderer."

Gran scribbled on her pad. "Digby Graves? More like Draggy Vibes."

Karen excused herself and went into the next room to check her single message. It must've come when she was in the MiG. Marcia's voice came on the line: "Hey, did you visit a tarot reader in the East Village the other day, name of Patricia Highsmith? Your card is there. Your fingerprints are, too. Person or persons unknown hacked her to pieces with a machete. It's seven o'clock Tuesday night. I'll be at my desk all evening. You'd better call me."

Hacked to pieces? If only Karen had gone to the police about Pat and her letters to the Billionaire Boys. But Pat had begged her not to, so Karen had put the idea aside. As Karen sat down numbly, Gran bustled into the room. "Say, about the First Caymans Bank. Maybe I can—"

"I've gotta go talk to Marcia in person." Karen snatched her bag from where she had put it in the hall and charged out the front door onto the sidewalk. She loped along the shadowy street and stabbed out Marcia's number on her cell to say she was en route.

Hands emerged from nowhere, grabbed her arm, and pulled her between two parked vehicles. Her cell phone clattered to the concrete. Karen found herself pinned against the back end of a van, very like the one on the Long Island Expressway. A wiry young man, clad in black with a soul patch on his chin, clutched her throat. Three others in black, two men and a woman, crowded behind him.

Karen tried to breathe, to speak. A small gurgle was the result.

"Do her here, Matthew?" the woman asked the guy holding Karen.

"Don't you listen, Miriam?" Matthew snarled at the woman, his face two inches from Karen's. "Open the back door to the van. Louis is waiting. He wants to do this himself."

Chapter Twenty

Had she been able to talk, Karen would have tried reasoning with them. Had she been able to shout, Karen would have called for help. Had she been able to break free, Karen would have run so fast that all hell's demons couldn't catch her. But they had caught her.

One of the young men behind Matthew opened the van's rear-end door, next to where Karen was pinned.

"Listen, bitch, you don't dare touch Louis," Matthew said to her, with the hot breath of a bad diet strong on her face. "We love Louis."

Matthew was much stronger than she was. Although her hands were free, she knew a move against him would be too late. He had the power to damage her windpipe quickly. Besides, his helpers were right there. "The door's open," Miriam said. "Put her inside already, Matthew."

He swiveled her head to her. "Hey, I'm giving orders here. Fuck you, Miriam."

"You tried and failed. Remember?"

"Oh, listen to her," Matthew said. "How many times have you had Louis, huh? Once? Twice, if he took pity on you."

One of the other Vampyrs threw up his hands. "Will you stop this, you two?"

They all sensed the presence of the men at the curb, two large, one less so. Then came the command: "Let her go, or we'll waste you."

Karen's frightened eyes flicked over to the sidewalk. Butch Strongville stood pointing his enormous .357 at them. Beside him were Ron and Jimmy, both leveling pistols at the Vampyrs.

Matthew's hand slowly disengaged from Karen's throat. He took a step back.

"Assume the position against the side of this van," Jimmy brayed.

Suddenly, a smaller revolver was in Matthew's hand. He aimed it at Karen's rescuers. "Not a chance, pig. We don't listen to swine like you." To the other Vampyrs, he said, "Get in the van. Now."

Three Vampyrs scrambled around the side, out of sight of Strongville and his men. Matthew stood his ground, his weapon trained on the bodyguards. Karen edged toward Strongville.

The van's motor roared to life. With gun arm still outstretched, Matthew backed into the rear of the van and slammed the door. The van wheeled away in a screech of tires.

Strongville put his arm around Karen. "Are you okay?"

For once, she didn't bridle at his touch. "This has

been a wonderful and exciting day." Then she felt that he was shaking. She gave Butch a look. "What are you doing here?"

Nervous sweat cascaded down his face. He smiled manfully. "You said you were going to your grandmother's, and I thought maybe I could convince to come out for a drink." The billionaire acted far from swaggering, however. He looked as if he needed a drink. "Your grandmother's address wasn't hard to find."

"Evidently."

"I got the plate numbers on their van," Jimmy said. "We can give them to the cops."

Karen moved out from under Strongville's arm. "The van will be registered to a guy named Warden Moxley of Buffalo. He's dead."

"Where can we take you?" offered Ron, who like Jimmy was unperturbed and unsweaty.

She peered up the block to ensure that her parents hadn't been attracted by the commotion. Some people were staring at them from windows. "To the police station. I need to see Detective Fink."

Riding in Strongville's car, Karen called her grandmother on the cell and, trying to keep the alarm out of her voice, told what had just happened. "They must have known where you live and that I visit you, Gran. God knows what these people will do. I can ask Marcia to put a cop outside your house. But I don't know if she'll want to, or be able to—"

"Don't let it bother you," Gran said, with the panache of a skilled party operative scheming to evade J. Edgar Hoover's minions. "I'll take your parents on a little surprise vacation. They'll be thrilled. Nothing too commercial, which would offend their political sensibilities. I'm thinking Woodstock. Hippie heaven, even today."

"I mean, Vampyr might not try to come into your house. Or they might. I—"

"The important thing is that you're okay. I won't tell Emma and Maury about your little street encounter. It would only upset them. Your father more than your mother."

"I love you, Gran. Very much."

"Love you, too, Regal Knick."

Karen plopped her phone back into her bag and brushed away a tear. Ron asked her if she was all right. She said she was. And she meant it.

The next morning, Karen sat at her desk, scouring her notes about the Billionaire Boys Club. After getting questioned last night by a male detective who was decidedly not Marcia Fink, she had sneaked back to her basement hideaway, where every little squeak outside kept her awake. She had turned on the lights once when she heard a loud and sinister scuttling sound. It was merely a huge roach with heavy feet and a bad attitude.

She was checking e-mail in her cubicle when the phone rang. It was Marcia Fink. "Sorry I couldn't be there last night to give you the royal welcome. But see, I had a queen-sized thirst, so we all went to the local cop bar. Anyway, you should've come to us about this poor chick, Highsmith. Too bad the girl now looks like steak tartare."

"I feel so guilty about this. Pat didn't want me to go to the cops, and I figured I could—"

"Don't beat yourself up too much. We've talked to her, too, before you. We knew she had a Vampyr connection. She has only herself to blame. You play, you pay, right?" Marcia put down the phone to call out a coffee order. "Anyway, we hadn't spotted that her handwriting matched the threat letters. Good job on that. You might make a decent Frank Vere after all."

"Marcia, I'll be getting more information—"

"But why you're still hanging around the Billionaire Boys is beyond me and beyond stupid. It's like vacationing in a war zone." The detective hung up.

The phone rang again right away. Tim's uncle, John Sands. She was delighted to hear from him.

"About what we talked about at the funeral," he said from his Philadelphia office, "I had my assistants dig out more. A bunch of documents. One set is from the SEC, about a guy named Edward Danton from Dewey Cheatham, who got charged in the 1980s with insider trading. Another set is from the federal prisons agency, about Danton when he was in jail. We did some work for a company that builds prisons and they have connections to . . . Well, never mind how we got them. I'm afraid the tale doesn't end well."

"What happened, Uncle John?"

"Danton killed himself. Rather gruesomely, I fear."

"Wow." Karen busily jotted notes on a legal pad.

"This is so nice of you. How will you get the documents to me?"

"Well, one of my assistants will send you them as an e-mail attachment. That kind of electronic wizardry is beyond me. I leave it to you younger folks."

"You're the wizard, Uncle John." At last, maybe she was getting somewhere. Just where, she hadn't a tiny clue. But somewhere.

Doing his best to hide the strain added by what Strongville had told him about the previous day, Frederick Morgan was passing beneath the Stomcox Massacre mural when he encountered Simon Dengler going in the other direction.

"You're going out?" Morgan asked his partner.

Dengler drew him out of earshot of the security men. "I got a message from the Caymans bank people that our records may have been compromised."

"What the hell do you mean by 'compromised'?" Morgan checked to ensure the bodyguards couldn't hear them.

"Someone from this office, using our passwords, has been accessing them. This happened in late April. And it took place in the middle of the night, long after any of us were still here." Dengler's eyebrows bristled like worried hedgehogs.

"You don't think . . . ?"

"I don't know what to think, Frederick."

Morgan started acting flustered. And he never acted flustered. "I'll get Heinrich on it right away. A full probe of who was in the building. We can't allow . . . I mean, this is outrageous . . . How in the name of . . ."

Dengler held up a silencing hand. "I'm going now to see Quince. I want to inspect what he has. I don't want him coming here or him messengering anything or talking about this over the phone any more than he has. We're dissatisfied with him anyway. This may be his funeral." Balthazar Quince was the personal contact at the Caymans bank for the RDS&M partners.

"I'll come with you. This, this, this—is very serious."

When their motorcade powered out of the Ludlum House underground garage and onto the city streets, a pedestrian of no particular distinction—besides his sharp vision—whipped out his cell phone and reported what he'd seen. "Dengler on the move," Byron reported. "Looks like Morgan is with him. Four cars. Lots of security."

"Good," Louis said on the other end. "You're my new favorite, Byron."

The bank occupied three floors in an anonymous domino of a Midtown office building. After the motorcade pulled up to it, large men hopped out of the armored autos and held open car doors for the two Billionaire Boys. Surrounded by a phalanx of security men, Morgan and Dengler crossed the wide sidewalk to the building's revolving door. A couple of bodyguards went through first and restrained people inside the lobby from spinning through the door when the two financiers were using it. The lobby was fairly busy and, as they crossed the floor, the bodyguards stayed alert for anything wrong.

George Sr. announced to the security man at the front desk that the two RDS&M partners were here to see Mr. Quince.

The officious front-desk toad in a blue blazer said he needed to see photo I.D. before they could be admitted to the elevator bank, which sat in a cul-de-sac behind a velvet rope. At the rope, another misshapen character in a blazer guarded the elevator bank like the entrance to a trendy dance club. At the end of the elevator corridor was a tacky steel door with a sign reading: "Stairwell."

"This is an outrage," Dengler declared to the desk man. "I don't carry photo I.D. That incompetent Quince." They hadn't been to the bank's office in a long time.

"Maybe we can get Quince to come down and identify us," said an ever-reasonable Morgan, who also never carried such a gauche item as a driver's license.

"I'll call up, but I don't know," the desk man said with the welcome of a Department of Motor Vehicles clerk. He slowly reached for the phone.

After waiting a few minutes, they were cleared to go up in the elevator. When Dengler asked where Quince was, George Sr. pointed to a wall-mounted camera.

They all crowded into the elevator corridor. The RDS&M security team shooed off other people waiting there. The size and steely purpose of the bodyguards prevented anyone from complaining out loud. Of the four elevators, one was already at lobby level, according to the floor readout above its closed doors. But it didn't seem to be working.

"Our fees are paying for the rent that funds these molasses elevators?" Dengler said.

Without warning, the lobby-level elevator's doors slid wide. Instead of passengers, several hissing canisters shot out of the elevator car.

The canisters erupted into clouds of choking white fumes. Dengler and Morgan and the bodyguards howled, screamed, retched, and fell to their knees. The burning gas set their eyes and throats afire.

A bunch of black figures danced through the burning cloud and grabbed the wailing Dengler. They hauled him toward the stairwell exit. One bent over Morgan, who could hear what he said through the gas mask: "Your turn is coming. I can't wait." Then he was gone.

Wendy came by to ask Karen if she was joining the gang for a foray that night to a friend's art opening. "Even Frank is going. I've promised to introduce him to women. Not that it will do any good, mind you."

"I might have a date tonight. Sort of. Kind of." She told her about Jeff Davis.

"Great. You need to wipe Tim off your shoes." Wendy's parrot agreed, repeating the phrase to drive the point home, and then some: "Wipe off your shoes, wipe off your shoes."

"My mother has set me up, though."

"Then it's a guaranteed success. She ought to know. She picked your father, didn't she? Hey, nice, handsome, smart men are hard to find."

"Because they all have boyfriends."

As Wendy and the parrot left, Karen turned back to the Uncle John documents. Edward Danton had been the numbers cruncher for the Billionaire Boys back when they weren't yet billionaires but were the leading lights of Dewey Cheatham's merger operation, the toast of 1980s Wall Street. Then the U.S. attorney charged Danton with using inside knowledge of pending deals, before they were announced, to buy stock—an illegal practice. He purchased shares in a target company and, once the deal was announced and its stock rose, sold for a profit. Karen found nothing about the Billionaire Boys themselves in Danton's indictment.

Danton's case was small time, however. He had only insider-traded a few deals for a $100,000 take. He financed his defense with his savings and those of his father, James, a college professor. After his sentencing but before he reported to the prison, the cops arrested Danton for threatening to kill his girlfriend, Mercedes, and himself. He apparently had been arrested in the lobby of her apartment building with a gun. That added another ten years to the three-year sentence he'd already received. Out of money, he used a public defender. Danton accused Morgan and his three other ex-bosses of setting him up. He claimed they had done far more extensive insider trading and had made him the fall guy; and they had planted a gun on him and delivered a fake message from Mercedes to meet him at her building.

At Iffewon Federal Penitentiary, Danton served time without incident. The file had several reports from a prison psychologist, who wrote that Danton seemed very depressed. "Subject says he never has made many friends, either here or in the outside world," the shrink wrote. Some hardcore inmates gave him a tough time. But then he struck up a friendship with an aged con man named Christopher Abbott, whom Danton somehow had known before. Abbott had clout at Iffewon and the bad guys left the young prisoner alone. The speculation was that Abbott had a great deal of hidden money that he used to bribe bad guys and guards.

Then Abbott got cancer. Danton visited his friend constantly at the prison medical ward. When Abbott died, Danton plunged back into depression. In his sixth year at Iffewon, he threw himself off the roof of the eight-story cellblock.

The booking mug shot of Danton was fuzzy. But his eyes had a quality that you wouldn't expect of a white-collar criminal, even one willing to commit murder-suicide.

On a hunch, she consulted the Boxerbelle FBI file. It confirmed that Louis Roman had served time at Iffewon during Danton's stay. She looked at the mug shot again.

No doubt here. His eyes were unmistakable.

She fished out the surveillance photo of Ward Mixon from the Met's security cameras, which Frank Vere had procured from his sources. She placed it next to the mug shot. Eddie Danton had a full head of hair in the late 1980s; Ward Mixon, according to Marcia, had fake hair and a moustache. Danton's and Mixon's facial contours were slightly different, which went beyond the effects of aging. Their noses also didn't match. But their eyes sure did.

Then she saw that she had a voice mail message. It was a pleasant male voice identifying himself as Jeff Davis and inviting her to a drink after she got off work. He suggested a bar down in Greenwich Village. How convenient for him, right near the New School so he wouldn't have to travel and she would.

She dialed his number. The message said, "This is Jeff. Leave a message, please." Matter of fact. Not obnoxious (one date from her single days had a message with "As Time Goes By" playing in the background and him saying in a bad Humphrey Bogart imitation: "Listen, sweetheart, if you don't leave a message, you'll be sorry. Not now, but some day, and for the rest of your life"). Not pompous (another date, a self-important blowhard, told his callers: "Do leave word and I'll try to get back to you when and if I can"). And not anal (like the fellow who instructed the morons who called him: "Spell your name slowly and distinctly and repeat your phone number twice, also slowly and distinctly").

"I'll meet you there at seven," she said to Jeff's machine.

Miriam pulled the blindfold off Dengler, who had been repeating, "I'll pay you any money you want. Don't hurt me."

He sat, hands bound behind him, on a chair in a pool of light cast by a single overhead lamp. The air was basement dank. His suit jacket was ripped. His tie was down. His eyes were bloodshot from the tear gas.

Several young Vampyrs, clad in black, circled him. They whispered among themselves.

Byron tilted his head and looked at Dengler as if he were a zoological curiosity. "You tore your pretty suit."

"I buy my suits at warehouse clearance sales," Dengler said, trying for that man-of-the-people style. "Why pay some fancy tailor like Frederick does?"

"You parasites took over a textile company and closed their plants and sent the work overseas, where the workers are exploited, paid a dollar a week," Miriam said in his ear, close enough to bite it.

"That was Butch's idea," Dengler said, then sobbed for a minute. "He hates organized labor. Don't blame me. I'm the good guy at RDS&M. I do the numbers. That's all. Ask anyone."

"You cheat on your taxes," Byron said.

"I'm a good citizen. I don't hurt anyone. I can give you money. Please."

"You hide your money with First Caymans Bank and Trust," Miriam said.

"Who told you about that?" Dengler said, momentarily snappish. "This is none of your business."

Byron smacked his face hard. "You're ours now. It is our business."

They all laughed. Dengler sobbed again. Then he realized everyone had grown silent. He looked up. A large man in a cape stood looming over him.

The other Vampyrs had fallen away.

"I'm Louis," he said. "And you're toast." Everyone laughed until he silenced them.

Sensing that this was the leader, Dengler said, "Listen, you and I can cut a deal. I'll give you whatever money you want. I'm very rich."

"Yeah, you're a real FOP. And you are one greedy, skinflint hump who craps on everybody else."

"I'm an honest businessman."

"No such animal. At least the other Billionaire Boys give some of their ill-gotten gains away to charity, even if only for their self-aggrandizement. See, money is like manure: pile it up in one place and it stinks; spread it around and it does some good."

"Well . . ." Dengler was flummoxed about how to answer.

"It's well-known how much you despise charities. You think a guy with no legs should pull himself up by his bootstraps. Kids are starving in Africa. And you don't care."

"Well . . . I can make you very comfortable."

"Today is going to be a big day of changes for you," Louis said. He turned around, and another light came on. There was a young woman, with bruises on her face, sitting at a computer work station. "Kyra here is good with computers. She had better be good today because she is working to restore herself."

"What are you talking about?" Dengler said. " "Do you want a million? I could wire-transfer you a million to any account on the planet in seconds. Caymans Bank can do it."

Louis nodded. "I do know that. We have had some expert outside advice on electronic banking ourselves. We are linked into your bank account in the Caymans, as well as to a number of worthy organizations who have been told they are about to receive sizable donations from you. Let's see, the first will be Save the Children Fund. Kyra, give them a billion."

That was when Dengler lost control of his bowels. His spiky eyebrows were halfway up his forehead. "What?" Then he screamed it: "What!"

Chapter Twenty-one

This was going amazingly well. Jeff Davis was indeed every bit as good-looking and nice as Ma had promised. In fact, he seemed a 1960s throwback, what with the denim shirt, the jeans, the work boots, and the longish, dirty-blond hair. At least he had no facial hair, which leftie men had long favored; Karen feared that men with beards were too often hiding something like a weak chin. Jeff had an easy-going manner, meaty forearms displayed by rolled-up sleeves, and a ready smile of straight white teeth. And despite the curse of a parental fix-up, he liked her.

"Yeah, I'm on a daddy-ship," he freely admitted. "My dad is the best indulgent parent going. He has financed my horizontal road to education." This meant that, after graduating from NYU with an English degree, he had spent years traveling and studying abroad. He had crewed on an Americas Cup contender, worked on a dig of a pharaoh's tomb, painted water colors in Montmartre, and climbed Mt. Kilimanjaro.

"What are you doing at the New School?" asked Karen, actually pleased to be asking dumb first-date questions of this interesting and attractive guy. She hadn't dressed up for the occasion: her shirt and slacks were work-place staples.

"I'm doing an interdisciplinary degree in psychology and sociology, focusing on ethnic diversity." He said this almost pompously, but then added: "I was inspired by my ex-wife. She had a mixed ethnic background."

"Mine, too. My husband is part German, part shepherd." Karen judged Jeff to be country-club WASP, a few rungs down the status ladder from old money like the Brattons.

He laughed and said, "No, really, Candace and I are still friends. She remarried, to a very nice guy."

Liking his ex-wife, not to mention her new man, was good. Karen doubted she would stay in touch with Tim, who would end up marrying some soulless, headband girl like Ashlea Kress. "Sociology, huh? Is that how you know my mother?"

Jeff hesitated for a moment, endearingly. "Your mother, as a practicing counselor of rape and domestic violence victims, addressed a class I took. Since then, she has brought me to loads of protests with your father."

"Ma is anxious to save the world, but deep down is afraid that it's impossible. Pop isn't as deep. He's just wildly indignant about everything. He hates capitalism, pure and simple."

"Your being a distinguished business journalist must get to him."

Flattery, yes. Delivered with the right note of admiring sincerity. Bring it on. "Well, I'm more like an extinguished journalist. I'm working on a big story now, hoping for a break."

"What's it on?" he leaned over the small table toward her, as if asking for the hiding place of the Holy Grail.

She leaned toward him. Their faces were six inches apart. She felt her knee touch his; she didn't move it for ten meaningful seconds. God, he had such welcoming eyes. "Have you ever heard of the Billionaire Boys Club?" He had.

After she told him the basic outline, Jeff sat back in appreciation. "This is dangerous stuff, Karen. And I thought climbing Kilimanjaro was daring. You got me beat."

"I hear that Vampyr has its hideout somewhere in Queens. Sounds like Long Island City, near the water. And that a rich man is underwriting them. Not much else is clear."

The weather between them had changed. Jeff took a pull of his beer, a tasteful brew imported from Iceland. Then he took another pull. He examined the grain on the tabletop.

"I have a good idea where they are," he said, barely audible. "This had to do with a girl I knew. She had just joined them, and she took me . . ." He took a swig of his beer.

"What's her name?"

He took a deep breath. "Kyra."

"Kyra." Karen's eyes widened. "Kyra Selden?"

"Uh, yeah. How do you—?"

"We had a run-in."

Jeff looked around the crowded barroom, as if contemplating fleeing.

Karen put a hand on his meaty forearm. "Take me there, Jeff."

"Why? Are you crazy?" He was no longer going for ingratiating.

"Very possibly. Take me there."

Balthazar Quince stood before Morgan and Strongville in their Ludlum House conference room, stammering his regrets. "No one knew you were coming. Not a soul. Really."

"Somebody has been hacking into our accounts at your bank," Strongville said with the force of a drill sergeant. "Somebody knows a lot of stuff about us, stuff that we're paying you to keep private." He jammed a cigarette into his mouth and lit it.

"We have preliminary indications that your accounts were accessed long after business hours from inside Ludlum House," said Quince, who had the long face of a sad dog. "If there has been a security breach—and I'm not saying there has been—then it is here, sir."

"I agree with Balthazar on that," Morgan said, as always the reasonable presiding officer. His eyes and throat still stung from the tear gas. "But I agree with Butch that it's troubling how they had your building lobby staked out and ready to spring a trap."

Quince spread his hands imploringly. "Our security is hired by the building and we are merely tenants. We're a bank, not a military garrison."

"They know our every move," Butch said. "How?"

The Wildlife Federation, Greenpeace, Rainforest Restoration, the Orphans Foundation, Hire the Handicapped—a list of worthy causes received billions from Simon Dengler, newly converted philanthropist.

As he watched his fortune fly away on electronic wings, Dengler bowed his head, his chin resting on his chest. His shoulders shook with grief. He barely registered that a Vampyr had captured his humiliating ordeal on a video camera.

"This," Louis informed the circle of his followers around him Dengler, "is justice." He gestured to a metal device, resembling a bear trap, which a young Vampyr held. "Here, Sidney is about to demonstrate a mechanism that holds people's mouths open. The capitalist pig Dengler is going to learn all about it. This is justice."

"I worked so hard for every penny," Dengler managed to say, eyeing Sidney and his sinister, torture-like device.

Louis's large hand cupped the ex-billionaire's chin, forcing him to look up at the head Vampyr. "You exploited people."

His lips slack, Dengler said, "You don't know me."

The camera stopped recording.

"I do." The voice came from outside the circle of Vampyrs.

Dengler's head jerked up and out of Louis's grasp. He recognized the voice, yet couldn't place it. "Who said that?"

Edward Danton walked into the pool of light and stood next to Louis, who towered over him and grinned fiercely. "I wanted to have a face-to-face reunion with one of you," Danton said. "It wasn't possible with Redmon. He had that crowd around. And I had to escape the Met."

Dengler's bristly eyebrows rose in surprise. The newcomer's face had changed, but not the voice or the eyes. "Danton? Eddie Danton?"

"You people betrayed me." Danton had told himself he'd keep the bitterness out of his tone. He could not avoid it, though. "You let me take the fall for you on the insider trading. And you set up the fake gun charge."

"You're dead," Denger said, in ghost-movie wonderment.

"Don't you wish."

"I never did anything to hurt you. It was the others."

"Bullshit, Simon. You were the one who roped me into your little insider-trading scheme, giving me a few crumbs. Hey, I needed the money. It was just a lark for you four."

Dengler exhaled in a burst to signify his bewilderment. "Frederick was the one who was after you. He wanted Mercedes. That was obvious. I thought what he had planned was wrong."

"You did nothing to stop it, did you? Tell me, who figured out the gun frame-up?"

Growing excited, talking louder and faster by the syllable, Dengler said, "Frederick was behind it all. Butch knows about guns, so he planted the pistol in your briefcase. But Frederick concocted that story that sent you over to Mercedes's building. Frederick called the police to arrest you there. He's the one. Not me."

"But you testified, after they arrested me in her lobby," Danton shouted, "that I had acted crazy and was going over to Mercedes's place to kill her and myself."

Dengler sighed. "And today," he said, slower now, resigned, "you're a radical?"

"I pay Vampyr very well for services rendered. The capitalist way, Simon."

"And the whole world will think Vampyr is behind our deaths, not you. Is that the idea?"

"You get it at last."

Louis put a big arm around Danton and steered him out into the darkness. "I got a capitalist question for you. We have left half a billion in his account. How about we send that to the account you set up for us in Switzerland? No one will miss it."

"Every bit of it goes to the charities I designated," Danton said, putting on a brave front. If he gave Louis so much money now, Vampyr's incentive to take on the two remaining Billionaire Boys would vanish. "I control that Swiss account of yours until our job is finished with the Billionaire Boys. You will be paid well at that point, Louis, and get control of the Swiss account. That's our arrangement."

Louis put a hand on Danton's neck, near his windpipe. "I'm your best friend. Maybe we should alter that arrangement. How about a nice preliminary payment?"

Ali appeared out of the gloom. "Get away from him, asshole," he said to Louis. The manservant's eyes flared in the darkness.

Louis gave Ali an appraising gaze, and released Danton. "Sure. For now."

Then Dengler's almost unearthly cry reached Danton: "You always were a loser. You didn't have the stuff at Dewey Cheatham. Half-baked analytics were the best you could do. Nobody liked you. We never would have made you an offer to join RDS&M. You loser."

Knowing that Frederick would be working late again at Ludlum House, Mercedes had a quiet dinner with her son, whom she wouldn't let leave the apartment. She asked about his schoolwork, and he told her how good the Dalton teachers were to e-mail him his assignments.

"How long am I under house arrest?" he asked his mother as the candlelight flickered across his impish teenage face.

"Your father says they are close to catching these awful people. It shouldn't be long now." She drank some more wine. She already had put away most of a bottle. Dinner alone with Bert had magic. Frederick so seldom appeared for a family dinner. If he did, he was on his cell phone half the time.

Bert was dressed in his Dalton blazer and school tie. She insisted that everyone dress for dinner. "Would they hurt you?" her son asked.

"No one will be hurt. Now finish your food."

"They want to hurt *him*, for sure." Bert lately referred to Frederick only as "him."

Mia entered the dining room, carrying a phone. "A call for you, Mrs. Morgan."

"Mia, I've told you: no phone calls at dinner time."

This rule, of course, didn't apply when Frederick was at the dinner table.

"It's Mr. Morgan. He says this is very important."

Mercedes thanked her and took the phone. With a glance at a perplexed Bert, she excused herself and moved to the hall outside, with its stripped walls, drop cloths, and wallpaper rolls, where the decorator soon would start work. "Frederick, what's the matter?"

Her husband was doing his considerable best to sound calm and in control. "The police are releasing this to the media now. Simon has been kidnapped." He gave her a terse account of their visit to the bank.

Mercedes put her hand to her forehead. "And you're okay?"

"I'm fine. We've got two men outside our apartment already. I'll send more." His voice started to break. He recovered and said, "I'm sorry, Mercedes." He hung up.

She wandered over to the library and stared dully out the window overlooking Park Avenue. Not for the first time, she wondered what life would be like if Frederick were gone. A horrible thought, she knew. But . . .

Mercedes pulled the letter out of her pocket. And once again, she re-read it.

My dearest Mercedes: I realize this will be a shock to you. I am alive. I will explain how and why when I see you. I've missed you terribly, all these long years. I still love you. Yours forever, Eddie.

Bert stood at the library door. "Is something wrong?"

"Wrong?" She fired up a smile for him. "No."

* * *

Jeff Davis's left eyelid had begun twitching. "This," he said, "is the place."

Karen squeezed his hand. "When were you here?"

"In the fall," he said hollowly. "It was getting cold. Very cold."

They stood on a deserted street corner in the Queens warehouse district, across the river from Manhattan's sparkling towers. Here, there was only darkness, broken by the occasional streetlight. In the light breeze, a crumpled newspaper tumbled down the oil-stained asphalt like a ghost without a home. Off to the south rose the skyway ramp of the Long Island Expressway, leading to the Queens-Midtown Tunnel. Cars sped along it and made shooing noises.

The two-story industrial loft building sat across the street from Karen and Jeff. It had long windows and betrayed no light from within. Vents snaked up its drab facade. An empty loading dock was to one side. From the street, the structure appeared to hold nothing living. There were several steel doors, solid and formidable as hell's gates.

Jeff droned his story as if reciting a trauma under hypnosis. "Kyra and I had been living together. We went to a lot of demonstrations. She was a spooky girl. She brought sharp objects to bed. She fascinated me and scared me. Maybe I was in love with her."

"Sharp objects?"

"She got into a fight with our landlord. He had trouble providing hot water. So she sabotaged his credit rating. See, she's a computer hacker. He found out and threatened to call the cops. Then she pulled a knife on him."

"So she took me here and told me she'd joined Vampyr and wanted me to come in to join, too." He swallowed audibly. "I was freaked."

A large door opened on the loading dock. They heard the sound of a well-tuned motor. A classy Ferrari rolled out and onto the street. The car glided past them. One person was inside. Even in the darkness, Karen knew him.

"Oh, God. That's Mixon. That's him, no doubt. Hoo boy." Karen fished in her bag for her cell phone. "Let me call my cop friend. You've got the exact address of this building?"

"No," Jeff said. "We're not calling any cops."

"What do you mean, we're—?" Karen saw that he had pulled a small revolver out of his pocket. "Oh, you asshole."

Several others, clad in black, had appeared behind them. One was Kyra, who had a bruised face and carried a large machete. They surrounded Karen. Kyra kissed Jeff on the mouth.

"Shit," was all Karen could say. If Karen weren't knee-knocking terrified, she would say this was the worst date of her life.

Chapter Twenty-two

They hustled Karen across the street—a tumbling newspaper briefly wrapped around her ankle—and up to one of the strong doors, which Kyra unlocked. Two of the young men held Karen firmly. Jeff lagged behind, so Karen couldn't see him. They entered a dank hallway and went down some dark stairs to the basement. At the bottom, in a large, ill-lit room, several more young Vampyrs awaited them.

Matthew had a gleeful and predatory expression. In addition to his unsightly soul patch, he had sprouted another eyesore, literally—a very large black eye.

"We got you now," Matthew said.

Each of them stared at her as if she were a Salem witch about to meet an extreme heat treatment. Karen's heart pounded wildly. Her breathing matched it.

"How about the boys take turns on her?" Matthew said.

Miriam held up her hands. "Whoa. Louis has said

nothing about a gang bang. You're such a sexist dirt hound, Matthew. You think the only position for women in this organization is prone."

Kyra had traded her machete for a knife. She stood in front of Karen, hefting it. "Louis wants her finger as a keepsake? That's *all* he has instructed us so far."

Henry, also bearing facial bruises, came into view. "She deserves it."

A grim-faced Jeff, the lone Vampyr not in black, had edged into Karen's line of sight. His gun was gone. "Whatever we do," Jeff said hesitantly, "let's be quick."

Hearing her fate discussed like that of a slaughterhouse cow, Karen found her gumption. "Oh, what a prince you are, Jeff. What are you going to tell my mother?"

This stopped Jeff. He examined his feet.

Then came a commotion. A crowd of other Vampyrs approached. In the lead, cloak draping his large frame, wearing black Jejune jeans, the bullet crease on his face, was Louis.

"Matthew gets points for this one—he thought up using Jeff. Congratulations, Matthew. You've started to redeem yourself." As Matthew beamed, Louis turned to Karen and caressed her cheek, just as he had in the *Profit* conference room. She glared at him and didn't flinch. "And Karen Glick here, the capitalist tool, has been out on a date. Looking good, Karen. You are hot tonight."

"Not for too much longer," Miriam said, which earned her a malevolent stare from Louis. She also examined her shoes.

"Matthew wants all the boys to rape her before we cut off her finger and all?" Kyra said. "Isn't that, like, against what we stand for?"

Louis, the god who handed down the commandments for this lost tribe, narrowed his eyes. "I don't think the boys should have her." He stroked Karen's cheek again. "But since she and I have had a kind of physical relationship, I'll take her. Get her clothes off."

"I've got an idea," Karen said to Louis, before her captors to each side could move. "If you're man enough, how about you and I fight? I've smacked you twice. Do you have what it takes to box with me?"

The idea made Louis laugh hard. His chest heaved and he stamped his feet. The others joined in with sycophantic guffaws.

"I'll clean your clock," Karen said. "Face-to-face this time. You won't be able to complain that I surprised you. What, are you afraid of a girl?"

Louis's laughter died, and so did that of the young Vampyrs. "Are you serious?"

Another Vampyr sidled up to Louis and said, "Dengler is ready for delivery."

"Put him in the van," Louis said, then swiveled back to Karen. "Are you?"

"What's this about Dengler?" Karen asked.

"Never mind," Louis said. He dropped his cape to the floor. He rolled up the sleeves of his black pullover to reveal powerful, muscle-packed arms. "Are you?"

"Yeah," Karen said, baring her teeth.

At Louis's signal, the two guys holding Karen fell away. She immediately clenched her fists as tightly as possible and moved sideways. The Vampyrs stood around them in a wide circle.

Louis didn't even bother to move or raise his fists. He kept his hands at his sides as he watched her with amusement. "You're a tough chick, huh?"

Karen hadn't thought through what her plan should be, or even if one were possible. She only knew that she wouldn't let these creeps have their way with her while she did nothing. Those hours from long ago in the Queens gym came back to her, and that time more recently shadow-boxing with Marcia in Mixon's empty apartment.

"I saw Edward Danton leaving in his Ferrari," Karen said, flashing on Frank Vere and Louis in the conference room. A good reporter asks questions always. "He's doing all this to get revenge on the Billionaire Boys, then blame it on you, huh?"

"Of course. What, did Frank Vere figure that out?"

Karen danced before him, taking quick air punches to let Louis know she was indeed serious about self-defense. "No, I did. I've found out a lot. The records show Danton jumped off the top of the Iffewon cellblock."

Louis pulled his head back to avoid her attempt at a face punch. "You know nothing. Guys die in prison every day. When you get access to Chris Abbott's hidden money, like Danton did, you can buy stuff. As in buy a dead body from the morgue and bribe the guards to throw it from the roof and say it's you. Then Danton waltzed out. Which you won't be doing tonight." His head zipped to the side to dodge her second shot. He was fast.

"You and Danton really believe you can wipe out the Billionaire Boys?"

"We've bagged two of them. When we're done, that dweeb Danton will drop into Mrs. Morgan's life, the old boyfriend back, the shoulder to cry on. His plastic surgery makes him look different from before, but not too much. Clever guy, huh?"

"How much is Danton paying you?" Karen said from behind her fists.

Tauntingly, Louis stuck his chin out. "Less than he should. But we'll change that." As Karen drew back to slug his chin, he backhanded her with amazing speed and force. She went reeling. The line of Vampyrs parted as she toppled to the hard concrete.

"Okay," Louis said matter-of-factly. He pointed at Jeff. "Since you're her big date for the evening, you get to take her clothes off. After I'm done, I'll stay for her finger." He pointed at Kyra and her knife. "Then I gotta go deliver Dengler."

Karen, her head buffeted by inner tides, rose unsteadily from the floor. "We're not finished here yet, you jackass."

Louis laughed again at her. "I like women beneath me with fire."

She shuffled up to him. "I liked you better in that ugly gunman's makeup."

Louis shook his head. "You're no knockout. But you'll do."

"You want a knockout?" Karen concentrated every erg of strength into the punch she landed in his stomach.

His eyes bulging, Louis bent over. His lips moved,

fishlike, and he fell to his knees. He grasped his midsection and gasped in agony.

"Get her!" Matthew yelled. He shoved Karen, who fell again.

That was when the already-dim lights went out. The Vampyrs cursed in puzzlement. Louis kept gasping. Karen, still dizzy, propped herself up on one elbow.

Next came the first gunshot and muzzle flare. More followed. Shouts and screams rose above the shooting.

Karen flattened herself against the cold, hard floor. She heard whizzing sounds above her. Bullets? Someone fell heavily beside her, twitched and then lay still. She groped in the darkness to find the person. It was a man, solid. She felt the fabric of a denim shirt and then wetness. Her hand crawled up to his neck. She felt for a pulse. None.

"Jeff," she muttered.

Around her, people ran and flailed and shouted.

Karen got on all fours and gingerly crept along the floor, hoping to find a wall or some other sanctuary. She came across another body, female this time.

At last her questing hands found the wall. She was bundling up against it when she sensed two large presences looming over her.

"It's Karen Glick," a man's voice said. "Let her alone."

Someone had opened a window to the street outside. The figures hovering over her took form in the half-light: large men wearing body armor and bizarre goggles, carrying short rifles.

Another of these armor-wearers peered out the window. "NYPD," he called out.

They all scrambled off in the other direction. In the light from the street, Karen could make out many shapes on the floor, islands of stillness. She didn't want to look at them. Karen edged along the basement wall, keeping clear of the Vampyr corpses, until she found the stairway she'd come down. She bolted up the steps and out into the street.

A carnival of police cars, roof strobes whirling and sirens crying, was blasting down the block toward her. It skidded to a halt with a squeal of tortured tire rubber. Cops poured out of the cars, weapons drawn.

Light-headed from Louis's blow and from the shock of seeing so much death, Karen stumbled onto the sidewalk. A cop said something threatening and garbled over a loudspeaker. She raised her hands, figuring that was what he wanted.

A troop of officers in Kevlar vests galloped up to her. The leader was Marcia Fink. "Are you okay?" the detective asked.

"That wasn't you guys doing the raid downstairs?"

"What raid?"

Frederick Morgan was pacing around his study when the call came. He eagerly snapped on his cell phone. "Yes?"

"The mission has achieved qualified success," Herman Heinrich droned on the other end. "Elimination of threat cohort has been effectuated."

"What do you mean by 'qualified success'?"

"Mr. Dengler's physical location remains undetermined at this point. A full inventory of eliminated threat individuals could not be accomplished due to the arrival of police personnel."

"You mean the police showed up?" Morgan cast his head about to ensure no one was standing outside listening. He shut the door.

"Our force had to implement exit procedure when it was ascertained the arrival of police personnel was imminent," Heinrich said with typical automaton verve.

"Did you get Louis Roman and Mixon, their leaders?"

"Identification of these individuals was not accomplished. One report maintains that a van departed their loading dock at a great rate of speed, right after our operation commenced. We are seeking more data."

"Some of them got away?"

"At this point in time, that remains non-confirmed. However, the presence of the reporter Karen Glick was established. Our force observed her being taken captive before commencement of the operation."

"Karen Glick?" Morgan exclaimed. "Is she dead?"

"She appears to have sustained little or no injury."

"Send someone for her. We'll bring her in and debrief her." Morgan passed a hand through his immaculate hair, tousling it. "And you have no idea where Simon is?"

"We are currently in search mode for Mr. Dengler."

"I want a full report in person at Ludlum House in a half hour. Notify Mr. Strongville to be present."

Thanking Heinrich before ending the call, Morgan tossed the cell onto a couch. He stood on his exquisite Persian rug and tried to think through the angles.

There was a soft knock on his door. Morgan crossed the room and opened it a crack. Bert stood outside in his pajamas.

"Is everything okay?" his son asked meekly.

"Everything's fine. Go back to bed."

"It's just . . . I'm scared for you, Daddy." His chin trembled.

Bert hadn't called Morgan "Daddy" in ages. Morgan found himself holding his son.

"Listen," Morgan said at last, his own voice husky with emotion, "I'll be fine. The cops are rounding up these horrible people. We'll be back to normal real soon."

By now a pro at giving police statements, Karen recited the evening's events to Marcia in the back of a police cruiser. Cops milled around outside, doing very little but looking as if they were intent on it.

"We'd put this building under surveillance but weren't sure," Marcia said. "Then came the gunfire. We're sure now, but we're late."

"You were right on time as far as I'm concerned."

"How are you holding up?" Marcia asked. "We've got a very good trauma counselor. You've been chewed up and spat out."

Karen shrugged. "I don't feel bad. Maybe this will hit later." Her mother would be a font of information and opinion on post-traumatic stress syndrome. But Karen didn't need any soothing. For now, Karen felt only anger . . . and sadness. In an odd way, she felt sorry for Jeff.

"You'd've made a good cop. I know guys who are in big firefights that lead to multi-body massacres, the blood up to their butts, and afterward they all tell jokes. Not bad jokes, either. Others break down into constant crying. I peg you for the first type."

"Whatever," said Karen, in no mood for joking. "Marcia, this Edward Danton character is behind the whole effort. I have no reason to doubt what Louis said."

Marcia nodded over her notebook and jotted down something. "This is all news to me. We've heard nothing about an insider-trading scheme involving the Billionaire Boys in the 1980s. We'll look into this. We'll try to get a recording of Danton's voice to see if it matches the recording you made of Mixon. Maybe there's one from Danton's questioning during investigations back then. It was a long time ago, so maybe we can't find one. He was careful about the fingerprints, as you know. But there's little doubt he's the money behind the whole circus, from the elephants to the clowns."

"How much money did Chris Abbott have? And how could Danton, in prison, get his hands on this stash once Abbott had died?"

Marcia laughed. "Prisons are as leaky as an old roof, even the federal pens. Someone always has his hand out. I'll bet Abbott had a system of couriers from the outside who'd bring him cash, which he'd spread around like Johnny Appleseed. Some prison guards—they like to call themselves 'corrections officers,' but they're prison guards—made a tidy side income getting seeded."

Karen tried getting into a comfortable position. The rear seats of police cars, where the suspects sat, weren't contoured for comfort like the seats on RDS&M's Gulfstream "But something troubles me. Remember how Danton, back at the Mixon apartment, claimed he didn't want to hurt me? But then Louis and his crew have done whatever they could to wax me? What if there's a rift between Louis and Danton? Louis is pissed that I've gotten in his way and smacked him. It's significant that they waited until Danton drove away tonight in his Ferrari before the Vampyrs took me prisoner."

"You gotta give Danton the brass hat award for thinking he can swoop in on the Widow Morgan and whisk her away on his white horse. Or Ferrari."

Karen delved into her bag, which the cops had returned to her from the Vampyr building. There was a blood stain on the side, which she chose to ignore. She fished out a piece of paper. "Here's a copy of the notes I took about Danton's background. Take it. But give me some more hard information back, okay? I'm giving you far more than you've given me."

Marcia examined the typed sheet. "I can give you informed speculation. I'm wondering about the aliases that Danton uses. The vans Vampyr has are registered to the dead guy from Buffalo, Warden Moxley. He was real, not made up. Maybe Danton chose him for a reason."

"You think Danton knew Moxley?"

"No. More likely that he wanted the guy's name.

We've got a Warden Moxley, a Ward Mixon the Met waiter, and Edward Danton. 'Ward' is the common denominator for the names."

"Why would Danton do that?" Karen asked.

"People who use second identities like to keep them sounding like their own. They're easier to remember. And if another person calls out their new name, they react. Meaning, if you switched your name, you might go for Kara or Carrie, not Desdemona or Hortense."

"Wait a sec." Karen took back the paper from Marcia. "Danton's mother's maiden name was Minox. You remember how my grandmother likes to do anagrams on people's names?"

"Do I ever. She called me Frick Mania. I didn't know whether to be pleased or insulted. She also called me Manic Fakir and African Mink."

"Nobody knows with Gran. She goes from shrewd businesswoman to nutty old lady in a heartbeat." Karen tapped the paper. "But look here. If you jumbled around the letters of Minox, you get Mixon. Now, Moxley isn't an anagram of either, but it's close. And Moxley was a real guy with a real history, which Danton needed to register the vans and the Ferrari. The Department of Motor Vehicles probably didn't know he was dead. Danton, I'll bet, went searching for the guy with a New York license who most recently died and had a last name like Minox and Ward in his first name."

"Plausible," Marcia said. "If Danton has had plastic surgery to alter his appearance slightly, what would his new name be?"

"A variant on Edward Danton, I suspect. Maybe with Ward in it somehow. I'll have to ask Gran."

Marcia opened the car door. "Go right ahead. I've got bigger fish to fry. Like Moby-Dick size. Like did all the Vampyrs die?"

"I hate to think this, but I kind of hope so."

"I can sympathize," the detective said. "We need to do lots of dental matches. Many of these kids have wealthy families, which means I'll be in a shit storm of high-priced family lawyers and politicians nosing into my investigation, trying to ensure that the poor, misguided brats aren't defamed in death."

"At first, I thought it was a police SWAT team that came in shooting."

Marcia shook her head. "We'd have given everyone in the Vampyr social club a chance to surrender. Whoever did this was out for slaughter, period. You're lucky they recognized you."

"I think they were wearing night-vision goggles."

"This was a top-notch, Special Forces–type operation. You can hire folks to do this for you. If you have big bucks. The Billionaire Boys will deny it and hide behind their lawyers."

"Where's Dengler? Did they have him in there?"

"No sign of him. We'll keep up the search. Why don't you go home?"

Karen hauled herself out of the car. Marcia had given her aspirin for her head, which still hurt from Louis's blow. She trudged out of the welter of police cars.

Waiting for her on the periphery of the cop jamboree was Ron. He had an avuncular smile for her, meant to look reassuring. It was. "Are you okay?"

"Ron, what are you doing here? How did you know about this?"

The bodyguard indicated his car parked down the block. "Let me give you a ride. Mr. Morgan and Mr. Strongville would like a word with you at Ludlum House."

Butch Strongville sat with face in hands as Herman Heinrich stood before the two remaining Billionaire Boys and recounted his mission in excruciating detail. The gruesomeness couldn't be softened by his bureaucratic jargon.

"We have ascertained, from a second eyewitness report from one of our operatives, that a van actually did evacuate the premises. It may have contained Mr. Dengler." Heinrich had hands clasped behind his back like a soldier at parade rest.

"Another subject," Morgan said wearily. "The night in April that someone here was accessing our accounts at the Caymans Bank. Who was on duty?"

"Only security and maintenance personnel. We are questioning every one of them." Heinrich, who never betrayed any feelings, gave Strongville a look bordering between pity and contempt.

Strongville lowered his hands from his face. "Don't change the subject, Frederick. Back to Vampyr. So they're not all dead? For God's sake, why not? How could you have let a van escape from a loading dock?"

"As you know from your own Special Forces background, Mr. Strongville," Heinrich said, with what seemed like condescension, "we only had a seven-man A Team."

"We've got breathing room until they send us a new threat letter," Morgan said.

"Do we?" Strongville pulled out a black envelope and slid it down the table to Morgan.

In white ink written with a familiar fine hand, the ripped-open letter was addressed to Butch. Morgan pulled out the black stationery inside. It had the same white calligraphy. Morgan felt an Arctic chill as he read.

Dear Billionaire Boy: You are the one who lays waste to working people's livelihoods. You are the one who makes families suffer, leaving good people destitute so you can enrich yourself. And all the while, you cheat on your taxes. You like to act the tough soldier, doing what is necessary. But you are a fraud. We will do what is necessary for you. Your death is soon. Vampyr.

Morgan put down the letter. "Don't worry," he said to Strongville. "We have them on the run. What's left of them."

The large doors opened and Al rushed over to Heinrich. Al whispered in his ear.

"Excuse me," Heinrich said. "We have a situation in the front of the building."

"A situation?" Morgan said. "What is happening?"

"It's Mr. Dengler," Heinrich said. "I advise your non-attendance." He nodded toward an ashen-faced Strongville. "Especially his."

Morgan clasped his hands together. "Is Simon . . . alive?"

Chapter Twenty-three

When his father sat down next to the bed, Danton jerked awake. "Damn, I wish you'd come more often during the daytime like a normal person."

"I'm not a normal person. I'm your father."

The wind blew the curtains around like wraiths. They were alone in the depths of the night. Danton sat up. "Where's Ali? He better not be out again."

"He's sleeping."

"He's not very alert sometimes. I don't like it that you can come skulking in here at all hours—and he's snoozing like a possum."

"The next thing you're going to say is: I pay him good money, for this?' "

"You're a real mind reader, James."

His father stroked his white beard. "So you've murdered another Billionaire Boy. You must be filled with a feeling of accomplishment."

"I don't feel very good, if you want to know."

"Don't tell me," James said. "Your conscience is getting to you?"

"Hardly." Edward told his father about how Dengler had called him a loser at Dewey Cheatham. "That's unfair. Dengler was convinced that everyone who works numbers is a moron except for him."

"My son the loser. That has a ring to it."

Edward swung his legs out of bed. "No, James. Not your son the loser—okay? I control a fortune worth $250 million. I live on Park Avenue."

"Where you can spy on your ex-girlfriend." James adjusted his knit tie. "But it's not like you earned this money. Chris Abbott stole the money."

"Hey, I deserved this money, James. Chris took me under his wing in prison. And when he was on his deathbed, I took care of him. So he gave me the passwords to his Swiss account."

"I don't care how many of his bedpans you emptied. The money is still stolen."

Getting to his feet and pacing, Edward felt his ire rise toward his high FOP ceiling. "Don't you dare disparage Chris Abbott to me. He was a better father than you ever were. He only wanted to help me."

James shook his head. "He only wanted to use you. He was a con artist. He needed a go-fer, and you were it."

"If I was, I made out pretty well. You never had any such money."

"No," James said. "I spent every dime on your insider-trading trial. When you got in that second mess with the gun charge, well . . . you were on your own."

Edward stood over his father. "James, I have always been on my own."

"You're telling me? As a kid, you never had any friends. Now that you're this rich poltroon of Park Avenue, do you have friends? Louis, the radical psycho? Ali, your servant? The people you pay to delve into the Billionaire Boys lives?"

"Keep it up, James. Let's go for the record on criticism of me."

James stood and headed for the door. "And you still haven't figured out why the Billionaire Boys are successful, have you?"

"Oh, here we go. You with your damn riddle."

His father paused at the threshold. "The reason they are successful is they are a team, albeit for a sordid pursuit like business. They are pals. Their different strengths complement each other. A super-salesman, a financial brain, a hard-driving negotiator, a consensus builder and conciliator. That last, Frederick Morgan, won your Mercedes from you for a reason, Edward."

Edward Danton stood on his fine floor and blinked. Then he said to his father, who had clasped either side of the door and leaned into it, head bowed, "Mercedes and I had a love that won't simply evaporate. She is not happy now."

His father's last words floated back, echoing: "Happy? Can you ever be?"

Danton awoke to find Ali tapping his shoulder. "Whatsa matter?"

"You were making noise in your sleep, boss," the servant said.

"Not the first time," Danton said. "Jesus, Ali. You know I have these nightmares about visits from my father. I told you to leave me alone."

Ali seemed vexed. "That's not the reason I woke you."

"Even in death he is a pain in the ass."

Like a procession of druids, Louis, Kyra, and Henry filed into Danton's bedroom. Louis flung his cape out in Dracula fashion.

"What are you doing here?" Danton scrambled out of bed.

"Nice pajamas," Louis said, indicating Danton's nightshirt.

"Get out," Danton demanded.

"No can do," the chief Vampyr said. "Looks like the Billionaire Boys found us and spent a little money on firepower. They missed the cool folks. So we're here."

"This is my private home."

"Call the cops then."

Ron brought Karen into Ludlum House. Several security types were gathered around the front desk, among them Herman Heinrich. Jimmy, eyeing Karen suspiciously, broke from the group to tell Ron: "He wants a meeting. Now."

"What's wrong?" Ron asked. He told Karen to wait and left with the others.

Karen took her seat. The two men on the desk scrutinized her like somebody's pet alligator. At least no one wanted to see elaborate credentials or conduct a body-cavity search. She began studying the Stomcox Massacre mural. Somehow, she didn't figure anybody would do a Vampyr Massacre mural, but you never knew.

Then Colin, Ashlea's young MBA helper, stumbled into view. He looked as if he had stuck his finger in an electric socket. His hair was wild, his mouth hung open, and his eyes were wide. He spotted Karen and jittered over to her.

"I can't believe it," he said, obviously needing someone to talk to.

Karen invited him to sit down, which he did like a passenger after a MiG ride. "What's the matter?" she asked.

"I can't believe it." Bent over, his elbows on his knees, Colin worked his jaw from left to right. "I can't believe it."

"I'll believe it. What's happened?"

Colin tried to compose himself. "A van drove up to the door. The back doors opened and a hand truck got shoved out. The van took off. The security guards saw there was something tied to the hand truck. Wrapped in plastic. They tore off the plastic. It was Mr. Dengler. And he . . ." Colin's chin hit his rep tie.

Karen put an arm around him. "And he what, Colin?"

Colin lifted his chin. "And he had dollar bills stuffed down his throat. He had choked to death on the cash. I knew he was greedy and miserly. And he was. But in a good way."

"Wow. That's awful." Evidently, some of them had escaped to deliver this thoughtful gift. Karen remembered the Vampyr telling Louis about Dengler and the van.

"That's not all. Ashlea just got a streaming video attachment on an e-mail." Colin expelled some air. "The video showed Mr. Dengler before he died and he . . ."

"And he what, Colin?" Karen put another hand on his shoulder.

"And on the video, he watched while they gave away all his money, electronic transfer, to charities. He really freaked."

An unsettled-seeming man with a long face scooted across the hall with an alacrity that Dengler would applaud. "Who's that guy?"

"Balthazar Quince, from First Caymans Bank and Trust. Vampyr somehow got Mr. Dengler's password for the funds transfer. But—you're not one of us. You're a reporter, right?"

"Guilty as charged, Colin."

To Colin, the bench heated up to 150 degrees, and he shot to his feet. "Then I shouldn't be talking to you. I'm so upset that I . . ." A pleading look seized his face. "Please don't tell anyone, particularly Ashlea Kress. Don't crack my rice bowl."

Karen sighed. "Your rice bowl."

Colin skittered away. Karen went back to beholding the gory glory of the Stomcox mural when her cell rang. She pulled it out of her blood-splattered bag.

It was Gran from Woodstock. "Did you hear on the news about the big shootout in Queens? All those damn Vampyr putzes got slaughtered like roaches."

Unlike the ones in her new place, which were invulnerable. "How are Ma and Pop?"

"Your father is in a sour mood, as usual. Your

mother is anxious about the state of mankind, as usual. And I'm driving them nuts, as usual."

Karen, of course, would spare Gran the tale of another brush with death. "I'm glad you called, Gran." She told her about how she suspected Edward Danton had changed his name via anagram, just as he had done with Mixon. "Could you come up with some alternatives for us to look into?"

"No problem. I can't do it now. There's a PBS special on the death of the Brazilian rain forest that Emma insists I watch. She wants me to give money to this bleeding-heart group trying to stop it. I say pave the damn place."

"Yeah, watching PBS specials is what I'd do on vacation."

"The reason I called," Gran said, "is that I've come to a decision."

"A decision?"

Gran slipped into a conspiratorial tone. "You see, I keep some of my money offshore in First Caymans Bank and Trust. Their New York–based hand holder is deeply in my debt. I found an apartment for his daughter after the kid got out of college. In Manhattan. At an affordable rent. Anyhow, I've arranged for him to talk to you about the Billionaire Boys' accounts."

Karen almost dropped the phone. "What? Why would he do that for me? He'll get in trouble with a capital T. I realize, the daughter and whatever, but—"

"Listen to me. The Billionaire Boys haven't been too happy with him. Who knows why with rich guys? They'll probably blame him for Dengler getting snatched. Quince knows he's on the way out. Other than a few drug lords and Mideast potentates, the Billionaire Boys are First Caymans' biggest depositors. Management will listen to them. So Balthazar figures he has nothing to lose by spilling his guts to you."

Fiona was striding across the Great Hall, intent on Karen as a hornet. "Thanks, Gran." She jotted down the banker's number. "I better go."

"Whom were you talking to?" Fiona growled, imperious upper-class English accent back in place.

"My sweet little old grandmother."

The surviving Vampyrs clustered around the large butcher-block table in Danton's otherwise empty kitchen. Danton used it to spread papers on, but the Vampyrs had swept those onto the floor. They were feasting on ordered-in pizza and beer, and puffing on cigar-size blunts, which they'd brought themselves. And they were listening to Louis's latest sermon.

"They may cut some of us down, but they will end up groveling before us. You saw how they shot me right before the lights went out. I got right back up and kept going." He patted his stomach, where the bullet supposedly had hit.

"Yesssssss," said the Vampyrs, choosing—as Groucho Marx had once put it—to believe him over their own eyes.

"Louis, may I talk to you?" Danton said from the door.

"Why not?" Louis and his flowing cape swept through the kitchen, past Danton, and into the empty living room, which was as large as a cathedral's nave.

Ali sat off to the side on the lone piece of furniture, a folding chair. "What can I do you for?"

"Karen Glick punched you in the stomach and knocked you to your knees?"

"What? Who told you those lies? I got hit with a Nazi bullet."

"A Nazi bullet?" Danton pointed at the balcony, where Matthew, high on weed, was spinning the expensive telescope around. "Could you keep him away from my telescope?"

"We need to unwind after those storm troopers did their little dance on us. We've got Byron posted outside Ludlum House on lookout. We're on top of things."

Danton tilted his head skeptically. "Well . . ."

"I'm your best friend." Louis put his large left arm around Danton's shoulders. "About that slight alteration in our financial arrangement. Since you refused to grease us with that spare half-billion of Dengler—"

"That was earmarked for the Cancer Cure Coalition."

"Our deal was that you'd pay us $5 million when we'd gotten rid of the Billionaire Boys. How about we get a bonus, another five? That would bring our total to $10 million."

Danton tried to slip out from under Louis's arm, but the Vampyr leader had a death grip on his shoulder and he couldn't move. "Your little disciples in the kitchen won't see a dime of it, right?" Danton said. "And they won't see you the moment the money hits your offshore account." Ali was within five yards of them now.

"Oh, shit." It was Matthew out on the balcony. He had tipped over the telescope, which lay on the tiled floor like a smashed insect.

Ali thrust his face up at Louis's. "You let go of my boss now, asshole."

"Sure enough." Louis lifted his left arm, allowing Danton to jump away. Then quickly, Louis's right hand pulled a pistol out from under the cape—a sleek sidearm with a fat sausage of a silencer affixed to the barrel.

Before Ali could react, Louis's gun had splattered his brains across the floor. The servant's body fell backward. A blood pool spread from his mangled skull.

"I didn't like him," Louis said.

"My God, my God, my God." Danton staggered backward and, as if his bones had turned to rubber, collapsed to the floor, where he sat with immense eyes.

Fiona, whose creamy English charm had long ago curdled, escorted Karen back to her office. Karen did her best to keep the blood stains on her bag away from Fiona's view. Fiona's office was as big as that of Bill McIntyre, *Profit*'s editor-in-chief, except Fiona's had antiques. And, of course, the obligatory painting of J.P. Morgan on the old-wood paneled walls.

"I've got to go to the loo," she announced from beneath the owl-like dark circles. "Mr. Morgan will call for you soon. Don't get into any mischief."

"Heaven forfend." Karen watched her leave, then promptly went through the half-open door into Morgan's sumptuous office. At the center was Morgan's mighty desk, once the property of his illustrious ancestor. Without touching, Karen perused the papers lying atop it in neat piles—most related to the Pulmon Tobacco deal.

A small sound outside brought Karen to full alert. Fiona couldn't be that fast, could she? If so, Karen needed a good cover story, like she thought she heard her mother calling, or old Ignatius Ludlum's ghost was chasing her, or . . .

Karen poked her head out Morgan's door. Fiona's office was deserted. There, through a closed door to the right, she heard tapping.

They said old Ludlum's ghost still wafted through the house as he searched for his missing heart. Karen wanted to believe a lot of impossible things: that Frank Vere could find a girlfriend, that her father could get his Ph.D., that Calvin Christian could cuddle a kitten. But she didn't believe in ghosts. Did she?

She opened the door, which turned silently on its fine brass hinges.

It was a dark room, lit only by a computer screen. The light from Fiona's office illuminated a man in a janitor's uniform, his rolling garbage can and mop beside him. He was bent over the keyboard of a PC and slipping a disc into the portal.

At the sight of Karen, the janitor looked up in fright. He had a round Slavic face. "Door was supposed to be locked," he said.

"I'm sorry. I thought—"

"Pasha, what are you doing here?" came Fiona's voice from behind Karen.

"I—I—I—I e-mail my family in Russia. Mr. Dengler said I can."

Karen knew a B.S. story when she heard one. "Why did you put a disc in, then?"

Pasha popped out of his chair and, knocking aside his rolling barrel, charged out of the room through the opposite door.

"There's our bloody spy," Fiona cried. She grabbed the phone. "Russian wanker. Me old dad said never to trust the damn Red rogues."

Ron let Karen into the Boys' Court of Star Chamber conference room. The appointments were impressive, especially the long table where a red-eyed Morgan and a chain-smoking Strongville sat. Jacob Cooke was standing before the two RDS&M partners, like a petitioner before the king. He summoned Karen to his side.

"So you caught Pasha spying." Morgan said this with the cadence of a man who needed two weeks' sleep.

"Yeah. Ron told me he escaped from the building before security could stop him."

"Sweet God in heaven," Strongville said. "Can't anybody do anything right around here? No wonder Vampyr knew our every move."

"We don't know he was with Vampyr," Morgan said, ever-reasonable.

"Was Pasha hooked up to your bank in the Caymans right now?" Karen asked.

"How do you know about First Caymans?" Strongville thundered.

After all that had gone down, Karen decided to go

for it. Even though she had no proof. And considering that she might never get proof, this was worth the shot. "I hear you've been stashing income in First Caymans Bank and Trust to avoid paying taxes on it."

"This is what I mean," Cooke interrupted. "First Karen Glick goes asking your wife, who is off limits, questions about personal problems in the distant past. Then she makes insinuations about your personal financial arrangements—"

"Jacob," Morgan shouted, silencing him. And shouting wasn't part of Morgan's standard repertoire. Turning back to Karen, he became more gentlemanly again: "We wanted to ask you about your experiences at Vampyr headquarters tonight."

"Those commando guys were yours, weren't they?" Karen said. "What are you doing with Dengler's body? Keeping it out of sight until you figure out how to spin this?"

Cooke's pot was really stirred up now. "More baseless charges," he brayed.

"Jacob, be quiet," Morgan said. Then to Karen: "Did Pasha send you financial documents about us?"

"Someone did. Seems likely Pasha downloaded the information."

Morgan's expression stiffened into that of a shrewd dealmaker. "And how," he said, "can you be sure that what you received wasn't a forgery?"

"Your tax records, which I also got, are real. I've had your signatures on them certified as genuine. I'm working on your bank statements."

"You're violating federal privacy laws," Cooke declared.

Strongville savagely stubbed out his cigarette. "I thought I could trust her. You told us, Cooke, that she was a pushover. Now she's coming after us like that Cassie Milton. We ought to fire your worthless fat ass."

Morgan leaned across the table. "RDS&M will no longer cooperate with you," he said to Karen. "If you print libelous untruths, we will sue you silly. You will leave Ludlum House now."

"Hey, Frederick," Karen said. "I've only saved your guys' fannies a couple of times." She showed them the bloodstains on her bag. "And your goons almost blew me to hell tonight for my trouble. How about owning up to what you've done?"

"We've done nothing wrong," Morgan said coldly.

Al and George Jr. strode into the room and each grasped one of Karen's arms.

"Let go," Karen said. They did. "The last guys to manhandle me were Vampyrs. I can find my way out." She stomped toward the magnificent door, flanked by the towering bodyguards. After crossing the Great Hall, Karen found herself on the street.

But not alone, although it was deep into the night.

Cassie Milton and her video crew were setting up outside, with Ludlum House looming in the background.

"What are you doing here?" Karen asked the TV reporter.

"Same back at ya," Cassie said. "We're doing a segment on tomorrow's early news about how Butch Strongville, who likes to brag about his military exploits, is a faker. He was a draftee in the early 1970s, who served as a supply clerk at the Special Forces school at Fort Bragg. He never went to Vietnam or Iran or the rest. He's no Rambo."

"No Rambo." And Karen went into the still night that seemed to crackle with danger.

Chapter Twenty-four

Karen trudged down the lonely side street, passing through lamp-lit stretches, then into midnight darkness. She had one hand gripped around the strap of her bag, hung from a shoulder, and the other shoved into a pocket. And her thoughts were a jumble. What to do? Would Balthazar Quince really come through? Who had sent her the damn documents?

One thing she didn't enjoy doing was walking alone at night on an empty street like this. Too *X-Files*. And she had disliked that show.

"Karen."

At the sound of her name, Karen jumped. She whirled around.

Miranda, the Morgans' social secretary, was loping after her. "I heard you were at Ludlum House. Sorry to scare you."

"Why should I be scared? Things are so calm lately."

Karen's fluttering heart subsided. It could have been Kyra calling to her, not Miranda.

Smiling gamely, Miranda said, "Mrs. Morgan would like to speak to you."

"Now?"

"Unless that's inconvenient."

"I live for inconvenience. Let's go."

They didn't have that far to walk to the Morgans' dazzling Park Avenue premises. A doorman, dressed like a hussar from the Napoleonic wars, greeted them. Inside the lobby, two linebacker types in suits—Karen didn't recognize them—treated her to the evil eye. Miranda gave them Karen's name and said she was expected. One of the bodyguards consulted a clipboard, then nodded them through. Karen hoped he wasn't checking with Ludlum House.

A building employee, clad in a flowery vest and red bow tie, manned the elevator. This was the old-fashioned kind of elevator with a handle that the employee used to navigate the car through its complex upward journey. The elevator was slightly larger than Karen's latest lodgings, and it contained no cockroaches, only English hunting prints. After a bunch of floors, the elevator came to rest and opened to reveal a marble-floored vestibule. Two more pituitary cases stood guard there; one was George Sr.

They entered the apartment, which resembled the Czar's Winter Palace. Karen gaped at the splendor—the flowers, the rugs, the mirrors, the furniture. Many of the walls were stripped, and Karen knew that the FOP set loved promiscuous renovation.

But the centerpiece of the eye-dazzling foyer had

not been removed from the wall: a large painting of water lilies.

"That's Monet," Miranda volunteered.

"Gobs and gobs of it," Karen said.

Karen followed Miranda down a long hallway that, while stripped, would beggar the Louvre in opulence. The social secretary showed her into a room filled with comfortable furniture. Mercedes sat on a couch, reading a piece of paper. A snifter filled with amber liquid sat beside her on the superbly crafted table. She had on a white T-shirt and shorts, which showed off her magnificent dancer's legs.

Mercedes rose with a smile to greet Karen, and Miranda discreetly retreated, closing the exquisitely lacquered doors behind her.

"I'm having brandy," Mercedes said. "Want some?"

"After the day I've had, sign me up."

Mercedes poured Karen a stiff one from a finely beveled glass decanter. "I tried to sleep, but couldn't. This kidnapping of Simon is horrible." She evidently hadn't heard the latest news.

"I'll drink to that." Karen also decided not to tell Mercedes about the raid on Vampyr headquarters, or about Cassie Milton's scoop on Strongville, the war wimp. Being the bearer of bad tidings tends to chill your welcome.

Rolling her snifter between her palms, Mercedes said, "On the Gulfstream, you asked me about Eddie. I think I can trust you. I need to get a perspective here."

"A perspective?"

"Let me show you a couple of letters." Mercedes

handed them over. "The second one came just today." Karen read them several times, the second one the most.

My beloved Mercedes: I know your life is very stressful right now. Maybe I can help you through this difficult time. You won't have to cry anymore. Meet me tomorrow at Bethesda Fountain in Central Park at 10 A.M. I can be of comfort. Yours, Eddie.

Comfort? This guy had his lines down. "So he's alive, huh?"

"They say he jumped off the top of a building at Iffewon prison, years back. When I got this first letter two months ago, I couldn't even open it. When I finally did, I was flabbergasted. I can't imagine what has gone on."

"Tell me about him back when you two were together."

"Oh, yes." Mercedes let out a big Texas laugh and sank down in the couch. "When my mother—and she was a real dance mother—sent me to this ballet program in Dallas that she'd scrimped to be able to afford, they called me Too Tall. And my entire dance career, I had to fight body type. Tall girls normally can't be in the white ballet, which wants little sylphs that float along like butterflies. Still, I kept at it. And I did well.

"Eddie and I were in the same class at NYU, although I didn't notice him. Eddie was shy and not one of the cool crowd. But then he became a Wall Street analyst at Dewey Cheatham and started making some money. And he asked me out. I have to tell you, there was a spark. I had been the Too Tall underdog of the dance world. He was the underdog of the Wall Street world. He was different from the other guys—sweet, loving, not a self-centered jerk."

"I've known at least one self-centered Wall Street jerk," Karen said.

"In those days, Frederick and his friends already had made names for themselves. They liked to dump on poor Eddie, but Eddie took it because he worshipped them—and he liked the income. Eddie kept buying me extravagant gifts, trying to impress me. I told him he didn't need to spend that kind of money. He didn't believe me. Caddy, certainly, was sniffing around me. So was Frederick. I only wanted Eddie, though."

"Good for you."

"It wasn't easy. I worried about Eddie. He had absolutely no friends, except for me. His basic shyness, I guess. He talked about marrying me and taking off overseas for an elaborate honeymoon. Despite my feelings for him, I have to say . . ."

"You had some doubts about him."

"He had this anger bubbling beneath him. Every once in a while, it would erupt, usually when he thought someone had slighted him, like a snooty waiter. I'm unsure where the anger came from. Maybe in reaction to his father, this English professor who disapproved of Eddie's going to Wall Street. The father, James, also disapproved of me. I was too non-intellectual."

Karen noticed that the Kenneth Cole bag at her feet had the blood stains showing. Mercedes wasn't a blood stains kind of gal. And the Kenneth Cole bag, two summers out of season, didn't belong on Park Avenue. Karen, who was happy the bag hadn't disintegrated already, toed it until the offending side faced away from Mercedes.

Mercedes was too into her story to notice. "Then came the insider-trading charges against Eddie. He was distraught. I told him we would face this together. He said Frederick and the others were part of the scheme and they weren't being charged. I asked him if the charges were justified. He said yes; he had done it to get more money for us. I told him I didn't need the money. He got crazy angry at me. He accused me of working with Frederick behind his back to make him the fall guy."

"Wow. I hate to say this, but Eddie was not the guy you want to cut off in traffic."

Mercedes poured herself more brandy. "Well, he got convicted. Then, right before he had to report to prison, they arrested him for threatening to kill me and himself with a gun. I never saw him. The cops arrested him in time in my lobby. He claimed Frederick, Butch, Simon, and Caddy set him up on that one, too. I was . . . shocked. After Eddie went away, Frederick came on in his suave way, and today I am . . . Mrs. Morgan."

Karen took the plunge on the rough question. "Do you love Frederick?"

"I want to say I do. For Bert's sake. Frederick has . . . It's complicated." Mercedes twisted her lovely face. "But Eddie has stayed inside me."

Karen examined the second letter again. "I'm struck

by one sentence. He says you won't have to cry anymore. Have you been crying lately?"

"Yes. Especially since I got Eddie's first letter. I've been confused and . . . I make sure I don't cry in public. I'm alone at home."

Karen took a thoughtful sip of brandy. Yeah, sure go for it. "Mercedes, you wanted my perspective. Maybe you shouldn't go to meet Eddie."

Mercedes was about to take her own sip and halted the snifter beneath her chin.

"Everybody thinks Danton took a dive off a building. That was a ploy he engineered, thanks to a pile of money he got from a rich con artist named Chris Abbott." Karen told a frozen-faced Mercedes what she'd found out about Edward Danton and Vampyr.

"I don't believe you," Mercedes said when she had finished.

"Mercedes, there's no way these Vampyr nuts could lay the ambushes they have without substantial funding. Think about it."

"Eddie Danton had problems, yet I can't believe he would commit . . ."

Miranda was at the door. "Phone call for you, Mrs. Morgan."

"Who is it?"

"Your husband."

Karen held up a finger. "Uh, Mercedes . . ."

Mrs. Morgan walked out to take the call. A few moments later, she reappeared. If her expression had been any colder, the room could store a week's provisions for Gallagher's Steakhouse.

"You want to ruin us," she said. "Get out of my house."

"See, your husband and the Boys haven't exactly been paying their taxes—"

"Get out of here before I call George Sr. and his men."

Once more, Karen made the long trek out of the FOPs' handsome halls and into the night. She crossed Park Avenue, hoping to find a taxi to take her back to her basement hovel, whose most distinctive wall decoration was a suspicious water stain. On the sidewalk, directly across the avenue from the Morgans' building, she saw a twisted mass of debris. Garbage simply isn't done on Park Avenue. She moved closer.

It was an expensive telescope and tripod, twisted oddly as if from a great fall. She craned her neck to take in the slumbering façade of the building facing Mercedes's apartment. She flashed on peeping Benny Slatz and his binoculars. And then on the books about telescopes in Mixon's Greenwich Village apartment. Could Danton or someone who worked for him have a vantage point in this building, used to spy on Mercedes? Only gentry with gazillions could set foot in such a building.

She couldn't exactly ask the doorman if a twisted ex-Wall Streeter, ex-con lived there. Doormen didn't usually spill secrets to reporters about rich, criminal residents.

Butch Strongville couldn't think or speak. Bob and Bill ushered him into his car in the Ludlum House basement and he rode like a coma patient for the short trip up Fifth Avenue. They slid safely into his building's underground garage.

Bob, who was Strongville's age, had been a bona fide Vietnam War hero; he had rescued two men from a burning Huey in 1972 and fought off a squad of North Vietnamese until they were rescued. The army had awarded Bob the Medal of Honor.

On the morning news in a few hours, Cassie Milton would tell the world that Baxter Strongville never even had been to Vietnam. Nor had he been a Special Forces daredevil who had tried to save the Iran hostages. Strongville had refused to talk to Milton outside Ludlum House, but Jacob Cooke had gone out to say, "No comment," and listen to her charges. After the obligatory libel suit threat, Cooke had returned to tell Strongville and Morgan what the TV reporter planned.

Cooke's brilliant idea was to call the cops about Dengler's body, news that would promptly be picked up and would overshadow Milton's exclusive about Strongville. Right.

Dazed, Strongville let the bodyguards guide him into the elevator for the trip up to his apartment. Bill and Bob spelled the two men already outside his door. Too addled to bid them good night, Strongville drifted inside and heard the door shut behind him.

The place showed the tastes of his last wife—what her decorator called "the Asian fusion look," having to do with bamboo, painted screens, and Buddha art. Strongville had regaled the decorator, whose sexual preferences would have precluded military service, about his missions in Southeast Asian jungles. The only time Strongville had actually been in Vietnam was in 1997 on a business deal.

Strongville stood in the darkness, unsure what to do.

Then a lamp flicked on. Louis Roman sat in a large rattan chair. "Hail the conquering hero," he said.

Several black-clad figures seeped out of the darkness and surrounded Strongville. One Vampyr reached inside Butch's suit jacket and extracted the .357 magnum from his shoulder holster.

"The gun's not loaded," this kid said.

When Strongville spoke, it was in a croak: "How did you get in here?"

Louis smiled. "When you study four guys as long as Edward Danton has, you learn all the ins and outs."

Chapter Twenty-five

Mercedes was back on stage, her every movement synched to the rock music, Twyla Tharp in the wings smiling, the audience beguiled. Her long legs flew into the air. Then suddenly she was in a white ballet—*Swan Lake*, gliding across the stage like a heavenly bird, the music soaring, the prince lifting her, the evil wizard approaching. And she and her royal lover ended their suffering by jumping into the lake and drowning.

She awoke gasping for air. Dreams of imminent death meant something. Well, she never had understood how a swan could commit suicide by jumping into a lake.

Frederick appeared at the bedroom door. "Are you all right?"

She squinted at him. He was in his usual Wall Street uniform of a suit and tie. "I had a bad dream. Have you been to bed?"

"No. I got in late. A lot has happened." He sat on the bed, close enough to touch her. He didn't. "Simon's body was found. And Butch—" Frederick broke down crying.

Mercedes put her arms around her husband, who covered his face with his hands. "It's okay," she kept telling him.

When he subsided, he pulled back. "It's not okay. They snatched Butch last night. From his *own apartment*. We had security at the door. We don't know how they got in or made off with him. And on the news this morning, that Cassie Milton . . ."

"We can work through this, Frederick." She tried to take his hands, but he bolted from the bed.

"What this means," Morgan said, "is that we're not even safe in our own homes. The only safe place is Ludlum House. I want you and Bert to move there today. If I could be sure they were only after me, I'd leave you here. But there's no telling what they'll do." He ran his hand through his immaculate hair, mussing it.

"As long as you don't have a letter . . ."

Morgan emitted a sound somewhere between a laugh and a sob. "Oh, I got mine early this morning. The bastards are closing in."

Mercedes swung her legs around and planted her feet on the floor. "May I see this letter, Frederick?"

Her husband adopted that look he had when about to fire someone. "No. Never. That will upset you."

She held her hand out, long tapered fingers fluttering. "I'm already upset."

Frederick slid a black piece of paper out of his inner

jacket pocket and handed it to her. Then he folded his hands before him, as if in prayer.

She felt her hands shake while she read it.

Dear Billionaire Boy: You are the last one, the master schemer, the worst of them. The others did the dirty work that you planned. Workers languish jobless, thanks to your plant closings. Honest toilers from less-fortunate nations are exploited. Poisons foul the air and water. All so you can make a dishonest buck. You brag about your descent from the hideous robber baron. That claim is as fraudulent as your tax returns. Your turn has come. Vampyr.

"What does this mean?" she asked. "Fraud, taxes?"

Morgan waved aside her question. "It means I'm the target. Herman Heinrich is close to finishing these devils off. We just have to stay safe in the meantime."

Mercedes checked the antique English clock that sat on her nightstand. It was slightly after eight. "You take Bert. There's a chore I must do before I join you."

"For God's sake, Mercedes, we're in danger. Don't give them a minute to spring an attack on us." His gorgeous tie metronomed as he ranted. "You can't."

She got out of bed and headed for the bathroom. "I'll join you shortly." The bathroom door shut him off. She leaned on it, her eyes closed, and waited for her husband to leave.

In a half hour, Mercedes emerged from her sanctuary. She looked good, but not too good. Little makeup, hair in a ponytail, capri pants, T-shirt. She examined the tiny wrinkles around her eyes. Kay-Kay called on the great god Botox to make those vanish. Somehow, Mercedes suspected, Eddie wouldn't mind her crow's feet.

In the study, Mercedes flicked on the plasma screen TV and briefly watched the news—about Simon, about the bloody raid on Vampyr's lair, about Butch. She knew she should feel afraid. She felt that and much else.

As she flicked off the picture with a stab of the remote, Miranda minced into the room. "They called to remind Mr. Morgan that the J.P. Morgan statue has arrived from Italy and will be mounted on its plinth in Central Park this afternoon."

"The good news never stops." She stopped short of berating ever-clueless Miranda.

"Where are you going now, Mrs. Morgan? I don't see anything on your schedule. Mr. Morgan took Bert and told Mia to pack clothes for all of you."

"I'm going to Central Park."

Balthazar Quince cleared his throat. He placed the last Caymans bank document atop the pile on the conference room table.

"I recognize every one of these papers," he said. "They're entirely accurate accountings of the Billionaire Boys' holdings. The one for Simon Dengler, of course, is out of date, his account having been almost cleaned out for various charities."

"I hate to say, 'I told you so,'" Karen told Eudell. "So I won't."

Her editor patted the back of Karen's hand. "You were right, honey. You showed me you can do investigative work. Congratulations."

Calvin Christian, touching his bow tie, wasn't as thrilled. "With due respect, Mr. Quince, isn't your motive in cooperating with us—suspect? RDS&M wants to have you fired. Doesn't that bias your evaluation?"

"I owe Ms. Glick's grandmother a lot, and not money," Quince said. "Maybe they will get me fired. I have made a lot of money and don't need to work. I like the sound of early retirement, to be frank."

"Honey," Eudell said to Karen, "you have such a kick-ass story that the Billionaire Boys won't be able to sit down for weeks."

"What's left of them," Karen said.

"Two of them are dead, one is missing—don't you feel bad about kicking them when they are down?" Quince asked Karen.

"Not one little bit," Eudell chimed in. "They're the big dogs. The average Joe can't get away with what they can. The average Joe doesn't have the minimum amount to qualify for your secret bank."

"In answer to your question," Karen said to Quince, "yes, I do feel bad."

Karen bade farewell to everyone and packed up the documents. She enlisted Monte the mail boy and his beloved cart to help her transport them to her desk.

"This is a whole lotta paper," Monte said. "Uh-huh."

Eudell came over to inquire how long Karen would take to write the story, and Karen told her she'd work into the evening to complete the job. When Eudell returned to her office, Karen sat regarding her blank computer screen.

"Congratulations." Karen looked up. Frank Vere stood beside her cubicle. He had a wise and kindly air about him.

"Do the Billionaire Boys—Strongville if he's still

alive, Morgan, and even Morgan's family—deserve what I'm about to do to them?" she said.

"You're getting qualms," Frank said.

"Maybe if these people were up on a pedestal like they used to be," Karen said. "Then maybe this would be easier. But they are suffering now. And I'm piling on. Maybe I don't have that killer instinct you need as an investigative reporter."

"You've got good instincts," Frank said. "And you're a good human being. You'll do what's right." The winner of multiple prizes and unanimous acclamation strolled away, leaving Karen confused and unhappy.

The phone rang. She expected Jacob Cooke, howling at her like a rabid coyote, threatening libel suits. It was her grandmother on the line.

Gran said, "I did a little anagram work on Edward or Eddie Danton. Want to hear this?"

"You bet." Karen pawed through the effluvia on her desk to find a pen and pad.

"Well, I can't get a real name for Edward Danton. There's Donated Drawn. Eddie Danton comes up with Detained Don and Tanned Diode."

Laying down her pen, Karen said, "Thanks for the effort anyway."

"But when I use only the last name, Danton, I come up with Tandon. That sounds like a real last name."

"Better than Sunshine Sami-Glick. I'll run this up the flagpole. Thanks, Gran." What the hell. Karen tried directory assistance for the Edward Tandon longshot. No such phone listing in Manhattan. Then, she called Marcia at work. The detective's voice mail gruffly invited you to leave a message, actually meaning: don't waste my time, maggot.

Karen related Gran's anagram work. "We know Danton's Ferrari—which I saw him driving in Queens—is registered to the late Warden Moxley at his Buffalo home," Karen told her old friend's voicemail. "But doesn't it make sense that Danton has a driver's license under his new alias? Or maybe he owns property under the new name. Is there a Tandon, perhaps Edward Tandon, on Park Avenue? You're a cop." On a hunch, she gave the Park Avenue address where she'd found the broken telescope on the sidewalk. "Who knows? Maybe there. You have quick access to this information. Let's invade some privacy."

Frank once had told her that driver's license data were forbidden to the public. And that wealthy property buyers often purchased under the name of a partnership or trust, thus concealing their ownership in public real estate records.

"I'll find you, Danton," she muttered. And Karen began writing her story.

Back in the 1980s, when Mercedes and Eddie were young and the world lay before them like an all-you-can-eat buffet, they would visit Bethesda Fountain. Eddie, who got a lot of his education from listening to the spouting of his smugly intellectual father, told her that Bethesda was a pool in Jerusalem that healed the sick.

George Sr., objecting to this jaunt, and a younger bodyguard named Abe trailed her as she strode across

Fifth into the greenery of the park in June, with its whirl of bikers, runners, strollers, and sunbathers. She trooped past the Boathouse and the line of Chinese massage artists, and emerged onto the esplanade with the fountain, topped by an angel.

Sitting on the lip of the fountain was the guy Mercedes once knew as an angel. Now he was bald but still slender. Despite all his tribulations, he seemed almost young, an MTV flashback. The shape of his face was a bit different. He smiled shyly. And his eyes flared at the sight of her. She never remembered Eddie's eyes as so intense.

He stood. She swept toward him. They embraced for a long moment. The fountain burbled. Then she drew back out of . . . embarrassment? The bodyguards were at her elbow. She told them to give her some space. George Sr. reluctantly agreed. She turned back to Eddie. They stood facing each other, eye to eye.

"Where have you been?" she asked him. "What happened to you?"

He wore a smile of crazed delight, a smile she found eerie. "I broke out of prison. I arranged it to look like I'd died," Danton said. "Never mind how. And I'm rich now, just as I always told you I'd be."

"Why have you stayed away all this time?"

Eddie caught the serious cast of her face. His smile edged into oblivion. "You had a new life. I had to change my name and my appearance, slightly, to stay free."

"Eddie, why are you showing up now?"

He frowned at her almost accusatory tone. "You're in trouble. That's why."

"Eddie, do you know a reporter named Karen Glick?"

His expression darkened. "You've spoken with Karen Glick?"

"Yes, and she thinks that you're behind Vampyr."

"Pointing the finger at me again, eh?" Eddie tried to summon up another smile, but the result was more of a snarl. "First I was guilty of inside trading."

"Which you admitted to me."

"Then I was the maniac out to kill you and myself. I planned no such thing. I was set up. You didn't stand behind me."

"Remember, Eddie. I did. You accused me of plotting against you."

Danton nodded vigorously. "Well, guess who ends up married to the great Frederick Morgan, latest in the fabled Morgan line?"

"I was hurting. He was there. You had shut me out. You were gone."

"You believe Glick, don't you?"

"Tell me whether I should, Eddie."

Hearing how the conversation had become sharper, George Sr. and Abe moved a few steps closer.

Danton shook his head. "I've done this all for you. And you accuse me."

"Eddie, please. Show me that Karen is wrong."

"Mercedes, I shouldn't have to show you. You should know in your heart that you belong with me, not with that pint-sized Ken doll who only wants a trophy wife."

Mercedes shook her head, too. "In his fashion, Frederick loves me. And Bert. I have a son with Frederick Morgan, Eddie. The years have piled up. I'm dug in."

Danton fixed her with those fierce eyes. "If Morgan is what you want, then good luck." He whirled around and angrily marched away.

George Sr. came to her side. "Should we apprehend this guy, Mrs. Morgan?"

But Mrs. Frederick Morgan found herself speechless. She watched Eddie Danton huff off into the morning.

What was right to do or say? She wanted to call out after Eddie. She couldn't.

Frederick Morgan sat staring at the bare top of J.P. Morgan's desk. Ashlea Kress was standing in front of his desk and talking. He heard not one word.

"Butch always called you 'Ashley,' not Ashlea," he said.

Ashlea struggled to maintain her composure and professional bearing. Her clothes and makeup were immaculate, her headband firmly in place, her diction flawless. "We need to deliver a counter-offer, sir."

Morgan looked up from the desktop. "A what?"

"To Naylor & Cross. They topped our bid. We need to respond to them."

"Our bid?"

"Yes, our bid," Ashlea said, as she would to a dotty old relative who might write her into his will. "As you know, we bid $22 per Pulmon Tobacco share. And now that Naylor & Cross has topped us with $25 per share, we need to deliver a higher bid."

"Oh? Yeah? Pulmon." Morgan hit the intercom and

asked Fiona if Mrs. Morgan were back at Ludlum House yet. She said George Sr. and Abe were bringing her in now. "And Bert?" The secretary said Bert was happily playing a video game upstairs in their quarters. Morgan thanked her and turned to Ashlea. "What were you saying?"

"Naylor & Cross gave Digby Graves a better employment contract than we did. If we can top them on the contract and deliver a higher bid for the stock, then we win."

Morgan swept his palm across the desk in a polishing motion. "My ancestor, the great J.P. Morgan, saved the world economy, more than once. The last time was in the Panic of 1907. He led a team of bankers to stop the catastrophe. He was a national hero."

Ashlea tried to bring her boss back to the present. "We need to find more capital for the Pulmon deal. I've been in touch with Dewey Cheatham on that."

"He wasn't a handsome man. Not an articulate man. Not a charming man. But when J.P. died, the world wept. An emperor had passed. Do you know that today they've mounted my statue of him in Central Park? I can't be there."

"As Mr. Dengler would say," Ashlea went on, her voice quavering at the mention of the dead, "we have to act at once."

"They called old J.P. 'the Napoleon of Wall Street.' If I die, what will they call me? The Louis XVI of Wall Street?" He focused his attention on poor Ashlea, who stood there struggling with her emotions. "What would Morgan do now, in my situation?"

"I . . . I . . . I can't cope with this." Ashlea ran from the room

Herman Heinrich lumbered into Morgan's office with Fiona squawking behind him that he had no clearance to enter. "Strongville has been found," he said.

"Is Butch all right?" Morgan asked, getting up. His leaned forward on his desk with his fingertips on its surface.

"No. His body was discovered at the Battery, amid the war memorials. They had painted him yellow. And shot him several times. It seemed like a firing squad."

"Butch is dead?" Morgan said, more in wonder than in shock. "Dead?"

Jacob Cooke slid around the immense slab of Heinrich. Fiona also emitted protests at his unauthorized entry. "We have another problem," the P.R. man said.

Morgan leaned farther forward on his desk, almost in the front leaning-rest position. "Another problem?" he said from somewhere in intergalactic space.

"Cassie Milton again," Cooke said. "She's about to do a standup in front of the new J.P. Morgan statue."

"My statue. Cast in Italy."

"She has this story that you are not descended from J.P. Morgan. That you have been faking your ancestry."

"Butch and me—fakes," Morgan said. "How about that?"

The public relations disaster didn't seem to register

with Heinrich, who only understood physical peril. "You and your family are safe in Ludlum House," he said.

"Safe?" Morgan said.

The clock hands revolved and Karen slid deep into the evening, writing the saga of the tax-cheating Billionaire Boys. After midnight, the newsroom cleaned out as people left to go home, floating away like spirits. The janitorial staff turned off the overhead lighting, and she switched on her desk lamp. Her cubicle shone, a lone island of light.

There was no sound except the tapping on her keyboard. She was almost done. The story was a gem, but needed some polishing.

Meanwhile, she needed some food. She could order a pizza, but the new building security rules required her to go down to the lobby to fetch it. So she grabbed her bag, got up, and headed for the vending machine room, an evil weight-gaining place she never dared visit. Not that the selections were that great.

What the hell was a Devil Dog anyway? She liked nice dogs that you could pet. And why would anyone, except maybe Bart Simpson, want to eat a Butterfinger? Candy made her break out. Then she saw those little goldfish-shaped crackers, which tasted as wonderful as construction paper.

That was when Monte glided past in the hall. Without his mail cart.

"Monte," she called to him, "what are you doing here?"

He stopped and seemed horrified to see her. "Oh, I came to pick up what I forgot. Uh-huh." Monte turned to go.

"What's good in these machines? Looks like a load of crap to me, with the nutritional value of earwax." Then Karen realized as she said this that it would go over poor Monte's head.

He looked at her beside the machines. "Don't know nothing about nothing."

You never really paid much notice to Monte. The mail boy was part of the newsroom scenery, delivering his packages and envelopes every morning.

But now Karen saw his eyes.

She had seen them before. Lucifer eyes.

Chapter Twenty-six

"You're Edward Danton, aren't you?" She said this in a voice so muted that only a dog could hear. She repeated it louder: "You're Edward Danton. Aren't you?" She flattened herself against a vending machine, unsure of what to do. No one else was on the floor.

"I'm not here with Louis," Monte said, now sounding like Mixon. "I want to make sure you are safe while you write."

Karen's laughter was involuntary and explosive. "Safe? After what you and your psycho pals have tried to do to me?"

"Listen, they did it against my orders. Louis hates you. I'm here to—"

"That's reassuring. Louis will take your money but not your orders."

"This is difficult for me. I started working here with the idea of planting the Billionaire Boys documents on Frank Vere. He'd run with this story. Then I found out he was forbidden to write the story because of . . ." He paused. "Of Mercedes."

"You think she'll fall for your scheme? You're dreaming, pal."

Danton's eyes flared and his voice rose. "You've screwed up the life I had planned with Mercedes. She told me how you defamed me."

"So she listened to me after all. Are you going to sue me, too?"

"No, but I'm tempted to let Louis deal with you. Instead, you have a big chance. I sent you the Caymans documents. Write your story and we'll leave you alone."

"It was you who Pasha worked for, huh?" Karen now was more angry than scared. "You should run, not walk, to the nearest loony bin."

"You're not getting much money out of your divorce. I'll pay you $1 million after you publish the Billionaire Boys tax story."

"Well, aren't you the Faustian bargain hunter?"

"Take the money. Who would know?"

"Forget it, Mephistopheles."

"You could buy whatever you wanted," Danton said. "Wouldn't you like to live like the people you write about? Wouldn't you enjoy living again in a luxury building like the one you shared with your husband?"

"No and no," Karen retorted. "I could have stayed in that life. I chose not to."

She realized that Danton was drawing closer to her.

The room was a cul-de-sac. She was trapped in there. And no one else was on the floor with them.

"Okay," Danton said. "Don't take the money." He took another step, and was close enough to touch her. "But the tax-dodging story will make you. You can say goodbye to the nice little features about CEOs' hobbies. You will be on a level with Frank Vere."

"I'm nowhere close to Frank Vere."

"This is the story you need."

"Do I?"

Danton now stood a foot away from her. "Exposing the Billionaire Boys. I've let Cassie Milton do minor pieces on that. I've saved the main story for you."

"To what do I owe the honor?" Karen's eyes darted about, searching for a way out.

"Because I like you. And you're tough. A good investigative reporter has a killer instinct. Cassie Milton would walk over her grandmother for a story like this."

"Nobody would dare try walking over my grandmother. They wouldn't live to tell the tale. Listen, I have to go."

Danton grabbed her arm. "I'm going to make you write the story."

With her free hand, Karen pulled her cell phone out of the bag around her shoulder.

Danton made to snatch it. Karen's bag tipped over and all kinds of garbage hit the floor.

He wrestled the cell away from her. "You're not calling anyone."

But Karen had dropped to her knees and picked up

one item that had fallen on the floor. The pepper spray.

She pointed it at Danton's face and pressed the button. Danton recoiled and backpedaled out of the vending-machine room.

"Come back here," she cried.

Danton, however, had sprinted into the darkened newsroom. She ran after him, spray in hand. All she heard was the sound of retreating footsteps down the fire stairs as the door closed behind him. She didn't know whether she had got him with the spray.

As dawn crept over Ludlum House with a sickly yellow tinge, Frederick Morgan stood beside J.P.'s desk. He could not touch it.

"Our family, you see, had been in this small Midwest town for a number of generations—farmers and tradesmen," he said, his beautiful tie yanked down and askew, his jacket off, a food stain on his handcrafted shirt. "Nobody ever did a genealogy on us. No need. We were nothing special."

"I don't have a way to spin this," Jacob Cooke said, slumping in a lovely old Victorian chair with lion's paw legs.

"When I came to New York, I had to make myself . . . special." Morgan examined the desk with its fine wood. "J.P. gave me magic."

"But the tax story Karen Glick is doing for the magazine," Cooke said. "That has to be false, right? We need a strategy to rebut that. Then we file a libel suit against *Profit*."

Morgan seemed to hear his P.R. man for the first

time. "The tax story? Oh, that's entirely true." He drifted away in a reverie. "We didn't want to share our money with the government, which had done nothing to earn it."

Cooke jolted to his feet, his belly bobbling. "You *what?* My God, you are committing suicide here."

"I can't face Mercedes. Or Bert. I'm lost, Jacob."

"Don't lose your nerve now. That's what they want."

"And I've lost Caddy and Simon and Butch."

Karen awoke the next morning, her head on her arms, which were folded atop her desk. Devil Dog and Butterfinger wrappers were scattered around, along with a few goldfish crackers.

Eudell stood over her, radiating disapproval.

Karen could have told the editor about how last night she had tried to alert building security in the lobby to stop Danton, but to no avail. The lone lobby guard sounded stoned, saying, "Who da guy running here? Hey, dude. He's gone."

So this morning, all she could manage through her sleepiness was to tell Eudell: "We won't have mail delivery today."

"Your story?" Eudell said.

"No," Karen said. "No story. Not this way."

Eudell gave a soul-deep sigh. "Honey, what the hell do you mean?"

With ostentatious care, Karen brushed the vending-machine debris into the wastepaper basket. Then she headed for the elevator. Others had started to arrive.

She took the regular elevator, not the service one.

She crossed the lobby in daylight, like a normal person, not a fugitive.

The Vampyrs clustered around the large table, swept now of its food and drink and dope. A large diagram of Ludlum House and several photos were before them.

Pasha, goggling nervously about him at the bizarre pack, had the look of a man whose head might fly off any moment. "Old Ignatius Ludlum," the janitor said, "he made this tunnel, so when radicals stormed in, he could escape. That how I got out."

"Heinrich's security storm troopers know nothing about this tunnel?" Louis asked, fixing Pasha with a terrifying stare.

"I never seen nobody use it," Pasha said with a rabbit's bravura.

Louis clapped the janitor-spy's shoulder. "Good." He addressed his followers. "Night strike. As planned. Get ready. We'll make their Stomcox mural look like a Pepsi ad."

"Yessssss," they said.

"Louis, I must speak with you." Danton stood in the large doorway.

His weird smile in place, Louis trailed Danton through the almost-bare study—where the wreckage of his home entertainment system lay, thanks to Matthew—and into the large, empty living room. "Your chinwag with the lady fair Mercedes in Central Park didn't go well?"

"About your request to double your money."

Louis made to drape his arm around Danton, but

Danton avoided him. "Now what's this?" Louis said. "I'm your best friend."

"Well, friend, I'll give you the $10 million you requested. Only if you take care of Karen Glick—when I tell you to."

"The $10 million was no request. And once we're done at Ludlum House, I want to blow this pop stand. One little problem for you: good luck getting rid of my young friends. They like it here. Except for Matthew, who trashed your entertainment system. He hated your music and movie collections. I mean, *Dangerous Liaisons*?"

"Okay then, $12 million. As soon as she publishes her tax story on the Billionaire Boys, you take care of her."

"You mean"—Louis cupped his ear—"kill her?"

Danton cut his eyes to the window giving onto the terrace and the Morgans' building beyond. He nodded.

"What if she doesn't publish the article? Libel risk, y'know."

"She'll publish it. She needs to."

"What do we do about the lovely Mercedes?" Louis's smile turned sly.

Danton's response was hoarse. "When you go to Ludlum House, take Mercedes, too."

The blue hour had come to Central Park. Karen sat on a bench opposite the freshly erected statue of the great J.P. Morgan, who faced east toward Ludlum House, where he and old Ignatius had discussed the fate of the world, which was intertwined with their own. Old J.P.'s statue looked strong and resolute.

Karen wished she felt strong and resolute. She had spent the day roaming over the city, eating street food like pizza, hot dogs, Italian ices. So not only was her hope of losing that winter pudge gone, her career was, as well.

At least no Vampyrs had flapped up to complicate her roaming and noshing. Maybe after that assault rifle party out in Queens, fewer were available.

Her phone, on vibrate, wiggled like a small animal in heat. She checked the caller I.D., having not answered or returned the storm of calls that had come in since she'd left the office. This one was from Frank. She hit the talk button.

"Now what do you do?" he said.

"Write my refutation of the theories of Stephen Hawking."

"What about going back to those personality pieces? Christian is telling Eudell that's all you should be doing. After you do a sympathetic color piece on the travails of the Billionaire Boys, that is."

"Christian should be fed to the lions. I've gotta go, Frank." She went back to studying J.P.'s statue, which was getting difficult to fully appreciate in the fading light. A night bird sang, probably one of his greatest hits, although Karen didn't recognize it.

Her phone, residing forgotten in her hand, had another case of the shakes. Caller I.D. showed Marcia's number at the police precinct.

"Hey, Mike Tyson, where've you been? As my mother would say, I got a hot flash." When Karen didn't respond, Marcia said, "You there?"

"I'm here," Karen said. "I'm preoccupied by important issues like whether I should buy a Diet Coke or a Coke Classic from a deli."

"Diet Coke's for wimps. Here's my news: There is an Edward Tandon, and he lives at the Park Avenue address you said to check out."

"Yeah? Are you off to arrest the bastard?"

"Me?" Marcia said with her blast of a laugh. "I can't barge into these rich and influential people's building with some wild accusation. I need probable cause. An anagram is not that. No offense to your Gran."

"Well, I might try, although my free pass into Park Avenue buildings has expired. Or I might go to that revival movie theater in the Village. They're showing *An Affair to Remember*, a bona fide chick flick. What I want to know is how Cary Grant can't figure out that Deborah Kerr is crippled. He's no dumbo."

"Neither are you. I mean, not all the time. That recording you made of Mixon, through the door at his Greenwich Village apartment? That is dead-for-sure Danton's voice, although a bit older. We found a recording from the 1980s at the SEC of his federal interrogation. If we catch him somehow, we can use it against him."

"Too bad nobody's going to arrest him."

"One more piece of hot news," Marcia said. "You unmasked Pasha Strolnikov, the janitor at RDS&M's office, right? The spy? Well, he turned up."

"Turned up how? You got him in for questioning?"

"Not quite. He turned up in the river. I guess the throwers thought he was dead. Well, before he went to that big broom closet in the sky, he did a little talking.

Not that he made much sense. Drowning and machete wounds do that to you."

Karen began looking uneasily about her. Perhaps she shouldn't be sitting out in plain view like this. "What did he say?"

"All we could make out was: 'Stomcox Massacre again.' Yeah, I sorta remember the Stomcox Massacre from eighth-grade history class. What was it exactly?"

On a whim, Karen wandered over to Fifth Avenue and Ludlum House. The sun had set by now. Ludlum House loomed there with a haunted-house majesty—the spooky gables, the leaded-glass windows, the Tiffany canopy over the front door.

Then Karen noticed that the front door yawned open. Even more odd, no guards hovered outside. Perhaps because this was after business hours.

She stepped up to the big door and peered inside.

No one was around. The front desk, where the inside guards sat, was empty. The Stomcox mural stretched above, still visible in its gory glory.

"Hello?" No one returned Karen's greeting.

She drifted into a hallway off to the side. Not one light was on. This place operated around the clock, with Ashlea Kress's MBAs like Colin toiling into the night over numbers. On the carved oak wall hung a portrait of J.P. Morgan that she could barely make out in the dimness. Next to it was a painting of Ignatius Ludlum.

She heard a noise down the hall. She squinted into the darkness. A spectral figure flitted into view, and vanished.

"Hello?"

Then she stumbled over the body. It was a large body, the size of a felled refrigerator. Brought to her knees, she found her face near its.

Herman Heinrich. Breathing for him, like for the folks in the Stomcox Massacre, was history.

"Holy hell." Karen bolted to her feet.

Hands grabbed her. She hollered in surprise and fright. Several dark figures surrounded her.

"Some nice luck," Matthew said into her ear.

He jammed a chemical-soaked rag against her nose and mouth, while the others suppressed her struggling.

After she lost consciousness, Karen saw Ignatius Ludlum passing through the hall. He told her he was searching for his heart, which had been stolen from him. She answered that she didn't have it. Ludlum said he'd take hers then.

Chapter Twenty-seven

When Kyra threw the bucket of water on her, Karen became very awake. She sat up from where she'd been lying and spluttered. She was in a large, well-appointed but otherwise unused kitchen. It had no utensils dangling overhead, nor anything in the glass-fronted cupboards. Then Karen realized she wasn't on a house tour.

"We're going to cut your finger off?" Kyra said. She held a wicked-looking knife.

"Really? How about this one?" Karen showed Kyra her preferred finger.

As Karen shook her head to clear it, Henry sauntered into view. "Where's Louis so we can start?"

Karen brushed her hair out of her face. "How about bring him in for another boxing match."

"That was pathetic last time," Henry said. "He smacked you silly."

"Huh? I landed one in his stomach that doubled him over."

"That was a bullet from the storm troopers?" Kyra said, with that maddening end-lilt that made every assertion sound like a question.

There was a pungent smell Karen knew well from college. "You say he got shot in the stomach, and he's walking around? Have you been smoking too much wacky weed here, Kyra?"

"Louis is very, very tough," Henry said.

"Then you must be very, very stupid," Karen said. When Matthew came in and whispered to Henry, she added, "Hey, when are you going to shave off that ugly soul patch, Matthew? Today would be nice."

"Well. Today is all you have left, and not much of it," Matthew said.

He and Henry hoisted Karen up by her armpits and half-walked, half-dragged her down a sparse corridor to a large room with many windows, a terrace beyond. The room was bare of furniture. Fighting to emerge from her grogginess, Karen took in the scene.

The Morgan family sat cross-legged on the polished floor. Their son was trembling. Mercedes had her arms around the boy; she looked into the vague distance, undaunted, defiant. Frederick Morgan slumped there, tie twisted, head bowed.

Louis stood to the side in his cape, his face alight with vast amusement. Two other black-clad Vampyrs were beside him.

And standing before the Morgans, like a fundamentalist preacher invoking hell and damnation, Edward Danton had worked himself into a lather.

"Look at me, Mercedes," he shouted. "You look at me."

She moved her head toward him. "Okay, I'm looking at you. Happy?"

"Happy?" he shouted with almost enough force to set off car alarms. "You said you loved me. You said you'd stand by me. But you were plotting to send me away, just like the son-of-bitch you married. You wanted the quick money, didn't you? You wanted to be the grand dame of Park Avenue. You betrayed me."

Mercedes shook her head.

"And you." Danton jammed an accusing finger an inch from Morgan's downward cast eye. "You let me swing for the insider-trading scheme. You let me be your damn fall guy. Then you framed me on that fake gun charge. You have no shame. You steal my woman, you screw everybody to the wall, you dodge your taxes. You don't deserve to live." He leaned over the crouched Morgan and screamed, "Filthy scum."

In the breathing silence that followed, Karen had her opening. "Hey, Danton—or is it Tandon?—aren't you being a little extreme here?"

Danton whirled around to confront her. "What? Extreme? After what they did to me? Extreme?"

"I mean, couldn't you have hired a clown to throw pies in their faces? Or maybe made up filthy limericks about them to post on the Internet? Humiliation followed by death, though—that's off the charts."

"Tell me you've written the tax story and I might let you live," Danton said.

"Yeah, sure you will. Hey, I'm not writing that story. Too bad for you." Karen figured she had nothing to lose. Besides, the lingering effect of the chloroform added a drunkard's boldness. "And these Vampyr idiots really think you're laying big bucks on them?"

"Money from Danton will go for our struggle?" Kyra declared.

"I'm glad you framed that as a question," Karen said. "See, somehow I think you dopes won't see a dime of it. Maybe Louis will. Not you."

Louis blatted out derisive laughter. "Kyra, it's time to cut off her finger."

Danton appeared to have calmed down. He held up a hand. "Before you do that, I want to show each of you in Vampyr my appreciation."

"What the hell are you talking about?" Louis asked.

"Wait." Danton trotted into the next empty room and came back bearing a silver tray with a wine bottle and seven glasses. "I want to toast you for a brilliant performance."

Louis shrugged. "Let's make this quick."

"You got a plane to catch, Louis?" Karen called.

Matthew told her to shut up and twisted her arm until she gave a bark of pain.

Danton placed the tray at his feet and stooped to uncork the wine. "This is a fine malbec." He sloshed some into each glass.

The Vampyrs hustled over to claim a glass. Kyra handed Louis his. Henry and Matthew shoved Karen face-first onto the floor, then swept over to snatch their own glasses. Danton held his glass aloft. They did the same.

"To Vampyr," Danton said. "The vanguard of

change that will halt the scourges of globalization, racism, militarism, and fascism. And to Louis, your intrepid leader—my best friend."

They drank.

Then Louis, hoisting his glass, added, "This is the finest group of humans ever to walk our planet. People with noble ideals. People who will go down in history as the ones willing to do what is necessary."

They drank once more.

"And that's not the best part," Louis went on. He had begun to slur, even though he'd had just two sips. "You are the most gullible rich kids I've ever scammed. Dumb, messed-up little dirtballs. You actually bought this donkey dung I fed you. The best thing you did was let me bang your brains out. Revolution, my ass. I'm taking the $12 million that Danton is forking over, and saying bye-bye to you. Good luck when the cops track you down. And they will. I'm grabbing the $12 million and buying my own island. The hell with you all."

The younger Vampyrs stood with their glasses, swaying and blinking.

Then Matthew said, "You expect us to forget that a girl beat you up? A Nazi bullet in your stomach, my ass."

The others joined in. Kyra accused Matthew of being a sexist pig for hitting on her, and said he was too ugly. Henry accused Kyra of sleeping with Jeff Davis, who given his name, likely was a racist. Kyra told Henry that Jeff was a better lover. Matthew told Henry he was a fag who should go back to the theater to be with the rest of them. They all bleated at Louis that he was a hypocritical swine, with his fancy jeans and Ferraris—as well as for his plans to bilk them out of the money.

Louis was the first to double over and crumple to the floor, where he writhed and then lay still. Matthew was the last.

Calmly, Danton, who had only pretended to drink, stepped over their fallen bodies. From inside Louis's spread cape, he plucked the sleek pistol with its fat silencer.

"The first Billionaire Boy, Caddy Redmon, I did myself," Danton said matter-of-factly as he approached the three Morgans, who watched him with wide eyes. "I didn't want the Vampyrs involved for a reason. You can see why."

"Let my son live, Eddie," Mercedes said. "He's done nothing to you."

"Oh, yes he did," Danton said. "He's been Morgan's son. That's plenty for me."

Morgan held out a beseeching hand. "Take me. I'm the one you want. You say you loved Mercedes. Show it. And let her have Bert. That's what's right." While muted, he spoke as if driving home one last deal.

"What's right?" Danton bellowed, exercised anew, losing track of Karen.

She rose from the floor, drew abreast of him, and landed a sizzling punch squarely on his nose. Danton reeled backward, blood gushing over his mouth and chin. He lost his balance and fell hard. His gun went skittering. Karen lunged for it.

At that moment, a far door cracked open. A phalanx

of cops in helmets and Kevlar vests surged into the room, their weapons ready.

Danton lay there, broken, bleeding, and sobbing. Frederick, Mercedes, and Bert were huddled, their arms around each other.

After the cops had absorbed the situation, Detective Marcia Fink, the leader of this pack, came up to Karen and took the gun. "That's what I like about female crime-solvers," she said. "They use their heads, not their fists."

Karen, holding her hand, which ached from its contact with Danton's nose bone, said, "I thought you didn't dare enter the Tandon residence."

"Yeah, after we got a report of suspicious activity at Ludlum House, we found the place wide open, and inside five of their security guys dead of gunshot wounds."

Karen flinched. "I was afraid that . . . Was one of them Ron?"

"There's no Ron on the list, which we've I.D.ed," Marcia said. "A little later, we got a report from an elderly resident in this building that strange young persons dressed in black were carrying an unconscious woman up in the freight elevator. That sounded like more than a group of hard-partying kids to me, particularly at Tandon's address. We had probable cause."

"Thanks for coming." Karen looked at the hugging tableau of the Morgan family.

"I'm sorry for what I did," Morgan was saying to his wife. "Will you forgive me?"

"Of course I will," Mercedes said. "You're my husband. But things can't stay the same, Frederick."

"I know they can't."

Young Bert kept saying: "Daddy, Daddy, Daddy."

Danton, handcuffed, watched them dully. The blood had flowed like a river down his chest. "You're still tax cheats," he muttered.

"Hey, Danton," Karen said. "Maybe the prison you'll draw will be Iffewon again. Reunion time."

"You've got yourself quite a story," Marcia said to Karen.

Karen grimaced. "I guess."

Marcia shrugged and walked over to Danton. "Ready for a trip to your friendly neighborhood precinct?"

"I want a lawyer," he said. "I can afford a good one. So watch yourself."

Mercedes moved off the floor, as she would from Twyla Tharp's stage, and glided over to Karen. "I want you to run the tax story," she said. "The truth must come out."

"The truth," Frederick said, penitent.

Karen looked from Mercedes to Frederick. "The truth."

Chapter Twenty-eight

The hammock swayed under the Hampton Bays stars. The house glowed with its welcoming warmth. The gang, filled with food and drink, was heading for bed.

"The tax story was good," Frank Vere said from his side of the hammock.

The usual chaste distance separated them.

"After Lynn okayed it from a legal standpoint," Karen said, "Christian looked like he was having an internal hemorrhage. I loved when Bill McIntyre, bless him, swept aside Calvin's last-minute objections. A libel suit? Hey, Morgan admits what he did."

Frank sighed contentedly. "An IRS investigation into RDS&M and Frederick Morgan, a Congressional inquiry into abuses by offshore banks that help American tax cheats—those are pretty good results from your first investigative story."

"Eudell's happy because we beat Cassie Milton and everyone else like a bad dog. My parents are happy because the capitalists took one in the choppers. And Gran is happy because she helped me track down Edward Danton."

"Her and her anagrams. Let's see, I'm either Freak Vern or Rank Fever." Frank stayed silent for a moment, much like the radiant star sweep overhead. "So. Are you happy, Karen?"

"Well, I'm a soon-to-be-divorced woman over thirty without a lot of money, but with good friends and, I hope, more investigations around the corner. On balance . . . yeah, I'm happy."

With their eyes still fixed on the stars, their hands moved to the center of the hammock and joined.